"A second case of murder nearly as close to home as her debut gives Sister Louise LaSalle another chance to show off her sleuthing chops."—*Kirkus Reviews*

Mayhem & Mass

"The possibility of romance between two of the characters provides a pleasant foil to Sister Lou's pursuit of the truth for the sake of her old friend . . . in this debut of a saintly sleuth with some very human failings."—*Kirkus Reviews*

"Although Sister Lou took the vow of obedience, she doesn't always play by traditional rules, as readers of this first-in-a-new-series will soon find out. *Mayhem & Mass* is a promising addition to the cozy mystery genre, and its protagonist is delightful!"—*Suspense Magazine*

"Kudos to Olivia Matthews, who has created a new 'hook' to draw in readers."—*Mystery Scene Magazine*

"A spunky leading lady—who just happens to be a nun. Lou will go to the ends of the earth to uncover the truth. The plot is fast-paced and believable . . . A worthwhile mystery series here that fans will adore."
—*RT Book Reviews*

Also by
OLIVIA MATTHEWS

Mayhem & Mass

Peril & Prayer

Alibis & Angels

A Sister Lou Mystery

OLIVIA
MATTHEWS

KENSINGTON PUBLISHING CORP.
www.kensingtonbooks.com

KENSINGTON BOOKS are published by

Kensington Publishing Corp.
119 West 40th Street
New York, NY 10018

All Kensington titles, imprints, and distributed lines are available at special quantity discounts for bulk purchases for sales promotions, premiums, fund-raising, educational, or institutional use. Special book excerpts or customized printings can also be created to fit specific needs. For details, write or phone the office of the Kensington sales manager: Kensington Publishing Corp., 119 West 40th Street, New York, NY 10018, attn: Sales Department; phone 1-800-221-2647.

KENSINGTON BOOKS and the K logo are Reg. U.S. Pat. & TM Off.

ISBN-13: 978-1-4967-0942-4
ISBN-10: 1-4967-0942-X

First printing: March 2019

10 9 8 7 6 5 4 3 2 1

Printed in the United States of America

Electronic edition: March 2019

ISBN-13: 978-1-4967-0943-1
ISBN-10: 1-4967-0943-8

To my dream team:

- *My sister, Bernadette, for giving me the dream;*
- *My husband, Michael, for supporting the dream;*
- *My brother Richard, for believing the dream;*
- *My brother Gideon, for encouraging the dream;*
  ♥ *And to Mom and Dad, always, with love.* ♥

This series is dedicated with respect and affection to the Congregation of the Dominican Sisters of Peace for inspiring me with their great courage, strength, determination, and joy.

Chapter 1

"You're giving up *coffee* for Lent?" Sharelle "Shari" Henson gaped at Christian "Chris" LaSalle. He sat across the table from her at the cozy Briar Coast Café on Sunday morning. "That's like giving up bathing."

Seated beside Shari, Sister Louise "Lou" LaSalle struggled with a smile as she watched the exchange between the young couple during brunch. Ash Wednesday, the start of the Lenten season, was just four days away. Sister Lou and her nephew, Chris, the vice president for College Advancement with the College of St. Hermione of Ephesus, had attended Mass before picking up Shari. Sister Lou and Chris still wore their sober Sunday finery. Shari had met them wearing a lemon yellow crewneck sweater, moss green jeans, and well-aged tangerine sneakers.

Chris sliced into a turkey sausage patty. His onyx gaze, which was so like his father's—Sister Lou's deceased brother's—dropped to Shari's white porcelain coffee mug. "I can see how you would think that. Is that your second or third coffee today?"

Shari's gaze dropped to her mug before returning

to Chris. "That depends. Are you counting the coffee I drank at home while waiting for you and Sister Lou?"

Sister Lou's eyebrows jumped. She sliced into her vegetable omelet as she contemplated Shari's coffee. They'd been in the café for less than an hour and already the newspaper reporter was on her second mug. Chris was still nursing his first coffee of the day.

Sister Lou was drinking chai tea, her hot beverage of choice. She'd need a refill soon. "Lent helps us recognize the things that we've become too dependent on; things that have taken hold of us in negative ways. By fasting from them during Lent, we're declaring that we won't let them control us anymore. That's why Chris's decision to give up coffee is an excellent one. It's also not the first time he's chosen to fast from coffee for Lent." Sister Lou gave her nephew an indulgent smile.

Shari's reckless cocoa eyes widened in horror. "You've done this *before?*"

Chris smiled as though he enjoyed Shari's dismay. "Several times."

Shari's winged eyebrows soared. *The Briar Coast Telegraph* newspaper reporter looked dumbstruck. "But I bought you that cappuccino maker for your birthday." They'd celebrated Chris's thirty-fourth birthday three weeks ago on January twenty-first.

Chris's perfectly proportioned sienna features softened with love and appreciation. "I'm using it now, and I'll look forward to using it again on Easter Sunday, April first."

Shari wrinkled her long nose. "It seems wrong to celebrate Easter Sunday on April Fool's Day."

"It kind of does." Chris returned to his toast.

Sister Lou was silent in her dissention. What did it matter that Easter Sunday fell on April first this year? She would be celebrating Easter and the joy of the resurrection. Sister Lou took a moment to relax into the laughter and chatter that ebbed and flowed from the tables around them.

Shari shoved her mass of unruly raven tresses behind her narrow shoulders. Her gaze settled on Sister Lou. Her diamond-shaped features—high cheekbones, pointed chin, and bow-shaped lips—conveyed a mixture of confusion and frustration. "What're *you* giving up for Lent?"

Sister Lou understood that Shari wasn't actually asking what she was giving up. Her young friend wanted guidance as to whether she should participate in some form of fasting during the Lenten season. Religious traditions were new to the reporter. Sometimes Sister Lou forgot that Shari hadn't been exposed to them from childhood the way she and Chris had.

Sister Lou shifted on her seat to face Shari. The bracing early February air of Briar Coast in upstate New York leaked through the window beside her. Despite her Southern California roots, Sister Lou didn't mind the chill breeze.

"The practice of exercising self-discipline is meant to draw us closer to Jesus Christ." Sister Lou touched the blue, gold, and white Hermionean pin she'd affixed to the right lapel of her pale blue blazer. "Our efforts remind us of how much we have to be grateful for, but we don't have to give something up to do that. During Lent, we're also encouraged to modify our behaviors."

Shari's brow furrowed with concentration. "You mean like being polite, not getting angry, and not cursing?"

Chris sipped his orange juice. "Being more intentional in what we do and say can improve the way we treat other people even after Lent."

Sister Lou drank more of her chai tea. The warm, sweet beverage had a cinnamon-like bite going down. "We're also encouraged to volunteer with nonprofit organizations like food banks, homeless shelters, and animal centers."

"Like the programs that your congregation sponsors." Shari referenced Sister Lou's congregation of Catholic sisters, the Congregation of the Sisters of St. Hermione of Ephesus. The reporter's expression brightened as she began to understand the bigger picture of the meaning and purpose of Lent.

Sister Lou took a sip from her nearly empty mug of chai tea. "That's right."

Shari's eyes sharpened with interest. "Are you giving something up or changing your behavior?"

Sister Lou finished off her omelet. She was sorry the culinary delight was over. "Both. In addition to giving up pastries—"

"You're giving up *pastries*?" Once again, Shari's voice reflected scandal and horror.

Sister Lou recognized the irony of making her announcement in a café that was full to bursting with the scents of chocolate, confectioners' sugar, cinnamon, and nutmeg. "I'm also recommitting to praying the rosary."

Shari gave her a blank look. "The rosary? What's that?"

Sister Lou fought against a smile. "I'll show you the next time you come to my apartment." There was a high probability that Chris and Shari had planned to do something together after Chris drove Sister Lou home. For that reason, she wouldn't commit the couple to visiting with her today.

"I'll hold you to that." Shari split a look between Chris and Sister Lou. "In the meantime, what should I give up for Lent?"

Chris seemed surprised. "You don't have to give up anything. It's optional."

Shari shrugged her narrow shoulders. "If you two are doing it, I want to do it, too."

Chris lowered his fork and gave Shari a steady look. "Making the decision to fast during Lent is a significant commitment."

Shari nodded. "I understand that."

Do you really? Sister Lou wrapped her hands around her cooling porcelain mug of tea and contemplated her young friend. Her goal wasn't to dampen Shari's enthusiasm. It was to ensure that Shari understood the solemnity of the tradition.

One didn't fast on a whim.

Sister Lou prayed for the right words. "I love your willingness to embrace something that's so important to Chris and me, but I want to make sure you're doing this for the right reasons."

"I'm not doing this just because of you and Chris," Shari assured Sister Lou. "I want to experience this, too."

Sister Lou smiled. "All right, then. Instead of giving up something, perhaps you can join me in modifying our behaviors."

Shari gave her a wary look. "You want me to do that rosary thing with you?"

Sister Lou almost laughed at the dread in the younger woman's voice. Perhaps now the reporter was getting a sense of the seriousness of this season. "Let's start small. Giving up something is far more fulfilling when there's a clear understanding of why you're doing it."

Shari glanced at Chris before returning her attention to Sister Lou. "Okay. What should I do?"

Sister Lou sat back on her seat. "This year, commit to learning more about the Lenten season, and its traditions, including fasting and reconciliation."

Shari looked disappointed. "Learn about Lent? That's it? For forty days?"

Baby steps. "It's a lot more than you may think."

Shari gave a decisive nod, then turned to Chris. "Can we go to a bookstore today so I can buy some books?"

Sister Lou cupped Shari's warm, slender hand where it lay between them on the table. "I have a booklet that I could give you."

Shari looked surprised. "To keep?"

Sister Lou squeezed Shari's hand before releasing her. "Of course, you can keep it."

"Thank you." Unshed tears sparkled in Shari's cocoa eyes. It was as though she still wasn't used to receiving gifts.

Sister Lou tossed her friend a grin to lighten the mood. "Maybe you can give up coffee for Lent next year."

Shari snorted. "I'd rather give up bathing."

Laughter—carefree, high-pitched, and feminine—filled the reception area of the Briar Coast mayor's office early Monday morning.

Mayor Heather Stanley turned away from her administrative assistant's desk and toward the sound of the levity. "Good morning, Kerry."

Kerry Fletcher's laughter left behind a radiant smile. The administrative assistant's light brown eyes sparkled and a faint blush dusted her milky cheeks. "Good morning, Mayor Stanley."

Heather had just placed a report on Kerry's desk, which was outside of her office, when her administrative assistant had appeared as though on cue. Kerry's new boyfriend, Jefferson Manning, was with her. Heather estimated that the couple had been dating for almost a month.

Jefferson worked for a conservative city councilman in Buffalo. In decent traffic, Buffalo's city hall was at least forty minutes from Briar Coast. Despite his comparatively long commute, Jefferson had been chauffeuring Kerry to and from work every day, and met her for lunch on occasion. That meant some days Jefferson wouldn't get to his job until well after eight a.m. and he'd leave his office before five p.m. His boss must have very forgiving office hours. Heather enjoyed a good love story as well as the next employer, but she wouldn't stand for such a blatant lack of commitment from her staff.

"Good morning, Mayor." Jefferson inclined his head toward her. His wavy golden blond hair was expensively cut to complement his sharp features. His dark brown eyes were watchful as though not quite certain of his welcome.

The clock above the office entrance they'd just walked through showed that there was still ten minutes before the eight o'clock hour. Jefferson was welcome for the next nine.

"Hello, Jefferson." Heather made a point of looking at her rose gold Shinola bracelet wristwatch, a gift from her well-off parents, before returning to her office.

Her three-inch navy pumps were silent as she crossed her office's thin wall-to-wall slate gray carpet. She rounded her well-organized walnut wood desk, which stood beside her matching rectangular conference table. Heather settled onto her padded, black faux leather executive chair. She logged back on to her computer and continued reviewing her e-mails. The accumulated flood of transmissions would have been so much greater if she didn't monitor her electronic in-box over the weekend. Still, judging by the time stamp on many of this morning's messages, she wasn't the only early riser.

Several minutes later, Kerry strode into Heather's office. The younger woman's curly strawberry blond hair swung around her plump doll-like features. Her navy blue coatdress skimmed her curvy figure.

Heather completed her final e-mail reply. She took a bracing drink from her second cup of coffee as she watched Kerry deposit a daunting bundle of mail into the black metal in-box that stood on the corner of the desk.

Heather fought the urge to ask her assistant to take the mail and bury it in the landscaping behind the town hall. "Thank you, Kerry."

The bright smile the younger woman tossed her way shimmered with the reflection of young love. It was also infectious. "You're welcome, Mayor Stanley. It's a lot easier getting to work on time now that I'm carpooling with Jeff. And we have so much in common since we both work for local government."

"That's nice, Kerry. I'm happy for you." Heather

kept her smile in place as Kerry gushed. "Let me know as soon as you've received the minutes from Friday's town planning meeting, please."

"Right away, Mayor Stanley." Kerry's curls swung as she turned to stride from the office.

Heather switched her attention to her physical mail. She bit back a groan. Whose bright idea was it for her to handle her own correspondence?

Oh, that's right. It was mine.

She grabbed a handful of correspondence off the top of the stack and started sorting through it. A plain white business envelope stood out from among the customized stationery, postcards, and oversized manila mailers.

The cheap envelope was addressed to her only by name, *Mayor Heather Stanley.* There was no stamp. No return address. Still the mail piece was eerily familiar. She'd received correspondence like this one last Wednesday.

Heather retrieved her black ink retractable pen from her desktop. It shook in her grip as she used it to open this latest mysterious letter. Dread weighted her muscles. With trembling fingers, she pulled out the plain white eight-and-a-half-by-eleven sheet of copier paper. It also had a disturbing familiarity. Heather read the brief message. Her heart lodged in her throat. This second note was verbatim to the first. *Outsider, if you know what's good for you, don't run for reelection. Leave Briar Coast.*

Chapter 2

The threat was direct, succinct, and chilling. The message left no hint of the culprit's identity. Who would send these anonymous notes?

Heather had dismissed the first one as a sick prank. Now that the threats were multiplying, what should she think? Why didn't they want her to run for a second term? How were these envelopes getting mixed in with her mail? Who was behind the threats?

Heather took a shaky breath. The scent of hazelnut reminded her of the still-warm mug of coffee faithfully waiting on her desk. She took another deep drink and a flare of anger and outrage incinerated her trepidation.

Who did this sniveling coward think he or she was? If this spineless troll didn't want her to run for a second term, he could tell her to her face instead of hiding behind plain paper and laser printers.

Just as she had with the first threat, Heather crumbled the letter and slammed it into the black plastic wastebasket beneath her desk. She did the same with the envelope. The mail piece didn't deserve the dignity of being recycled. Heather saw red. Her pulse raced. Her breath quickened. She'd long ago vowed not to be intimidated by anyone ever again. She wouldn't allow anything—or anyone—to allow her to break that promise to herself, especially not this gutless vermin.

The knock on her open office door made her jump. Heather's head jerked up and her gaze found her chief of staff, Arneeka Laguda, framed in her doorway.

Arneeka looked concerned by Heather's reaction. "Do you need me to come back in ten minutes?"

"No, please come in." Heather pulled her chair farther under her table and sat straighter. "I was deep in thought about something unrelated to our meeting."

Arneeka strode into the office past the tall walnut wood bookcase against the wall. She sat on one of the three black cloth guest chairs in front of Heather's desk. Her gold hijab, the veil traditionally worn by Muslim women, which covered their head and chest, complemented her olive complexion as well as her navy ankle-length skirt suit.

"The most critical event on your schedule for today is your budget meeting with the Board of Education." Arneeka's almond-shaped dark chocolate eyes pinned Heather to her chair. "Do you have everything you need for that meeting?"

Heather drew her manila folder on the Briar Coast Board of Education's proposed budget from the black wire incline file on her desk. Stalling for time, she opened the folder and studied the first sheet of paper.

She'd discussed the data with her finance and management director, and had spent hours reviewing it on her own. Despite that, none of the information made sense this morning. Heather fisted her right hand. The two written threats she'd received had rattled her more than she'd wanted them to. Her hands itched with the need to pummel the spineless worm who'd sent them.

She closed the folder and met Arneeka's gaze. "I'm going to ask Opal to attend that meeting in my place."

Opal Lorrie, her administration's director of finance and management, had developed the numbers and was keenly aware of the figures' impact on the Board of Education as well as the town.

Surprise widened Arneeka's eyes in her round face. "Is something wrong?"

Heather frowned, immediately defensive. "No. Why?"

Arneeka looked dubious. "It's not like you to have someone attend a meeting in your stead."

The younger woman had worked on Heather's election campaign for a year. She'd been chief of staff for the past four years of Heather's five-year term. During that time, Arneeka had come to know her very well.

Heather worked harder to appear relaxed and in control. She didn't want anyone to know about the threats, not even members of her staff. She couldn't afford to seem vulnerable. "I know it's out of character for me, but as you noted, this is a critical meeting. Opal knows the numbers inside and out. She'll do a better job with this meeting than I could."

"Will you let Opal know or should I?"

Heather couldn't read Arneeka's expression. Did her chief of staff buy her reasoning? "I'll call her."

"All right." Arneeka stood. "If there's nothing else, I'll get back to work."

"You are working, Arneeka, and I appreciate your help."

"Whatever I can do to be of assistance." Arneeka's full, red lips curved in a gentle smile, then she disappeared beyond Heather's door.

Heather turned to stare at her computer monitor. That's what she needed; someone to help her find the coward behind the threats she'd received. Someone who wasn't in her administration. Someone who was discreet. Someone she could trust.

"How did you get that nun to help you with your news stories?" The male voice came from behind Shari Monday morning.

For the moment, Shari ignored the interruption. Her fingers flew over her computer keyboard in her cubicle at the *Telegraph*'s office. She had plenty of experience tuning out meaningless background noise, starting with her years in the foster care system and then her work in previous newsrooms. She couldn't risk breaking her train of thought as she added critical details to her story on Briar Coast's upcoming budget battles. The background information came courtesy of Opal Lorrie, Briar Coast's director of finance and management.

Of course she had to remain impartial. She had a responsibility to cover both sides of the conflict. But from where Shari sat, there were definite rights and wrongs. She hoped her readers would recognize that, too.

Shari saved her computer file before spinning her gray padded chair to face her uninvited visitor. She'd hoped that her surprise guest had grown bored and left. Sadly, her hopes had been in vain.

Harold "Don't Call Me Hal" Beckett stood at the threshold of her cubicle. He was the newest reporter on the *Telegraph*'s staff. He also was the most irritating. Shari paused a moment to fantasize about erecting a force field that would prevent the rookie from entering her cubicle. Ever. Again.

"Why are you here, Hal?" Shari used the rookie's hated nickname. She'd hate it, too. It was a creepy reminder of the crazy computer from the movie *2001: A Space Odyssey*.

"How many times do I have to tell you not to call me that?" Harold sounded tense.

"Are you yelling at me or just trying to be heard above the newsroom noise?" Shari raised her voice as well, pitching it above the clacking keyboards, shouted conversations, and ringing telephones.

Harold glowered. "How did you and that nun start working on news stories together?"

Shari ignored his question. "Sister Lou's not a nun. She's a sister. Nuns are cloistered. She's not."

"Whatever." Harold leaned back against her gray cubicle wall and crossed his arms. "How'd you get the setup?"

The rookie looked like he was prepared to hang out in her cube for a while. That was when it occurred to Shari that she could work on her patience for Lent. She immediately dismissed the idea, though. Committing to that specific goal would be setting herself up for failure.

Shari scowled at the twentysomething recent graduate of the State University of New York at Buffalo. Not for the first time, Shari wondered how the Texan had ended up first in Buffalo and now in Briar Coast. She'd add that to her list of Questions About Hal, which included the source of his perpetual tan.

Harold was perhaps five-foot-nine or -ten, not counting the assist from the two-inch heels on his black wingtips. He was slim—almost thin, with narrow shoulders under a plain white cotton shirt. His long, thin legs were encased in skinny navy slacks. His matching suit jacket was probably still in his cubicle. His curly dark brown hair looked finger combed.

Shari jerked her chin toward his red power tie. "Is that silk?"

"Yes, it is." Harold smoothed the material lovingly.

"Who wears silk in a newsroom on purpose? Aren't you afraid the newsprint from the papers will stain it?"

Harold's smug expression turned sour. "Are you going to answer my question?"

"No. Go away." Shari spun her wheeled chair back to her computer. She reached for the white porcelain mug her boss, Diego, had given to her as a gift. The mug had the question, CAN I QUOTE YOU? stenciled in black type across the side. It was her third coffee of the morning. The warm hazelnut scent comforted her.

"Why not? Are you afraid you'll lose your cushy beat?" Harold's taunt hit its intended mark.

Cushy? Shari's hands shook with her rising temper. She carefully returned her mug to her tan modular desk. Shari relived the anguish she'd felt after her previous boss had fired her for pursuing her first murder investigation. She flashed back to her fear when she and Sister Lou had chased down a murder suspect less than three months ago.

Shari met Harold's eyes over her shoulder. "What makes you think I have a *cushy* beat?"

"Come off it." Harold rolled his light brown eyes.

"It's obvious from reading those reports that Sister Lou told you exactly what to write. You just put your byline on the stories. I wish that I had a sweet deal like that."

Harold's stupidity rendered Shari speechless—but not for long.

"Do you often speak when you don't know what you're talking about?" Shari knew the thoughts running through her head were inappropriate for the upcoming Lenten season. She had less than three days to clear them from her mind.

That wasn't enough time.

Shari watched, incredulous, as Harold sauntered even farther into her cubicle.

He slouched onto her guest chair. "You don't think that other people have figured out that all you're doing is waiting for Sister Lou to give you a guaranteed front page article and all the information you'd need to write it? People aren't stupid."

"I can think of at least one person who is." Shari considered the intruder in her cubicle.

Thanks to Perry O'Toole, the newspaper's former managing editor, Harold had had an internship with *The Briar Coast Telegraph* throughout his six-year college career. Perry had given Harold a lot of leeway as an intern. He'd ignored Harold's missed deadlines and reworked the worst of his articles. According to the reporters who'd been on staff at the time, Perry's leniency toward Harold had hurt the *Telegraph*'s image and damaged the staff's morale. Nevertheless, the former managing editor had given Harold a full-time job after the young man's graduation. Perry probably thought his generosity would curry favor with Harold's very wealthy and very well connected parents. It hadn't.

Despite Harold's comparatively charmed life, he

never appeared satisfied. Take their exchange this morning as an example. Instead of covering his assigned beat—the upcoming election ballot issues—Harold was prowling around, looking for a way to pounce on Shari's stories.

Not as long as there was breath in her body.

Resentment left a bitter taste in Shari's mouth. "I helped Sister Lou and her nephew, Chris, with those murder investigations and brought those stories to the *Telegraph*. No one *handed* anything to me. And no one *ever* does my work. Can you say the same?"

Her words didn't have an effect on Harold. Jealousy continued to mar his thin face. "I've been working here longer than you have. I was an intern each of the six years I was in college, but Diego didn't care. He still gave *you*, an outsider, the prime stories."

"Diego didn't *give* me anything, Hal." Quick, short breaths helped Shari keep her tone under control. Her cubicle's familiar scents of hazelnut coffee and fresh newsprint from the day's *Telegraph* and its chief competitor, *Buffalo Today*, were calming. "Now get out of my cube and work your own beat."

Shari again turned her back on the rookie reporter—but he didn't leave.

"My beat sucks."

"Your beat's what you make of it." Shari had learned that as a cub reporter, covering community meetings and neighborhood events in Chicago. Everyone wanted the police beat or politics, but newbies had to earn those.

"The election is almost a year away." Harold's grousing was working Shari's nerves.

Diego had assigned Harold to cover the candidates and ballot issues for the September primary and the

November general election. Shari would have sold a limb to have had that assignment when she was fresh out of college.

Shari unclenched her teeth and faced the rookie again. "Neither the primary nor the general will come any faster in my cubicle, so leave. Now."

Harold gave her another baleful glare before rising. Shari watched to make sure this time he left.

Newsroom gossips were obsessed with Harold's Norman Rockwell–esque upbringing. He came from a politically well-connected family with deep roots in Texas. How did it feel to know you had a home? How did it feel to belong somewhere?

And if his family and home were in Texas, what was he doing in Briar Coast, New York? Granted Diego and Mayor Heather Stanley were transplanted Texans who'd made their home in Briar Coast. Nevertheless, Shari added this entry to her mental list of Questions About Hal.

Shari returned to her computer but struggled to get back into her story. Her exchange with Harold had been more unsettling than she'd realized. The rookie had made it clear that he was after her beat. Shari didn't doubt that if Harold wanted to, he could take it from her. Media outlets salivated to have reporters with pedigrees like his. Shari couldn't let her guard down.

Chapter 3

Heather looked up at the knock on her open door late Monday morning. Opal Lorrie, her director of finance and management, stood in the threshold. Heather rose and circled her desk to meet Opal halfway.

She felt a chill in her office—or was she imagining it? Either way, Heather believed another cup of coffee would help her once she and Opal were done with their briefing. "Thank you for taking the Board of Ed budget meeting for me. I hope I haven't disrupted your day too much."

Opal shook her head, causing her bone-straight brown tresses to swing behind her slim shoulders. Her hair was a shade or two lighter than Heather's chestnut brown. A smile softened her peaches-and-cream expression even as her large brown eyes remained serious. "I should be thanking you. You've given me a good excuse to skip two meetings that I don't need to attend. I've asked Penelope to sit in on the third one for me." Opal referred to her direct report, Penelope del Castillo, the town's finance manager.

The nagging regret that had been plaguing Heather for most of the morning disappeared. "I'm glad I could help, even if it was unintentional." She checked her wristwatch. It was almost nine a.m. The meeting was scheduled for ten. "You're much more familiar with the numbers. You'll do a better presentation of the proposed budget than I could and you'll have better answers to any questions they may have." Especially since the latest threat she'd received that morning still had her rattled.

"I'm comfortable with the information, but I wasn't expecting to go to this meeting." Opal gave Heather a sheepish smile. "I don't think my gray parka will set the right tone and I don't have my car with me."

Heather eyed the other woman critically. Opal was slim and stood about five-foot-eight or -nine inches tall in her black flats. She'd accessorized a heavy brown knit sweater and brown slacks with chunky gold earrings and a matching necklace.

"You look great." Heather crossed to her black metal coatrack in the corner of her office beside the bookcase. She freed her scarlet wool winter coat from one of the hooks, then returned to Opal. "But you're right about your parka. Borrow my coat."

"Are you serious?" Opal's brown eyes sparkled. "I love your coat."

"So do I." Heather smiled, offering her coat to Opal. The garment was *wonderfully* heavy in Heather's arms, reminding her of how warm and cozy the coat was even on the coldest winter day that upstate New York could offer. "Try it on."

"You don't have to ask me twice." Opal shrugged into Heather's coat. "Oh, so warm. What do you think?"

"It's a little long since I'm taller than you, but other than that, it's a good fit."

Opal's eyes twinkled with mischief as she pointedly dropped her gaze to Heather's three-inch pumps. "You know, I think I need more professional-looking shoes."

Heather propped her fists on her hips. "Stop while you're ahead."

Opal chuckled. "Can't blame a woman for trying. I love your clothes, especially your shoes."

"Thanks. Well, that part's settled." Heather circled her desk and pulled open her right bottom drawer. She retrieved her purse and dug out a set of keys. The metal was cool to her touch. She offered the keys to Opal. "Take my car."

Opal's brown eyes widened. She repeated her previous question. "Are you serious?"

"Of course I'm serious."

"Thank you." Opal accepted Heather's keys. "My fiancé brought me to work. My car's in the shop."

"It's not a problem." Heather remained standing behind her desk. "I trust you. Besides, you're doing me a favor. We really need the Board of Ed to understand the figures and impacts that we're facing. Unless they can come up with a better cost-saving plan, we need them to support our austere proposal."

Opal wrapped her fingers around the car keys and met Heather's gaze. "I know these preliminary budget meetings are important, especially since our opponents will use these numbers against us in the election."

The muscles in Heather's neck and shoulders tightened. Her gaze dropped to her wastebasket. The metallic taste of fear coated her tongue. "I haven't decided whether I'm going to run for reelection."

Opal laughed. "Everyone knows that you're going to run again. You love this town as much as I do, and I was born and raised here. You just moved here seven years ago."

Outsider. The word played on a loop in Heather's mind, growing louder. "Does it bother you that I was elected mayor even though I'm not from Briar Coast?"

"Of course not." Opal seemed surprised. "I worked on your campaign. I saw up close and personally that you love this town and the people who live here."

"I do." Heather's voice was low. She allowed herself to drop onto her chair.

"Is something wrong?" Opal's dark eyebrows knitted with concern.

"No, I just . . ." Heather shook her head. "I want to do what's best for Briar Coast and our community."

"You are. Believe me. And on the few occasions when you've needed to make a different decision, you've had five very confident women on your executive team who've been happy to let you know." Opal's smile softened the pronouncement.

Heather had already determined that the person behind the gutless threats was a coward, too afraid to confront her, even in writing. That description didn't fit anyone on her staff.

Her gaze was drawn to the walnut wood conference table in the corner of her office beside her desk. That's where they held their executive meetings, with everyone freely expressing their policy opinions.

Well, everyone except Kerry. Heather had to prompt her assistant to share her thoughts. The young woman didn't seem interested in politics, which made Heather curious about why Kerry had applied for the job—and what Kerry and her politically ambitious new boyfriend talked about.

"You're right." Heather returned Opal's smile. "The fact that you're all outspoken is one of the many reasons I hired all of you. Thanks, Opal."

"Of course. And thanks for the loan of your coat and car. I'll bring them both back safely." Opal turned toward the doorway. "In the meantime, there are some tasks that I want to complete before the meeting."

Heather frowned as she watched Opal disappear through her doorway. If the threats weren't coming from someone on her staff, how were the unmarked, unstamped letters getting into her mail?

Hours later, a movement in Heather's doorway claimed her attention. She paused in the middle of a tense telephone conversation with the Briar Coast Town Council president.

Kerry stood just inside her office. She was in the company of two Briar Coast County sheriff's deputies, one male and one female. The deputies gripped their brown felt campaign hats in their fists. They wore matching heavy brown faux leather jackets over their identical uniforms of tan shirts, black ties, and spruce green gabardine pants.

Her administrative assistant looked puzzled, but the deputies' somber expressions sent chills up Heather's spine.

"Ian, I'll have to call you back." Heather cradled her beige telephone receiver without waiting for the council president's response. She rose to her feet, giving Kerry a reassuring look before turning to the deputies. "Good afternoon, deputies. How can I help you?"

"Madame Mayor, I'm Sheriff's Deputy Fran Cole." The female deputy gestured toward herself with the hat she held in her right hand. She then waved the hat to indicate the tall, bald man beside her. "This is my partner, Sheriff's Deputy Ted Tate."

Sheriff's deputies didn't pop into her office on a regular basis. What was going on?

Heather took a deep breath in an effort to manage her increasing anxiety. The scent of the late winter day seemed to have followed the deputies into her office. "I know who you are, Deputy Cole, Deputy Tate. I congratulated both of you on your investigation into Autumn Tassler's murder three and a half months ago." Although everyone in Briar Coast knew the lion's share of the credit belonged to Sister Lou, a member of the Congregation of the Sisters of St. Hermione of Ephesus.

Deputy Ted Tate beamed as though pleased that the mayor remembered them. "Thanks, Madame Mayor. Could we speak with you in private?" His pale gray gaze settled pointedly on Kerry.

Ted's request escalated Heather's discomfort. What could they need to speak with her about in private? Heather glanced at her wastebasket, which held the letter she'd crumpled and discarded that morning.

"Of course." She summoned a smile for her administrative assistant. "Thank you for your help, Kerry. Could you close the door, please?"

Kerry nodded before leaving, pulling the door closed behind her.

Heather gestured toward the cushioned chairs in front of her desk. She waited until the deputies were seated before settling on her chair again. "What's this about, Deputies?"

"Your finance and management director, Opal Lorrie." Fran's bottle green eyes watched her closely. The deputy's unruly ash blond hair was scrapped back from her thin milky features and gathered into a bun at the nape of her long neck. "Madame Mayor, I'm sorry to inform you that we found Ms. Lorrie's body in the Board of Ed's parking lot less than an hour ago."

Heather gasped. Her right hand slapped against her open mouth, covering her parted lips. Her ears were buzzing. Her eyes were bulging. Her muscles trembled with shock. "Opal?" She forced her friend's name out on a pant. "Are you sure it's Opal? What happened?"

In the back of her mind, Heather had begun to wonder about Opal's return. She should have been back by now. Heather thought that perhaps the meeting had run long or her finance director had stopped for lunch. The Briar Coast Café wasn't far from the Board of Education's building.

Ted ran his large right hand over his clean-shaven head. His narrowed eyes set in his wide, craggy face were as watchful as his partner's. "It looks like she stumbled on her way down the steps leading to the parking lot. She fell and broke her neck."

"Stumbled?" Heather frowned at the deputies. "But Opal was wearing flats. How could she have stumbled in them?"

Fran shrugged her narrow shoulders. "It's possible. If she was rushing down the steps, she might have missed her footing."

"Rushing?" Heather didn't buy it. But what was the alternative, that Opal had been pushed down the stairs? By whom? Heather's gaze was again drawn to her wastebasket.

"Her body was found at the foot of the stairs." Ted sounded dismissive. "From all indications, it appears that she tripped on her way down. The scene looks like an unfortunate accident."

"We're very sorry for your loss," Fran added. "We were told by some of the witnesses that Ms. Lorrie was on-site for a meeting you were supposed to attend this morning."

"That's right." Heather blinked away the sting of tears. She sniffed, catching the scent of the Italian dressing she'd poured on the chicken salad lunch she'd rushed through earlier. "It was a meeting to discuss the Board of Education's preliminary budget numbers. I was supposed to attend but asked Opal to go instead. She has—had—a much better grasp of the numbers than I do."

Fran nodded. "A couple of people at the meeting mentioned that Ms. Lorrie was wearing your coat."

Heather felt another chill along her spine. "That's right. I loaned her my coat and my car to get to the meeting. Her car's in the shop. Her fiancé drove her to work."

Opal's fiancé. Heather's heart hurt. This tragedy will destroy him and Opal's family.

"We can drive you to the Board of Ed to get your car, if you'd like," Fran offered. "We recovered Ms. Lorrie's umbrella and handbag. We'll need to get those to her next of kin. You can have your coat back."

"No, please leave that with Opal." Heather waved a dismissive hand. "I'll provide you with the emergency contact information from her employment forms so you can notify her family."

Another pain contracted in her chest as Heather thought about Opal's parents, brothers, sisters, nieces, and nephews. They were all so close.

"We'd appreciate that." Ted reached forward, offering Heather his plain white business card, which featured the Briar Coast County Sheriff's Office logo centered at the top.

Heather took the card from the deputy. "You mentioned that you found Opal's umbrella and her handbag. Was her briefcase with her?"

Heather flashed back to the memory of Opal stopping by her office on her way to the budget meeting. The other woman was still beaming at wearing Heather's coat. Her long dark hair had swung behind her shoulders as she'd circled to model it. It had fit her so well. At the time, the finance director had balanced her bag on her right shoulder. She'd carried her umbrella in her right hand and her briefcase in her left.

"We didn't find a briefcase with Ms. Lorrie." Ted exchanged a look with Fran.

Fran nodded in agreement. "Maybe she left it in the meeting room."

"Maybe." But Heather knew Opal hadn't forgotten her briefcase. It would have held important notes. Opal wouldn't have left those behind.

Could that be what had happened? Her finance

director had realized she'd forgotten her briefcase. She'd turned, intending to hurry back up to the conference room, but tripped on a step instead. Heather still didn't buy it. Her gaze again slid to her wastebasket. Opal's tragic death couldn't possibly be connected to the threats Heather had received.

Could it?

Chapter 4

Shari wrapped up her interview with Arneeka Laguda, the mayor's chief of staff, and stepped into the corridor in time to see the sheriff's deputies leaving the mayor's office down the hall. The pair crossed to the double glass doors that led out of the office suite.

Why had the deputies met with the mayor? Curiosity spurred Shari down the hall, but Fran and Ted were too far for her to catch their attention.

She quickened her steps and stopped in front of Heather's administrative assistant. Kerry's walnut wood desk sat behind a raised white Formica counter on which stood a lined sign-in sheet, a black ceramic pen-and-pencil holder, and a square crystal bowl of mixed candies.

Shari pocketed a handful of the sweets. "Hi, Kerry. Why were the deputies with the mayor?"

Kerry shifted her attention from the glass doors through which the deputies had exited to Shari. "I don't know. They wanted to meet with her privately." Kerry sounded as curious as Shari felt.

Shari glanced at the open door to the mayor's office. "Does she have a few minutes for me?"

Kerry clicked her computer mouse and her monitor's image changed to reveal a very colorful electronic calendar. She scanned the screen. "Maybe ten minutes. Her afternoon's pretty full."

"Thanks, Kerry." On the sign-in sheet, Shari scribbled her name, and the date and time before circling Kerry's work area. She knocked briefly on the mayor's open door, but Heather didn't hear her.

The mayor's office was spacious, much bigger than Diego's office at the *Telegraph*. The moment Shari crossed into the room, a heavy, solemn silence engulfed her. It hovered over the space like a dark entity and mocked the bright, natural light from the afternoon sun that shone through the open venetian blinds.

Heather had turned her chair, putting her back to the door. Her thick chestnut hair fell in straight tresses past her shoulders. She appeared to be staring out of the window beside her desk. Shari stepped back. Should she intrude on this moment with the mayor or quietly slip away?

What would Sister Lou do?

Shari stepped forward. "Excuse me, Mayor Stanley. May I have a few minutes of your time?"

Heather jumped at Shari's first words. With her back still to the door, the mayor lifted her hands to her face. What was that sound? Was the mayor sniffling?

Finally, Heather spun her chair around. "Sure, I have a couple of minutes. How can I help you?" Her voice was thick with tears.

Shock struck Shari like an electrical charge. Heather's

violet eyes were red. Her porcelain cheeks and the tip of her elegant nose were pink. The flush was even more vivid against her navy suit jacket.

Concerned, Shari crossed the room in long, brisk strides. She gripped the back of the middle padded guest chair. "Deputy Cole and Deputy Tate just left your office. I wondered—"

"Opal is dead." Heather looked dismayed to have blurted out the news of her finance and management director's death to a newspaper reporter. Her lips trembled. She pulled a tissue from the box beside her desk and turned away to dry her eyes.

"Opal?" Shari's mind went blank.

Heather nodded her confirmation, apparently too overcome to speak.

Shari's eyes stung. She collapsed onto the visitor's chair. "But . . . I just spoke with her. This morning. She verified numbers for my budget article."

The comment was too ridiculous. Shari knew it. She'd tried but she couldn't stop the words from spilling from her mouth.

"I know." Thankfully, Heather didn't sound put off by Shari's inane response. She dried her eyes with the tissue in her left hand as she offered Shari the box with her right. "I can't believe it, either."

Shari leaned closer to accept a tissue. If Opal's death was affecting her so strongly, she couldn't bear to imagine the pain Heather felt. She searched her mind for words to express her condolences. "I'm so very sorry for your loss. Opal was very kind and very smart. She was always patient with me when I called for information for a story."

Heather's unsteady smile softened the expression on her elegant features. "She had a surprising sense of humor and playfulness beneath her studious demeanor."

Shari took a steadying breath. The scent of Italian salad dressing tickled her nose. The mayor must have had another working lunch. "Can I ask what happened?"

Heather balanced her elbows on her desk. She pressed the heels of her hands against her eyes. Her long, slender fingers trembled. Shari had never seen the iron-willed public servant so shaken, so vulnerable.

The mayor sat back, lowering her hands to her lap. Her eyes were damp. She pulled another tissue from the box and wiped her nose. "Opal attended the budget meeting for the Board of Ed this morning. The deputies think she fell down the stairs on her way back to the parking lot."

Shari noticed an odd note in Heather's voice. Did the mayor doubt the deputies' theory? The law enforcement officers had been wrong before. In fact, they'd been wrong a lot. "What makes the deputies think it was an accident? Was it the position of the body?"

The atmosphere in the room shifted. Grief became something tense and angry. The expression in Heather's violet eyes hardened with suspicion. "Are you interviewing me for a story?"

"What?" Shari was startled. "No."

"I thought you were genuinely saddened by Opal's death."

"I am—"

"I thought you really cared about my team as *people*."

"I do—"

"I should have known you were just after a story." Heather spat the accusation as though the words were rancid meat. "What's that old newspaper saying? 'If it bleeds, it leads.'"

Shari stiffened on her chair. The attack surprised her. "Excuse me, Mayor Stanley, but your reaction is out of proportion to this situation—"

"Get out."

Shari's eyes widened. "What's wrong?"

"What's wrong?" The mayor's tone was almost a growl. "What's wrong is that while I'm mourning the loss of someone I considered a friend, you're exploiting that grief for a story."

It was understandable that Opal's death would have traumatized the mayor. She hadn't even had a chance to tell her staff yet, but Heather's reaction to Shari's innocent question seemed extreme. Shari was concerned for the mayor's emotional state. She considered the other woman's blazing eyes, flushed cheeks, and thinned lips. She could hear her quickened breaths. How would Sister Lou handle the mayor?

Shari was a convenient target. Was that the reason the mayor was lashing out at her? "I'm not exploiting your grief. I'm sharing it. Opal's death has affected me. A lot of other people in the community are going to feel the same way. She was well respected and well liked in Briar Coast."

Heather looked away. She took a shaky breath before meeting Shari's eyes again. "I don't have time to discuss this further. My staff needs to hear about Opal, and I want them to hear it directly from me."

Shari stood. "Opal's death is a great loss for our community. I'm going to cover this tragedy to honor her memory. I'm sorry if that offends you."

If looks could kill, Shari would have been struck

down in the mayor's office. "Do what you think you have to." Heather's tone was dismissive. She leaned forward as though trying to see around Shari and raised her voice. "Kerry?"

Shari looked over her shoulder as Heather's administrative assistant appeared in the doorway.

Kerry looked from Shari to the mayor. "Yes, Heather?"

"Could you get everyone together, please, and ask Penelope to join us?" Heather gestured toward the conference table in her office. "We need to have a staff meeting."

Kerry disappeared again.

Shari turned back to the mayor. "I'm sorry that I upset you. I didn't mean to. You have my number if you—"

"I won't need it."

Shari felt as though Heather had bitten her fingers. She walked out of the office in more confusion and with more questions than when she'd entered. What was it about Opal's accident that prompted such a fierce reaction from the mayor? She seemed to feel guilty about Opal's death. But why would she?

Heather rose from her seat behind her desk as Kerry led the rest of her executive team into her office Monday afternoon. The short procession ended at her conference table. Grief and dread weighted her body. In contrast, her team's movements were brisk as they moved to their usual seats around the table. Their body language expressed confidence that they could handle whatever emergency had brought about this unscheduled summons.

The lump in Heather's throat scalded her. They had no idea.

Heather crossed her office to close the door. Her movements were stiff and awkward. She sensed their curious stares as she collected her box of tissues from her desk.

"Thank you for dropping everything without notice to meet with me." Heather took her seat at the head of the table.

Chief of Staff Arneeka Laguda was on Heather's left. Tian Lu, the communications director, sat beside Arneeka. The petite woman adjusted the jacket of her black pantsuit, which she'd coupled with a white blouse. Yolanda Barnes, senior legal counsel, always took the chair at the foot of the table, directly across from Heather. Her warm brown features were unreadable. Kerry's chair was on Yolanda's left and closest to the door. She seemed nervous as her gaze bounced between Heather and the table's surface. Penelope had taken the seat to Heather's right. That had been Opal's usual seat.

Kerry leaned forward, drawing Heather's attention. "I don't think Opal's back from the Board of Ed meeting yet."

Heather's administrative assistant spared a quick glance for Penelope. As the statement left her lips, the look in Kerry's powder blue eyes transitioned from confusion to shock and finally denial. Heather struggled with those same emotions. She blinked back more tears. Her cabinet—her friends—needed her to be strong.

Heather looked around the table at her small but mighty team. With the exception of Penelope who Opal had hired after the election, everyone had worked together since the early days of Heather's campaign. They were as close as a family. How would she find the words to tell them that they'd lost a valued member of that family?

"I received devastating news a few minutes ago. I'm still trying to process it myself." Heather met the eyes of each person at the table. "I'm so sorry to have to tell you this. Our friend Opal is dead."

Had her words been too blunt? Should she have taken more time to ease into the tragic news?

Had Opal's death been her fault? Heather shivered in reaction to the wayward thought.

Shock blanked the expressions around the table. After a brief, stunned pause, their responses were swift and stark as they spoke over each other.

"What? When?" Yolanda's brown eyes widened in disbelief.

"This must be a mistake." Arneeka shook her head as though trying to reject the news.

Heather slid the box of tissues to Arneeka. Her chief of staff took a tissue, then passed it down the table to the others.

"I can't believe it." Kerry's hand jerked up to cover her mouth.

"She's dead?" Tian's almond-shaped ebony eyes pleaded for a retraction. She took a tissue, then shoved it toward Yolanda.

"What. Happened?" Penelope spoke between sobs. Her wide brown eyes were wet in her round, youthful face. Her dark brown hair was scraped back into a bun at the nape of her neck.

Heather drew a steadying breath. Her office still smelled of the light Italian dressing she'd used on the salad she'd brought from home. Sunlight poured into the room from the windows behind her desk to dance incongruously above the conference table.

"A short time ago, two deputies came to my office to inform me of Opal's . . ." Heather stopped, shaking her head. She just couldn't say the word again. Not now. She continued. "Opal had attended the Board of Ed's budget meeting this morning. The deputies think she fell down the stairs to the rear parking lot after the meeting."

The meeting she was supposed to attend. Heather's gaze was drawn to the black plastic wastebasket under her desk.

"She slipped?" Tian's startled interjection broke the heavy silence.

Heather brought her attention back to the table. "The deputies said her neck . . . was broken in the fall."

A collective gasp rose up from the table. Heather cupped her hand over Penelope's left forearm as the other woman sobbed quietly beside her.

Yolanda used a tissue to dry her tears. "Has her family been notified?"

Heather swallowed past the lump that was burning her throat. "I just left a voice mail message for Deputy Fran Cole with Opal's parents' telephone number and home address."

Kerry sniffed, wiping her nose with one of the tissues. "I'll make arrangements to send Opal's family flowers from all of us."

"That would be very nice. Thank you, Kerry." Heather wiped a stray tear from her cheek. "I'd also like to send her fiancé a condolence card."

Kerry made a note on her writing tablet. "I'll take care of that, too."

"Thank you." Heather turned back to the rest of

the group. "Please speak with your staffs right away. They need to hear from us before they hear or read about it in the media. I'll send you information on our available grief counseling services. The sessions are confidential and voluntary, of course, but I encourage everyone to consider contacting a counselor. We've known Opal for years. We may not even realize how deeply her death is affecting us."

"If I should get any media calls, how should I respond to their questions?" Tian wiped her nose.

Heather's mind flashed back to Shari's pseudo-interview. "Let's get ahead of this, please. Could you prepare a statement explaining that we're all grieving Opal's loss? Our thoughts and prayers are with her family and fiancé, of course. She was our friend as well as our colleague. But the media should direct specific questions to the sheriff's office." She squeezed Penelope's forearm before letting her hand slip away. "Penny will be our interim director of finance and management."

Yolanda's eyes softened with compassion. "Penny, let us know if there's *anything* we can do to help you."

That kind of empathy was characteristic of her team. It always reinforced for Heather that she'd brought the right individuals together to serve Briar Coast. And it always went to her heart. "This is a difficult time for everyone in our office, but we'll get through it together. Let's keep our doors open for each other."

Arneeka sniffed. "Whatever we need, we'll be there for each other."

"Any questions or final thoughts?" Heather looked at each member of her team. It seemed that they were still processing this painful event. "Please let me know if I should meet with your individual staffs or if we need to bring everyone together. Whatever you think would be best."

Heather's heart broke as she watched her friends leave. Their movements were heavy and uncertain. Their shoulders slumped. She forced herself to turn away from the sight and cross back to her desk. As she dropped onto her chair, her gaze fell to the waste-basket beside her calves.

She had no reason to believe the threatening messages that had been sent to her had anything to do with Opal's death. Still she couldn't shake the nagging sensation that the two were somehow linked. She dug through the used tissues, soiled napkins, chewing gum wrappers, and the orange peels from her midmorning snack until she spotted the crumpled note and envelope. She smoothed the items, then shoved them into her purse, which she kept locked in her bottom desk drawer.

Now what? How would she prove—or disprove—a connection between these threats and Opal's death?

Chapter 5

"Afternoon, Shari. Cup o' joe?"

Deputy Ted Tate's offer stopped Shari midstride as she approached the deputy's desk Monday afternoon. Her gaze swung to the homey and pristine coffee station in the quaint little cottage that masqueraded as the Briar Coast County Sheriff's Office.

The bullpen's silver marble flooring and sunny yellow walls created a bright and cheerful environment. However, in the six months that she'd known Ted and his partner, Deputy Fran Cole, they'd done their best to make her feel unwelcome. Now the taciturn Ted was offering her coffee. Their relationship had undergone a complete one-hundred-and-eighty-degree shift since they'd worked together to catch the Briar Coast Cabin Resort owner's killer, and Shari had given them perhaps more credit than they deserved in her *Telegraph* article.

Shari noted Ted's disarmingly sincere expression. Her editor had wanted her to be on better terms with the deputies, but it was never a good idea for a journalist to get cozy with the people on their beat. It would result in biased coverage, which would be unfair to her readers.

"No thanks, Ted." Declining coffee was difficult, but if the deputies' java tasted as good as it smelled, she'd lose all objectivity.

Shari exchanged a nod of greeting with Fran, whose desk backed up to Ted's. There wasn't even a speck of dust on Fran's desk. Her manila folders were neatly filed on her credenza. Pens and pencils stood in a black plastic holder. Her coffee mug waited within easy reach of her right hand as she typed on her computer keyboard.

In his opposing space, Ted's desk looked like the victim of a burglary. Pens and pencils rolled across various layers of papers and manila folders. A dried coffee mug ring lay like a memento beside his computer keyboard. He seemed to be making some inroads on the chaos, though. His bronze nameplate was now visible on his desk. Shari hadn't realized he had one.

"Then have some pie." Ted gestured over his shoulder toward the coffee station with his cracked and stained cream ceramic mug. The scent of warm apple pie floated around the room. The pastry sat in a bakery box branded with the cursive blue logo of the Briar Coast Café.

Shari gestured toward Ted who sat slumped on his gray cushioned swivel chair. The deputy's tan shirt and spruce green gabardine pants seemed a bit loose on him. "Have you lost more weight? What's your secret to resisting the desserts you guys get every day?"

Ted reached under the small mound of papers and folders on his desk and pulled out an orange. "Fruits and vegetables, but I'd rather have pie."

"You're doing great, Ted," Fran chimed in with encouragement before returning to whatever she was typing on her computer.

Ted blushed. "Thanks, Frannie."

Shari hadn't missed the admiration in Fran's bottle green eyes. She didn't think Ted had missed it, either. "*Frannie?*"

Ted's blush deepened. "That was a slip." He shoved the orange back under the pile of papers on his desk.

Fran ignored their exchange. She hit a few keys on her keyboard before giving Shari her attention. "Have a seat."

"Thanks." The invitation to sit was another first for Shari in the sheriff's office.

Shari unfastened the black buttons of her midcalf-length, emerald green wool winter coat. She folded the coat on the back of the gray fabric guest chair before sitting. The office was cozy and warm compared to the frigid February temperatures beyond their doors.

Fran gave her a curious look. "Are you here about Opal Lorrie's death?"

Shari crossed her right leg over her left and shifted to face Fran. "Has her family been notified?"

"We just called them." A cloud moved over Fran's thin features. "They were devastated, of course. And now they have to tell their other kids." Fran rubbed her eyes with the fingertips of her right hand as though trying to ease the heartache of the sympathy call.

Shari swallowed to relieve the tightness in her throat. "I'm so sorry for their loss."

Ted swallowed a drink of his coffee. "We all are. You writing a story on it?"

Shari didn't sense the usual hostility from Ted

when he asked that question. "Opal was a well-known and well-liked public servant. People will want to know how she died."

"Accident." Ted balanced his right ankle on his left knee. He took a drink from his coffee mug. "She fell down the stairs to the Board of Ed's rear parking lot."

"You won't get much of a story from that." Fran gestured toward Ted. "This death isn't your usual murder investigation."

Shari pulled her reporter's notepad and a pen from her oversized brick red handbag. "This story's value will be in paying tribute to Opal as a public servant and perhaps offering readers some cautions about slip-and-fall accidents."

Ted made a face. "That's not much of a story."

"Was Opal wearing heels?" Shari couldn't recall Opal ever wearing high heels. With her shoe fetish, Shari would remember that.

"She was wearing flats." Fran confirmed Shari's supposition.

Shari glanced toward the front of the bullpen where a large picture window allowed a flood of natural light to bounce off the bright yellow walls. "It's cold, but most of the ice has melted from the sidewalk." She returned her attention to Ted. "Are the steps in disrepair?"

Ted took a deeper drink of coffee. "No ice at the scene. Steps were fine."

Shari looked from Ted to Fran. "Was there anything unusual about the scene?"

"I don't think so." Fran shook her head. "Nothing seemed out of place. Everything looked normal, except for Opal's body, of course."

Ted shrugged his burly shoulders. "Nothing."

Shari rubbed her brow to ease the frown developing there. "Then what caused Opal to fall?"

"Tripped." Ted sounded like he was stating the obvious. Perhaps to him, he was. Shari was starting to wonder.

"Falling is the second leading cause of accidental deaths, not just in this country, but around the world. Traffic accidents are the first." Fran leaned back on her chair. "It's unfortunate and tragic, but Opal's death was a freak accident."

Shari could buy that, except . . . "Briar Coast's municipal buildings are usually pretty well maintained, especially in the winter to keep people safe. Has anyone else ever died from a fall down those stairs or any municipal building stairs?"

Fran looked to Ted, then back at Shari. "No."

"It's good to see you again, Mayor Stanley." Sister Lou greeted the public servant with a handshake and a smile. She'd been called to the congregational office's reception area late Monday afternoon to collect her unexpected guest.

"Please call me Heather, Sister Lou." Heather's hands were exceptionally cold. It was as though she'd carried the black leather gloves clenched in her left hand when she should have been wearing them.

Or perhaps Heather's poor circulation had been brought about by whatever was weighing on her mind. The mayor's expression was strained. Her smile was stiff. What had caused the haunted look in her wide violet eyes?

"Thank you for that compliment, Heather." Sister Lou released the mayor's hand.

Heather gave Sister Lou an apologetic look. "I'm sorry to interrupt you."

The uncertainty in Heather's voice was another cause of concern. The mayor was known to be unapologetically assertive, forceful, and arrogant. What had caused this uncharacteristic vulnerability? "Let's talk in my office."

"Thank you." Heather's relief was tangible.

Sister Lou waved good-bye to the sister on duty at the office's front desk. Heather fell into step beside Sister Lou as they walked the short distance down the wide hallway to Sister Lou's office. Fluorescent lighting danced against the pale gold walls. Their steps were muted against the thick warm rose carpet. Their path took them past conference rooms, offices, administrative assistants' desks, and a breakroom. Most of the doors were open, allowing Sister Lou to catch parts of murmured conversations and laughter.

At her office, Sister Lou stepped aside and gestured for Heather to precede her across the threshold. She closed her door as the mayor shrugged out of her royal blue cashmere winter coat. Heather folded the garment over the back of the well-cushioned powder blue guest chair to the right of the walnut wood desk and settled onto the twin chair beside the wall. Sister Lou reclaimed the powder blue executive chair behind her desk.

"How can I help you, Heather?" Sister Lou offered an encouraging smile.

Heather leaned forward to set her black faux leather purse on the floor beside her feet. She straightened, flexing her shoulders beneath the navy jacket of her conservative pantsuit. "I need your help to find out who's been sending me threatening messages."

Sister Lou inhaled a quick breath. She caught the sweet, comforting scent of white tea potpourri from the bowl on the bookcase beside her. Her eyes widened in shock and concern. "Someone's threatening you?"

Heather's gaze was direct and emotionless. "I've received two letters that were obviously meant to intimidate me. They were sent anonymously, of course, by some coward, so I haven't taken them seriously. Until today."

Sister Lou tensed. "What happened today that changed your mind?"

"I received the second threatening letter this morning." Heather's voice trembled. She took a moment and a deep breath before continuing. "Opal, my finance director, attended a meeting for me. Now she's dead."

Sister Lou gasped. Her right hand flew to cover her mouth. "Oh, dear Lord. I'm so sorry."

"The deputies believe she fell down a short flight of stairs." Heather's gaze lowered to her clasped hands on her lap.

Sister Lou rose and circled her desk. She sat sideways on the guest chair beside Heather's and took the other woman's hands in hers. Even though her office was warm, Heather's slender fingers were cold and trembling. "I'm so sorry for your loss. Opal Lorrie was a wonderful person with a promising future. She'll be missed by so many people."

Heather's head was bowed. Her hair swung forward to mask her profile. Sister Lou didn't think the mayor had heard the words she'd spoken. She had the sense that Heather had turned her attention inward. Sister Lou felt the other woman's grief as her own. Tears fell from Heather's eyes and landed on the back of Sister Lou's hand as she held the grieving woman's fingers.

"She was driving my car. Wearing my coat." Heather seemed to be speaking to herself.

Sister Lou tightened her hold on Heather's hands. "Are you saying you don't believe this was an accident?"

"I'm sorry," Heather mumbled, using her fingertips to wipe her tears from the back of Sister Lou's hand.

"There's no need to apologize." Sister Lou drew back her hands. "Do you think the person behind these anonymous letters is responsible for Opal's death?"

Heather lifted her head to meet Sister Lou's gaze. Her eyes were pink and wet with tears. "Yes, I do. I can't prove it, but I can't believe that she just tripped."

"Have you shared your suspicions with the deputies?"

"What am I supposed to tell them?" Heather stood to pace Sister Lou's office with jerky, impatient steps. "That I think the anonymous coward who's been sending me threatening letters pushed a member of my team down well-maintained municipal steps to her death? They'll think that I'm crazy."

Sister Lou tracked Heather's movements. "They won't think that. You're the mayor."

Heather sent Sister Lou a skeptical look from over her shoulder. The public servant spun on her navy heels to pace away from the large rear window. She turned her back to the late winter scene of barren trees and evergreen bushes. The access road wound its way past rolling lawns just beginning to emerge from the snow.

The mayor stopped beside Sister Lou's desk. "I want you to investigate Opal's death."

Sister Lou's eyes stretched wide. Her lips parted. "Me? No, Mayor—Heather. If you suspect Opal was murdered, you should inform the deputies of your concerns."

"Why? You're the one who investigated the last two murders in Briar Coast."

Sister Lou ignored the mayor's comment. "Who informed you of Opal's death?"

"Deputies Cole and Tate came to my office."

"There you have it." Sister Lou spread her hands. "Those deputies investigated the last two murders as well. You should speak with them."

"Let's not be coy. If it wasn't for you, the wrong person would have been charged with murder in both cases." Heather spun away from Sister Lou to resume her pacing. "The truth is you're a much better investigator than our sheriff's deputies."

"I disagree."

"Besides if I go to the deputies, news of these threats will spread all over the sheriff's department and then all over town." Heather stopped to stare out of the rear picture window. She hugged her waist as though trying to hold herself together. "People will think that I'm weak for letting these cowardly threats rattle me."

"You won't appear weak." Sister Lou was appalled by Heather's suggestion. "If there's any question that Opal's death wasn't an accident, you should insist that the deputies do a thorough, professional investigation."

Heather turned away from the scene beyond the

window to confront Sister Lou. "Why won't *you* do the investigation? You did the other two."

Sister Lou swallowed a frustrated sigh. She empathized with Heather's grief. She was still coping with the very recent death of one of her dearest friends. But she wasn't a detective. She was a sister and a community organizer. Wasn't that enough? "I looked into those two cases because the deputies believed the congregation was involved in both murders. I needed to prove that we weren't."

"Those cases prove that you have better instincts for solving homicides than the deputies."

Sister Lou held up her right hand, palm out. "It proves that I know the members of my congregation." She lowered her hand to her lap. "And may I remind you that, on more than one occasion during my investigation of Autumn's murder, you insisted that I let the deputies do their job."

Heather dragged her right hand through her hair. "I was wrong then. I'm asking for your help now."

"This is out of the realm of anything I've been involved in before. I'm not a trained investigator. I'm sorry, Heather, but I must insist that you involve the deputies."

An expression of disappointment flashed across Heather's face before she masked it. She crossed to the guest chairs and collected her purse. "Thank you for hearing me out, Sister Lou. Enjoy the rest of your day."

Sister Lou caught Heather's hand as the mayor reached to retrieve her coat from the back of Sister Lou's chair. "Are you going to speak with Deputy Cole and Deputy Tate?"

"No, I'll handle it myself. Thank you."

Sister Lou watched the mayor march out of her office. She was concerned about Heather's dilemma, but what could she do to fix it—short of getting involved herself?

Chapter 6

"What are you doing?" Shari crossed the mother-house parking lot Monday evening to confront Harold Beckett. The *Telegraph*'s rookie reporter was tracking her movements like gum on her shoe.

Harold's knee-length black Burberry cashmere coat probably cost more than Shari made in a month. He leaned back against his BMW sports car. Light from the nearby parking lot lamppost glinted off its silver paint.

He crossed his legs at the ankles and his arms over his thin chest. "I'm joining you and Sister Lou for dinner."

His confidence stole Shari's breath. Her palms itched to smack the smug expression from his face. She thrust her fists into the pockets of her winter coat to minimize temptation. "Why?"

"I want to meet your friends." Harold sounded so reasonable as though he had the right to expect the introduction.

Shari's hot temper protected her from the cold. If only she had a way to protect herself from people like

Harold; people who used their false entitlement to make others—like her—feel small. After decades of searching, she'd finally found a place where maybe—just maybe—she could fit in. A place where she felt wanted. And normal. Now here comes another Harold, trying to take it away from her. This time, she wouldn't let him. This time, she'd hold her ground.

"Go home, Hal." Shari relished the flash of irritation in his brown eyes at her use of his hated nickname. "I'm not playing your games."

A chill wind blew past her, seeping into her emerald green wool coat and ruffling Harold's dark hair. The quiet winter evening carried the scents of pine trees and the smoky hint of wood burning in a nearby fireplace.

"Where's your sense of Christian charity?" Harold's grin split his face, but never touched his eyes. He reminded Shari of a silent movie villain. "Now that I'm a full-time member of the *Telegraph*'s staff and not just an intern, I should familiarize myself with members of the community that we report about. And I thought that Easter would be the perfect time to meet members of the Briar Coast religious community, wouldn't you agree?"

"No, I wouldn't." Shari stepped back. She didn't want to catch any of his crazy. "You can't invite yourself to dinner at someone else's home, especially not at the last minute. That's rude."

"They're not going to turn me away." Harold shrugged. "What about that line in the Bible, 'I was hungry and you fed me'? If we walk in together, it'll be fine."

Who did Harold think he was toying with? The sisters wouldn't be so easily duped. They'd take one look at his salon-styled hair, cashmere coat, and Italian wingtip shoes and know that Harold wasn't in need of their charity.

Shari adjusted the strap of her brick red handbag on her shoulder. "I'm not walking with you into the motherhouse."

"Why not?"

"I don't like you."

They locked gazes. Shari matched her grit against his ego. She sensed that Harold wasn't willing to give in. Neither was she. Shari'd had enough of people using her. Her series of foster parents had used her for money. Former coworkers had used her to do their work. Previous bosses had used her ideas to make themselves look good. She was done with all of that.

Harold broke the standoff. "Did you use Christian LaSalle to get close to his aunt?"

Shari stretched the fingers of her right hand in her pocket. She turned away before temptation got the better of her. "Go home, Hal."

She kept a brisk pace as she walked to the motherhouse's front door but strained to hear any movement behind her.

What if Harold followed her inside? What if Sister Lou didn't turn him away? What if Harold started spending time with the congregation and the college? With his traditional upbringing, it would be easy for Harold to find a place among the friends Shari was starting to consider family. They would see that he was normal. And they would realize she was not.

Shari let herself into the motherhouse, relieved that Harold hadn't followed her. She greeted the sister at the front desk before signing the visitor's log. As she made her way to the dining room, Shari replayed that day's various encounters with Harold. If he wanted to cover local crime, why wasn't he harassing the deputies? Why was he fixated on Sister Lou and her team?

"You said no to the mayor?" Sister Carmen Vega's incredulous tone made Sister Lou feel worse.

Dawn was more than an hour away. Sister Lou jogged beside her good friend and exercise companion from the motherhouse to the grounds of the College of St. Hermione of Ephesus on what must be the darkest and coldest morning of the year. It was even darker and colder than it had been yesterday.

But Sister Lou still preferred to jog early in the morning. She loved the faint metallic smell of winter and the scent of pine from the nearby tree line. She could hear the deep silence of the season and feel the moisture in the chilled early Tuesday morning breeze.

Tuesday. Fat Tuesday. *Mardi Gras.* Carnival. The day observant Catholics—and their not-so-observant friends—indulged injudiciously in their favorite foods and beverages in preparation of the Lenten fast, which would begin the next day, Ash Wednesday. Sister Carmen considered it her Christian duty to partake of as many pastries as possible. In support of her friend, Sister Lou planned to join Sister Carmen on a lunchtime bakery shopping spree at the Briar Coast Café.

Sister Lou looked at her friend, noting how vivid Sister Carmen's lime green insulated vest and teal tights appeared in the light from the lampposts that tracked the campus. As usual, Sister Carmen's eye-catching outfit contrasted sharply with Sister Lou's choice of slate gray vest and black tights.

"If Mayor Stanley's right and someone murdered Opal Lorrie because he mistook Opal for the mayor, then the mayor's life is in danger." Sister Lou's words generated puffs of air that floated like smoke in front of her. "If that's the case, Heather doesn't need an amateur sleuth. She needs professional protection."

"'Heather'?" The lampposts caught the twinkle in Sister Carmen's coffee brown eyes as they laughed at her from beneath the fold of her knitted orange winter hat.

Sister Lou's cheeks grew warm in the cold breeze. "She asked me to call her that."

"Can *I* call her 'Heather'?"

"I don't know, Carm. I'll ask her."

At the base of one of the vintage lampposts that ringed the college oval was the familiar feline figure of Unnamed Calico Cat. She'd finally returned to the campus. Sister Lou was almost weak with relief. She'd begun to worry when she hadn't spotted the calico during the winter months. How was she finding food? Where was she staying warm? Sister Lou should have realized the cat could care for itself. It was a survivor.

As Sister Lou drew closer to the calico, she realized the cat was grooming herself. She waited until she was in the cat's line-of-sight before nodding her head in greeting. She waited a beat for a similar gesture from Unnamed Calico. Instead the feline gave her a look of shock and outrage. She rose to her paws and stalked back across the oval, weaving her way around the mounds of unmelted ice on the grass. Sister Lou couldn't blame the feline. One's toilette was a private occasion.

"You're right, Lou." Sister Carmen tugged her hat more firmly over her ears and her riot of curly raven hair lightly threaded with strands of gray. "Mayor Stanley would need professional protection if she's in danger, but you won't know for certain unless you investigate."

"I'd rather concentrate on our marathon training and on my community outreach program—on almost anything other than amateur sleuthing." Perhaps she was exaggerating, but she'd made the right decision in turning down the mayor's request.

Hadn't I?

"Speaking of our training, we've got our second long run this Saturday, eleven miles." Sister Carmen's observation made Sister Lou groan. Sister Carmen laughed. "The ten miles we ran Saturday for our first long run wasn't so bad, was it?"

"Yes, actually. Yes, it was." Sister Lou crested the incline as Sister Carmen kept pace with her. "Ten miles is double our usual distance. Saturday will be even farther."

"Only one mile farther. You can handle it." Sister Carmen's laughter was breathless.

"I suppose I could." *I have to stop underestimating myself.*

They were gaining ground on the college's residence halls. The trio of redbrick Federal-style buildings circled an asphalt parking lot. Most of the windows were dark but a few students were getting an early start on their studies.

Sister Lou blew into her black fleece gloves. "At least I'm enjoying our Friday morning beginner yoga classes."

They'd committed to a fifteen-week training schedule in preparation for their Memorial Weekend marathon. Sundays through Thursdays, they continued their daily five-mile jogs. They'd registered for the free beginner yoga classes the college offered every Friday morning at five thirty. Saturdays were for their long runs. It was a well-planned if ambitious routine.

After jogging around the residence halls, Sister Lou turned with Sister Carmen toward the oval at the center of the college. Stately trees and academic buildings in the same architectural style as the residence halls outlined the campus's well-manicured lawns and pedestrian walkways.

On the second of their three laps around the oval, Sister Lou watched as a familiar group of female student-athletes appeared. The nine young women, members of the college's track and field team, ran in a tight formation. Sister Lou greeted them with a sedate wave and a warm smile. In response, the runners cheered and waved with exuberant support.

"Keep training, Sisters! Good luck on the marathon!" The chorus of well wishes came as members of the team raced past Sister Lou. Their voices echoed around the oval, shattering the cold silence with warm enthusiasm.

Sister Lou smiled at their cheers and whoops of encouragement. She watched as Sister Carmen gave the student-athletes her usual red carpet wave and paparazzi smile. The St. Hermione students had nicknamed her and Sister Carmen the Running Sisters. News that they were training for their first marathon had spread like wildfire from the motherhouse to the college. Sister Lou gave Sister Carmen a suspicious look. She knew at least one of the sources of that leak.

"It's not so bad being the only old ladies in the yoga class." Sister Lou watched the student-athletes race toward the dirt path that led to the center of Briar Coast. "Everyone is so encouraging and supportive. It probably helped that you told all of the other participants that we're taking the class as part of our marathon training."

"Probably." Sister Carmen was unrepentant. "I think you should reconsider helping Mayor Stanley."

Sister Lou blinked at the abrupt change of topic. "Why?"

"This case could give you a chance to save a life."

Sister Lou felt a wave of sorrow sweep over her. She and Sister Carmen started their third lap around the oval. "But if Heather's right, it's too late to save Opal."

Sister Carmen slowed as though she also was weighted by grief. "I know and I'm so sorry about that. But, Lou, the mayor's still alive."

Shari sighed as she settled onto her chair at her tan modular desk in the *Telegraph*'s office early Tuesday morning. She savored the first sip of her third cup of coffee and waited for her computer to wake up. She'd had two cups of caffeine before she'd stepped foot outside of her apartment. How could Chris even consider giving up this pleasure for forty days and forty nights? Shari still couldn't wrap her mind around that rash decision. Was he having second thoughts now that Ash Wednesday was less than twenty-four hours away? Shari snorted. *Probably.*

Her ringing telephone interrupted Shari in the middle of her musings. She secured her ceramic coffee mug in her right hand before leaning forward to answer the summons. "*Telegraph.* Sharelle Henson."

"Good morning, Sharelle. It's Becca Floyd." The

voice of the managing editor of *Buffalo Today*, one of their rival newspapers, had become familiar.

"Hi, Becca. You've started your day early." Shari's gaze swept to the clock in the lower right corner of her computer monitor. It was eleven minutes before eight o'clock. Becca must be really dedicated to her job. Or was the managing editor checking in with Shari to see whether she was just as committed? Shari swallowed a bark of laughter with her next sip of caffeine.

"I read your article on the death of Briar Coast's finance and management director." Becca's voice carried a trace of synthetic commiseration. Middle managers often manufactured various emotions to bond with the rank-and-file. Shari gave this particular middle manager points for effort.

"Opal Lorrie." Shari wanted Opal's name to be remembered. She'd done too much for their community to be reduced to a title.

"Yes, the poor woman. What a terrible way to go."

Shari felt another cloud of grief roll over her. "Briar Coast is mourning Opal's death. It shook a lot of people in the community, especially since it was so sudden. I knew her personally and liked her a lot."

There was a brief pause on the other end of the line as though Becca was distracted by something else. "Well, I just wanted to compliment you on another solid article. It was well reported."

"Thank you." Shari shifted on her gray cushioned swivel chair.

Things could get awkward if Becca continued to call every time Shari had a byline in the *Telegraph*. What if she had a byline and Becca *didn't* call? The thought made Shari's mind stutter.

"Are you going to investigate it?" Becca's question was a good one.

"I don't know yet." Shari took another sip of her coffee. She frowned. It was starting to get cold. Bummer. "It depends on the results from the sheriff's deputies' final report on the scene."

"Well, I look forward to reading whatever you find out."

A movement in Shari's peripheral vision drew her attention. She glanced over her shoulder to see Heather Stanley march past her cubicle like a vengeful wraith. The mayor's movements were stiff with anger as she stormed down the hallway. Was she on her way to confront Diego over whatever she'd interpreted as the latest challenge to her authority? Poor guy.

Shari returned to her conversation with the *Buffalo Today*'s managing editor. "Becca, I've told you I'm not interested in leaving the *Telegraph*. Although I'm flattered by your attention, why do you keep calling me?"

Becca's low chuckle traveled down the phone line. "You're direct. I like that."

"And I'd like a direct answer to my question." Shari's tone was dry. She took a deeper drink of her coffee. Was she wrong to want a fourth cup so soon?

"All right. I'll give you one." Becca still sounded amused. She also sounded confident. "I'm hoping to convince you to at least come in for an interview with *Today*. Take a tour of our offices. Meet some of our staff. See what we can offer you. I'm sure you'll be impressed."

Shari smothered a chuckle. That wouldn't take much. She raised her eyes to see above her high cubicle partitions. The *Telegraph*'s walls and ceiling were stained with age and neglect. The space was cramped. The gray wall-to-wall carpeting was thin and worn. The stench of newsprint made her almost dizzy by the end of the day. The computer software was several versions behind and the photocopier was outdated. It didn't even do color.

Shari lowered her gaze to the mug in her hand. She'd bet the coffee tasted better on the other side, too. "Thanks, but like I said, I'm happy with the *Telegraph*."

"Are you sure? I believe you'd be impressed with our pay as well."

"The *Today* staff get *paid* to do this? That *is* impressive."

Becca's laughter sounded forced. "The management team discussed the range we'd be able to offer you."

The managing editor named a salary that made Shari's eyes stretch wide. Becca was killing her. Just killing her. Even with the wage increase the *Telegraph* staff had received at the beginning of the year, the salary Becca mentioned would have a significant positive impact on Shari's lifestyle.

Still Shari wasn't interested in leaving Briar Coast. "You're right. I'm impressed, but as I said, I'm happy here. There aren't a lot of people who can say that."

"All right. Well, you can't blame me for trying." Becca gave a deep sigh. "I wish you the best, Sharelle. I hope Diego knows how lucky he is to have you."

"Thanks. Good luck to you as well." Shari frowned as she cradled her telephone receiver.

Becca had sounded very comfortable dropping Diego's name. Did the two newspaper editors know each other? Shari supposed it wasn't so strange that journalists in nearby markets would be acquainted with each other. After all, she was acquainted with Becca.

But that's because the other woman was trying to offer her a job.

Shari turned her frown in the direction of Diego's office. How was he acquainted with the *Buffalo Today*'s managing editor? Had their rival newspaper also offered Diego a job? If he chose to leave the *Telegraph*, it was his business and his right—and it would tick her off.

She took another deep drink of her coffee, this time draining the mug. Shari's days at the *Telegraph* may be numbered, though. If that rookie Harold got his hands on her beat, Shari would absolutely leave the *Telegraph*. Maybe she'd been hasty in turning down Becca's offer.

Chapter 7

The *Telegraph*'s office was a blur to Heather as she marched past the flustered front entry receptionist and several stunned reporters Tuesday morning. The heels of her three-inch black pumps drove into the thin gray carpet as she wound past the copy editors' desks, reporters' cubicles, and conference rooms. Loose papers fluttered and fell in her wake. Heather gritted her teeth and clenched her fists when she realized Shari was on the telephone. She felt as though steam was rushing from her ears. She saw red as her mind spun in search of a new target for her temper. The answer came to her.

Diego DeVarona.

Heather set her course for the newspaper editor's office, which was all the way in the back of the main floor.

She stormed into Diego's office and slammed that day's *Telegraph* onto his walnut wood desk. The explosive act caused nearby papers to dive off the table's surface and onto the floor.

Diego looked up at her. His coffee brown eyes were expressionless. His voice was flat. "Something wrong?"

Heather leaned over his desk and drilled her finger against the newspaper at the exact spot where the headline for the article on Opal Lorrie's death was printed. "You had no right to run this article on Opal's death."

"We're a newspaper. We had every right. Opal Lorrie's death is a terrible tragedy and I'm sorry for the town's loss. But it's also news." Diego's quiet, reasonable tone was like gasoline on Heather's flaming temper.

His words were maddening. His calm was maddening. Everything about him was maddening. Had it always been that way with him?

Heather drew a deep breath. Diego's sandalwood scent filled her senses, temporarily confusing her. And that was maddening. Heather straightened, stepping back to clear her head.

It was warm in Diego's office. Or was that her temper? It had been on an incendiary course since she'd read the headline to the article about her finance and management director's death. Heather unfastened the big silver buttons on her royal blue cashmere winter coat. Emotions swamped her as she remembered lending Opal her scarlet coat. That coat was still with her friend. Heather couldn't imagine wearing it again.

She jabbed her index finger toward the newspaper she'd left on Diego's desk. "Shari Henson's article makes a big deal about Opal driving my car and wearing my coat. She had no right to do that."

Diego gave her a confused look. "Shari didn't make a big deal about those things. She just mentioned them. They're interesting details."

"It's no one else's f—"

"Those references to your loaning Opal your car and your clothes make you look human. You should thank Shari. The public needs to know the mayor has some humanity. People have wondered about that."

Heather inhaled a sharp breath at the attack. "That's bull."

The newspaper editor was nonresponsive. Diego leaned back against his faded gray faux leather executive chair. He crossed his arms over his broad muscled chest, which was wrapped in a snow-white shirt. His black-and-red-striped tie brought to mind the franchise colors of the Houston Rockets professional basketball team. She and Diego were Texas transplants. That's all they had in common. Wasn't it?

Heather scrutinized her opponent. Diego's relaxed pose didn't fool her. She found the intense scrutiny in his eyes and met it with a flare of fury. The newsman hadn't changed much since they'd known each other in El Paso almost fourteen years ago. He was still as cunning as a fox and as sneaky as a snake.

Heather stood akimbo. "*Thank* Shari Henson for writing that article? It'll be a cold day in—"

Diego raised his right hand, cutting off her colorful analogy. "I get the picture."

"I'm only in here ripping *you* a new one instead of *her* because she's on the phone."

Diego shook his head with what Heather interpreted as a mocking smile. "Your image could use the warming up, Heather, especially if you're going to run for reelection."

Heather's muscles trembled. She hated that anonymous threats from an obvious coward made her react this way to the thought of remaining in office. How dare the spineless worm behind those notes have any power over her?

She noticed the curiosity in Diego's eyes. He knew something was wrong. The fact that he was able to read her so well even after they'd spent more than a decade apart made her even more furious. She angled her chin and took her self-disgust out on the editor. "Instead of wasting all that space chasing after a story that isn't news, you'd do better using it to promote the town's annual spring fund-raiser. Why don't you do some good in the community? For once."

Instead of appearing offended, Diego looked even more concerned. "Why are you really so upset about the story on Opal's death? What aren't you telling me?"

Heather swung her right hand toward her copy of the *Telegraph*, which was still prone on Diego's desk. "Why should I tell you anything? It'll only end up in your crappy paper."

"Not if you don't want it to."

The concern in his eyes was her undoing. Heather was weakening. She wanted to share her fears, her suspicions—and her guilt. With him. She stiffened her resolve. "Am I supposed to trust a *journalist*?"

"You can trust me, Heather. You know that. We were friends once."

Heather arched an eyebrow. "With our history, I'd either have to be desperate or a fool to trust you again."

Diego cocked his head, still appearing unfazed by

even her strongest insults. "Opal was wearing your coat and driving your car. Are you afraid that her death wasn't an accident? Do you think someone mistook her for you?"

The blood drained from Heather's head. Her ears buzzed. Her pulse picked up. If Diego could put those details together, would other people realize it, too? That's what she'd been afraid of when she'd read Shari's article. Had the meddling investigative reporter left her exposed and vulnerable?

"That's absurd." Heather's voice was breathy. Had Diego noticed? "Why would you even suggest that? Why would someone want to kill me?"

Diego rose and circled his desk to stand an arm's length from her. "Heather, if you're in trouble, you should report your concerns to the deputies."

Heather stepped back, needing distance between them. "I don't know what you're talking about. And neither do you."

Diego turned back to his desk. He pulled one of his business cards from its cardholder and rescued his pen from beneath Heather's newspaper. He wrote something on the back of the card before returning to Heather. He pressed his business card into her palm. His hand was large, firm, and warm against her skin. "This is my personal cell phone number. Take it in case you change your mind about needing help."

Heather withdrew her hand from his grasp and took another step back. "I don't need your help."

Diego frowned. "Heather, don't let your pride and ego get in the way and hurt you again. Do you remember El Paso?"

Heather gave him a scathing look. "How could I forget when you're a constant reminder?"

She spun on her heels and marched out of Diego's office. If only it was that easy to put the past behind her.

Shari's dark thoughts must have conjured Harold. The rookie reporter walked uninvited into her cubicle minutes later.

"How did you find out about the finance and management director's death?" Harold stood just inside her cubicle, holding the *Telegraph* in his right hand.

"Her name was Opal Lorrie." Shari spoke over her shoulder.

"How did you find out?"

This time, Shari waited until she'd finished replying to the e-mail message on her computer screen before spinning her chair to face Harold. "It's called working your beat. You should try it sometime."

"What do you mean?" Confusion clouded Harold's small brown eyes.

Shari gave Harold a considering look. The recent college graduate must subscribe to the philosophy that you dress for the job you want, not the one you have. Based on his appearance this morning, his goal must be to own the newspaper. His black dress pants, champagne linen shirt, and plum silk tie looked like they came from a high-end men's clothing store. Were they gifts? No one at the *Telegraph* could afford such expensive clothes, not even after their pay increase.

Shari crossed her arms and legs. She swung her right foot, shod in black boots with three-inch heels, a perfect match to her black pantsuit. "Didn't they teach basic journalism at your school?"

"Of course they did." Even Harold's perfect salon-styled hair seemed ruffled by her question.

"Then you should be working your beat instead of taking up space in my cubicle." Shari turned back to her computer.

But Harold didn't leave. "Does this story have anything to do with what you're working on with Sister Lou?"

Shari met Harold's gaze over her shoulder. "What makes you think I'm working on a project with Sister Lou?"

"Aren't you?" His smile taunted her.

"That's none of your business."

"Come on. Just tell me. I could help you." Harold's wheedling made him even more annoying.

"Could you work your own beat? Perry gave you the election issues before he left." Shari referenced Diego's predecessor, Perry O'Toole, the worst boss she'd ever had, which was really saying something. "You should be glad Diego didn't take it away from you when he became editor-in-chief. I would've."

Harold frowned. "Why would you have taken away my beat?"

"Oh, I don't know. Maybe because you're not working it." Shari dripped sarcasm. "You should be thanking your lucky stars that you're not doing general assignments like most rookies."

Harold uttered a short, sharp laugh. "General assignment? I'm too good of a reporter for general assignment. That would be a waste of my talents."

"You can't just make a claim like that. You need to back it up, and so far, you haven't."

"Who were you on the phone with earlier?"

Shari may find words to express how appalled she was by the intrusiveness of Harold's question. Eventually. But she wasn't interested in expending that mental and physical energy at this time.

Instead, she took a deep breath and lowered her voice. "Get out of my cubicle. Now."

Tension drained from Shari's neck, shoulders, and back as Harold made his way out of her cubicle. She slumped deeper onto her cushioned chair. Harold wasn't going to give up. With his prying, one day she'd wake up to find he'd become a member of Sister Lou's amateur sleuth team, leaving her once again on the outside looking in. How long after that would it take them to realize she was a fraud?

"As I've told you before, Ian, I'm firm on the no-tax-abatement policy." Heather spoke into the hands-free earbuds attached to her cellular phone Tuesday evening. The traffic light turned green, permitting her to continue her drive home from her town hall office.

Her debate with Briar Coast Town Council president Ian Greer—she refused to call it an argument—had begun on her office phone. She'd called him back on her cell phone once she'd attached her earbuds so that she could take their disagreement on the road. This wasn't the first time they'd had this conversation, though. She and Ian had discussed this proposal at least twice before. Either the town council president enjoyed the sound of her voice or he was hard of hearing.

"It's only for three years, Heather." Ian continued

to use the timeline for his unpersuasive argument. "And it would allow us to attract new businesses to our town. I thought we'd all want that, especially in an election year."

"Do you have me on speaker phone, Ian?" Heather made the abrupt diversion in their conversation. "I hear a lot of road noise in the background."

"I'm driving while we're talking. You don't want me to drive with one hand, do you? That's not safe." The council president sounded offended.

Heather ignored his question. "Is anyone else in the car with you?"

"No, I'm alone." Ian's hesitation was telling. He clearly hadn't given her an honest answer.

Heather rolled her eyes. How many people were in the car with him as he debated the tax abatements? "I don't care how long or short the contract term would be. I'm not giving companies that are new to our community a tax break. It wouldn't be fair to increase our residents' tax burden, regardless of the election cycle."

"Haven't you noticed that young people are leaving Briar Coast in droves to find better-paying jobs?" Ian sounded snotty. "Don't you want to attract new jobs to our community?"

"They'd have to be exceptionally well-paying jobs for all of our residents." Heather activated her garage door's remote control opener and rolled forward into her garage. "We can't expect the people of this town to accept an increased tax burden just to be able to offer businesses a tax cut. How would you justify that?"

"We would justify it with new jobs."

"And what about the businesses that have always

paid their fair share of taxes?" Heather closed her garage door. "How is that fair to them?"

"We would explain the benefits to the town—"

"I'm not explaining anything," Heather interrupted as she climbed from her car. She unlocked her side entrance to let herself into her little Cape Cod home. "Corporations should pay their fair share of taxes, Ian. That's the bottom line."

"You're making a mistake, Heather."

"If you and the other council members want to promote tax breaks for corporations, go ahead, but I'm not supporting this." Heather dropped her briefcase and purse at the foot of her staircase on her way to her kitchen.

Ian's sigh was equal parts frustration and disappointment. "All right, Heather. You've made your position perfectly clear."

"I hope so, Ian. You and I have other things to discuss like increasing our education budget to bring our schools' technology into the twenty-first century."

Heather froze at the entrance to her kitchen. In the center of her blond wood table lay a plain white envelope that hadn't been there this morning.

"We don't have—"

"Ian, I have to go." Her gaze swept the room. Was the intruder still in her home?

Heather disconnected the call without waiting for Ian's response. She kicked off her shoes. Rushing to her butcher's block, Heather grabbed the biggest knife in the collection. If the intruder was still in her home, he must have heard her come in.

A stream of swearwords chanted in her head.

She'd made a lot of noise between her phone call

with Ian, and dropping her purse and briefcase beside the staircase.

More swearwords.

Heather's heart pounded in her ears. She couldn't catch her breath. With her cell phone in one hand, ready to call the sheriff's office, and the butcher's knife in the other, Heather did a swift and silent reconnaissance of the living room, dining room, and small powder room on her main floor.

Nothing.

She crept upstairs with as much stealth as possible to walk through the three bedrooms and two full baths. She even checked her half basement.

Alone. She seemed to be alone. She hoped she was alone. That was small comfort considering whoever had broken into her home had felt emboldened enough to let her know they'd been in her space.

Heather returned to her kitchen and her poison pen pal's latest communication. Her hands shook as she picked up the cheap white business envelope. As usual, there was no stamp or return address. She knew nothing about this stalker, but he seemed to know a great deal about her. Where she worked. Where she lived. The temperature in her kitchen dropped. Her body grew cold.

Heather rested her cell phone on the kitchen table. The muscles in her shoulders and back were stiff as she used the butcher's knife to cut open the envelope. Her hands still shook as she extracted the familiar single, plain white sheet of copier paper. She unfolded it to read this third message. It had a new twist: *Outsider, Opal Lorrie wasn't supposed to die. That threat is just for you. I'd only wanted to scare her. But murder's even easier the second time around.*

Heather crumpled the note in her right fist. She was equal parts terrorized and enraged. *How* had he broken into her home? How *dared* he break into her home?

She bowed her head and placed her hands on her hips. Heather felt the impression of Diego's business card. It was still in the pocket of her skirt suit from this morning. Heather pulled out the newspaper editor's card again. She'd read it so often throughout the day that she could recite his cell phone number from memory. Backward. She found an unsettling comfort in knowing Diego had cared enough to give her his number. Perhaps a part of her even wanted to call him, but El Paso had been a long time ago.

Heather shoved Diego's card back into her pocket and called the sheriff's office instead. She needed professionals to perform a search before she'd feel safe in her own home again.

The call was answered after the first ring. "Briar Coast County Sheriff's Office. How can I help you?"

"This is Mayor Heather Stanley. Could you send a couple of deputies to search my house, please? I'm afraid someone may have broken in. I found . . ." She looked at the crumbled envelope still in her fist. Despite Diego's and Sister Lou's advice, she wasn't ready to tell the authorities about her stalker. "My front door was open when I got home."

"We'll send someone over right away, Mayor." The voice on the other end of the line was brisk.

"Thank you. I'm at Twelve Sixteen Siena Way." Heather disconnected the call.

She glanced at her fist again, temporarily at a loss. Forcing her muscles to move, Heather smoothed out the letter and returned it to its cheap and creepy envelope. She shoved the threatening message into her briefcase to join the one she'd received yesterday. Heather shrugged deeper into her coat. She'd wait for the sheriff's deputies in her garage. She wasn't about to wait inside. Heather pulled out her cell phone again. While she waited, she'd call the local locksmith. It was time for new locks.

Chapter 8

Less than an hour later, Heather was jogging through her neighborhood. It was after seven o'clock Tuesday evening. The streets were dark and deserted, leaving her alone with her thoughts. She ran along the side of the street. The asphalt was easier on her knees than the sidewalk, and there were very few cars parked along Siena Way.

It had taken about half an hour for the locksmith to change her locks and a little longer than that for the deputies to search her home. The two young women had been reassuringly thorough. They'd searched areas that she hadn't considered, such as the attic in her house and the one above her garage. They'd tugged on every window to make sure they were locked. Checked every closet and under all the beds. Walked her home's perimeter, and circled the bushes in her front and back yards.

Heather shook her head. Not checking those places herself still made her feel stupid, but not as stupid as she'd felt when she realized the spare key she'd kept hidden beneath the planter on her front porch was missing. That must have been how the villain had gotten into her house in the first place. She'd had the locksmith make three sets of her new keys. She'd keep the first set with her. The second set she'd hide in her office, and the third she'd give to Kerry for those rare occasions when she'd need her administrative assistant to take something to her house or retrieve something from it.

Footsteps sounded behind her. The sound sent a warning signal to Heather's brain. The echoes traveled down the tendons of her limbs. She forced her muscles to relax. She couldn't allow herself to jump at every noise, flinch at each shadow. Heather shifted closer to the curb. The new arrival now had room to pass on her left. The footsteps drew nearer. Were they faster?

Heather attempted a casual glance over her left shoulder. She didn't want to appear spooked.

Suddenly the runner slammed into her. He swept her up into his arms and kept running. Heather screamed long and loudly. It was an ear-piercing shriek of shock and terror. Her assailant dropped her onto the street. Heather's head bounced once against the asphalt.

Everything went black.

"Thank you, but really, I'm fine." If Heather repeated those words often enough, perhaps her head would stop throbbing hard enough to make her teeth rattle. At the very least, perhaps the nurse would go away.

She'd been horrified when she'd regained consciousness and realized she was prone in the middle of the street surrounded by emergency vehicles, medical professionals, and well-meaning neighbors. The medical technicians had poked and prodded her, and peppered her with questions while they carried her into the ambulance. All the while, her neighbors had shouted words of encouragement, caring, and support. It had been like an official town event. Heather had been embarrassed to find herself crying silently on the gurney, overcome by her neighbors' concern and kindness. This was one of the reasons she loved Briar Coast. Heather had given the EMTs a stern look. Hopefully, they'd understood her silent message: What happened in the ambulance stayed in the ambulance.

Now she lay in a hospital bed Tuesday night at the mercy of an overzealous, older nurse. The health care professional's poking and prodding were making Heather crazy.

"Do you feel dizzy?" Her nemesis barked the question as her chubby hands checked Heather's pulse.

Heather winced at the loud noise. "No, I don't." She mentally added a few swearwords to her reply.

"Nauseous?" The nurse adjusted the thin white sheet and pale blue blanket that covered Heather.

"No. My ears aren't ringing, either, and you can hear that my speech isn't slurred."

The nurse lowered Heather's wrist and straightened to her full height. Tuffs of gray-and-blond chin-length tresses had escaped the other woman's hair clip. She squared her broad shoulders and pinned Heather with a glare from her frosty blue eyes. "When did you get your medical degree, Doctor Stanley?"

Heather wouldn't lie, not even to herself: the gruff nurse intimidated her. She hid her unease behind a scowl. Heather glanced above the nurse's impressive bosom at the name badge pinned to her cotton-candy pink uniform blouse. "You didn't vote for me, did you, Nurse Jones?"

Nurse Jones stared down her broad nose at Heather. "As a matter of fact, I did. That doesn't mean I'm going to fawn all over you as though you were a member of One Direction."

Heather gaped at the older woman's reference to the popular British boy band. Had that been a joke? How did the nurse know about One Direction? Did she have grandchildren?

The image of the tough, intimidating health care professional dancing to pop music made her smile. "Thank you for your support."

"You're welcome." The response was grudging, which made Heather appreciate it even more.

Nurse Jones turned to leave just as Diego and Shari hurried into the room. Both journalists wore identical expressions of concern. They stopped just inside the room.

Diego was dressed as casually as Heather had ever seen him in dark khaki pants with a lightweight cranberry knit sweater and black canvas shoes. His salt-and-pepper hair was rumpled as though he'd run his long, blunt fingers through it over and over and over again.

In contrast, Shari looked as though she'd arrived fresh from the newspaper's offices. The investigative reporter wore a tidy grape skirt suit with matching three-inch stilettos. The hem of her skirt fell to mid-calf. Her riot of raven curls seemed to vibrate around her shoulders.

Heather understood why Diego had shown up at her hospital room. She'd called him after the hospital had admitted her for observation. She'd regretted the momentary weakness as soon as she'd disconnected their call. But what was Shari doing here? Had Diego called her? If so, why? She was young enough to be his daughter. In fact, she was young enough to be their daughter.

That was a disconcerting thought.

"The mayor needs rest." Nurse Jones's brusque demand broke Heather's train of thought.

Diego's gaze moved from Heather to the scowling medical protector. "We won't stay long."

Nurse Jones glared at them for several silent seconds. Finally, she gave an abrupt nod, then marched toward Heather's visitors. "I'll be back in ten minutes. If you aren't gone by then, I'll remove you."

The whole Nurse Jones experience stunned Heather. She stammered a few swearwords as the nurse left her room. "I can see her doing that."

"So can I." Diego's full lips curved into a sexy half grin.

"Me, three." Shari joined Diego beside Heather's bed.

Diego watched her closely. "What happened? When you called, all you said was 'I'm in the hospital. Can you come?' Then you hung up."

Heather turned to Shari. "I'm not giving you an interview, if that's why you're here. You're not turning this into a—"

"Circus?" Diego cut her off.

"I was going to say . . ." Heather rolled her eyes. She received twin expressions of dismay in response to her choice of modifiers for "circus." They were a couple of babies.

Shari arched a winged eyebrow. "At least your charm hasn't been affected by whatever's landed you here."

Diego raised both of his hands in what was probably meant to be a reassuring gesture. It failed. "Shari's not here for a story. I asked her to come because I thought you might be more comfortable with another woman present."

And the reporter was the only woman he could think to invite? Note to self: Diego wasn't dating. Heather didn't know why that revelation pleased her.

But it did.

She looked up at him from her propped position on the bed. "I told the EMTs that I tripped and fell off the sidewalk onto the street while I was jogging."

"That's not what happened." Shari made it a statement rather than a question.

"No, it's not." Heather met the investigative reporter's eyes and forced herself to make the admission she hadn't wanted to face. "I was attacked."

"By. Whom?" The concern in Diego's voice was reassuring. Maybe Heather had been right to call him.

"I don't know." Heather shook her head. That was a mistake. It reawakened the percussion instruments that were rehearsing Led Zeppelin's "Immigrant Song" on the right side of her head. "I think it has something to do with the threatening notes I've been getting."

"Someone's been sending you threats?" Diego stepped closer to her bed. His voice increased in volume, urging Heather's personal percussion section to perform an encore. "Who? For how long?"

"Careful, Diego. Remember the mayor's concussion."

Heather's gaze dropped to the hand Shari had rested on Diego's tricep. There'd been a time when she would have felt comfortable making such a gesture toward the newsman. But that was many years and several bridges ago. "I don't know who's been sending the letters."

"How many have you gotten? When did this start?" Shari's voice was gentle as though she was compensating for Diego's agitation.

"I've received three letters since last Wednesday." That had been shortly after eight a.m., February seventh. She wasn't likely to forget that date.

"Three?" Diego's interruption was incredulous.

"What do they say?" Shari asked.

Heather ignored Diego's interjection and answered Shari's question. "The first two were the same. They read, 'Outsider, if you know what's good for you, don't run for reelection. Leave Briar Coast.'" Heather recited the message from memory. They were short—and hard to forget. She ignored Shari's quick intake of breath and Diego's expletive. "The last one was different. 'Outsider, Opal Lorrie wasn't supposed to die. That threat is just for you. I'd only wanted to scare her. But murder's even easier the second time around.' I received that one this evening. It was waiting for me on my kitchen table."

"Someone broke into your house?" Diego's agitation was on the rise again. "And then you were attacked while you were jogging in your neighborhood?"

"Yes." Heather shivered as she relived her fear. "I was less than a block from my home when someone came from behind me, literally lifted me into his arms, then dropped me on the street."

"And you didn't report that to the deputies?" Diego dragged his right hand through his short salt-and-pepper hair. "For pity's sake, Heather, why not?"

Heather felt an uncontrollable surge of irritation. "Because I won't be intimidated. I'm not going to let this coward think he can scare me or that I'm taking him seriously because I'm not." She capped her mini-tirade with a stream of ear-burning expletives. It was cathartic.

Diego broke in again, matching her vexation. "You should."

Shari rested her hand on Diego's arm again. "Did you report the break-in?"

This time, Heather remembered not to nod. "Yes, and the deputies did a thorough search. They didn't find anything, and nothing had been taken. Whoever broke in just wanted to intimidate me." She sent another glare in Diego's direction. "They failed."

Diego heaved a sigh as though forcing himself to relax. "You should report these threats to the deputies. Give them the letters and tell them you think they're connected to tonight's attack."

Heather's curse was short and sharp. "And in case that wasn't clear enough for you: no." She angled her chin as she scowled up at Diego. "My opponents will jump all over this like sharks, rushing at chum in the water. They'll use these threats to paint me as weak and vulnerable."

Diego spread his arms, incredulous. "Who cares?"

"I do," Heather asserted. "How am I supposed to be effective in office if people second-guess my every decision, wondering whether I'm making a

'safe' decision because someone wants to kill me?"
Her voice hiccupped, breaking her final expletive into
syllables. Embarrassed, Heather dropped her head
into her hands.

"Heather—"

It was her turn to interrupt him. "Leave me alone.
I'll figure this out on my own."

"No, you won't." Shari's voice was firm. "We'll
help you."

"And we'll start by finding you somewhere else to
stay." Diego crossed his arms over his broad chest.
"You're not safe in your house. Someone's already
broken in. You can stay with me."

Heather arched an eyebrow. She selected another
swearword from her inexhaustible mental supply. "I'll
check into a hotel."

Diego frowned. "You shouldn't be alone."

Heather snorted. "Well, I'm not staying with you."

"I know the perfect place for you to stay." Shari
grinned. Her eyes twinkled with mischief. "But you'll
have to give up cursing for Lent."

"It was a wonderful homily, wasn't it, Lou?" Sister
Barbara's hazel green eyes twinkled behind her silver-
rimmed glasses. Her Hermionean pin sat just below
the right shoulder of her mauve pantsuit.

Sister Barbara was a hugger. The congregation's
prioress wrapped Sister Lou in a brief embrace of
affection as Sister Lou joined her in the tiled lobby
outside of the motherhouse chapel after morning
Mass on Ash Wednesday.

Most of the sisters, including all of the congregation's
leadership team, had attended the seven fifteen Mass.

They preferred to get their ashes early. Application of the ashes was a solemn Ash Wednesday ritual that welcomed the Lenten season. The ashes were applied to each person's forehead in the shape of the cross. As Father Ryan O'Flynn had applied the ashes to each participant's forehead, he'd quoted Genesis chapter three, verse nineteen, "Remember that you are dust, and unto dust you shall return."

Most people—including some Catholics—seemed disconcerted when they saw the ashes on her forehead. But the ashes gave Sister Lou a sense of contentment. They symbolized her repentance for her sins and readiness to grow in faith in preparation to celebrate Easter.

"I always enjoy Father Ryan's homilies. He manages the right balance of humor and solemnity." Sister Lou's gaze located the celebrant in the sea of sisters.

As usual, the middle-aged priest's thinning salt-and-pepper hair was in need of a trim. He crossed the lobby in the company of several sisters, presumably on their way to breakfast in the dining area. Their joyful laughter danced back to her.

Sister Lou returned her attention to the prioress. Behind Sister Barbara, towering leafy potted plants framed the floor-to-ceiling picture window.

Beyond the window, the courtyard was stark with winter's stamp. Mounds of melting snow dotted the mid-February landscape. Small evergreen shrubs lined the perimeter and circled barren trees. In the center, a ring of Burberry bushes surrounded a white plaster statue of St. Hermione of Ephesus. Her face was lifted to the sky and her expression was so intent Sister Lou could imagine the saint in conversation with God.

Sister Barbara wrapped her arm around Sister Lou's waist and started them down the hallway away from the chapel. "I can tell you have something on your mind, Lou. I'm listening."

"Shari Henson called me late last night."

They turned the corner at the end of the hallway. Sister Barbara let her arm drop from Sister Lou's waist. "The young newspaper reporter. Is she all right?"

"Yes, she's fine. Thank you for asking." Sister Lou smiled, remembering the congregation's Fat Tuesday celebration yesterday evening. Shari and Sister Carmen had once again bonded over the chocolate mini-cupcakes.

Halfway down the hall, Sister Lou pushed open the metal door that led to the subterranean passageway that wound its way between the motherhouse and the congregational offices. The space wasn't long. The motherhouse wasn't far from the offices.

Sister Lou stepped aside as she held the door open, allowing Sister Barbara to precede her. "Mayor Stanley needs our help."

Despite being underground, the space was bright and cheerful. Its pale walls displayed dozens of vibrant, original artwork—paintings, wall hangings, and mounted sculptures—lit by fluorescent bulbs. Some pieces had been donated by patrons of the congregation, but the majority were original art by congregational members who used their talents to express their love for God.

Sister Lou matched her steps to Sister Barbara's brisk strides. The passageway was comfortably cool in deference to the art. Their low-heeled shoes tapped against the pale blue concrete floor. Sister Lou was comfortable speaking openly in this space. They were alone since most of the sisters preferred to walk outside to get to the congregational offices—unless the weather was unbearable. In contrast, Sister Barbara preferred the convenience of the passageway. Sister Lou thought the prioress also loved to view the art.

"Of course." Sister Barbara inclined her head. "If the mayor needs our help, we'll do whatever we can to help her."

Sister Lou had anticipated the prioress's response, but Sister Barbara wasn't yet aware of what the congregation was getting into.

Do I know what we're getting into?

Sister Lou adjusted the strap of her navy purse on her right shoulder. "The mayor has asked to stay in one of the motherhouse's guest accommodations. She's been receiving threatening letters. While she was at work yesterday, someone broke into her home. The person left a third letter on her kitchen table. Then later last night, someone attacked her while she was jogging near her home."

"Oh dear." Sister Barbara's eyes widened behind her glasses. "Is she all right?"

"She had a mild concussion, but she'll be fine with some rest." Sister Lou pushed open the door at the end of the passage. It opened onto the offices of the Congregation of St. Hermione of Ephesus. Her private office was a short distance down the hallway to the left. Sister Lou turned away from it to accompany the prioress.

Sister Barbara tossed Sister Lou a quick grin as she

led the way to her office. "Mayor Stanley doesn't seem to be the kind of person who knows how to rest."

"No, she doesn't." Sister Lou thought of her recent encounters with the town official. The young woman seemed to have boundless energy, drive—and determination.

Who felt so threatened by her that they would terrorize and physically harm her?

"Of course she can stay with us." Sister Barbara crossed her office's threshold and settled onto the powder blue cloth-cushioned chair behind her L-shaped walnut wood desk. "She shouldn't remain in her home and she definitely shouldn't be alone, at least not until her assailant is found and taken into custody. Here, she'll be surrounded by people and we have excellent security."

Sister Lou took one of the three matching guest chairs in front of Sister Barbara's desk. The other woman's office always smelled pleasantly of cinnamon and peppermints. "Thank you, Barb. Mayor Stanley has agreed to make a donation to cover the duration of her stay."

Sister Barbara interrupted Sister Lou with a wave of her hand. "Let's worry about that later. We have no idea how long it will take to resolve this unfortunate situation, but she can stay here for as long as she needs to. Her safety is our greatest concern."

"Thank you." Sister Lou smiled with relief. "There's just one more thing. Mayor Stanley doesn't want anyone to know about the threats she's been receiving or about her attack. The only people who know are Shari; Chris; Diego DeVarona, Shari's editor; you;

Carm; and me. She's insistent that no one else know about the threats or attack."

"I understand." Sister Barbara leaned into her desk. "I take it this means she doesn't want to go to the deputies, either?"

"No, she doesn't." Sister Lou was still unclear about the mayor's reasoning behind that decision.

"Will you and your team handle the investigation?"

Sister Lou leaned back against the thickly cushioned chair. "When Mayor Stanley originally asked for my help, I turned her down. I'm not a professional investigator. I do community outreach." *That's my charism. These investigations are luck.*

Sister Barbara's piercing gaze held Sister Lou's. "I understand why you would be reluctant to take on another investigation. They're dangerous. But, Lou, you have a gift for them."

Sister Barbara's pronouncement shocked Sister Lou. "I disagree. These investigations are out of my skillset."

"You've already successfully led two investigations. Each time, you saved innocent people from being charged with crimes they didn't commit."

Sister Lou spread her arms in a helpless gesture. "I have no idea how to even begin this one."

"You didn't know how to start the others, either." Sister Barbara leaned back against her chair. "You'll figure this one out, too."

"One person has already been killed." That knowledge drove a fission of fear through Sister Lou.

Sister Barbara grew solemn. "I realize that these investigations are dangerous, but trust that God gave you this gift for a reason."

When did we agree that I had this gift? "I'm also concerned about Marianna. She won't give up until she discovers the reason Mayor Stanley is staying with us."

Sister Barbara waved a negligent hand. "We can handle Marianna."

Sister Lou gave her prioress a dubious look. *No one could control Marianna.*

Chapter 9

Later Wednesday morning, Sister Lou met with the rest of the congregation's leadership team for their daily meeting in the small conference room. Today's meeting had been rescheduled to a later time to accommodate the seven fifteen Ash Wednesday morning Mass.

Sister Barbara sat at the head of the oval-shaped walnut wood conference table. Sister Marianna sat to the prioress's right. Sister Marianna's blue, gold, and violet scarf complemented her royal blue blazer and a crisp, cloud white blouse. Sister Lou recognized the scarf as one of the original handmade designs by Sister Katharine "Kathy" Wen. The proceeds benefited the orphanage in Haiti that the congregation sponsored.

Sister Paula Walton sat beside Sister Marianna and across the table from Sister Lou. Sister Paula's red hair glowed as it curled above the shoulders of her white skirt suit. Sister Angela "Angie" Yeoh sat to Sister Lou's right between her and Sister Barbara. Her pale gold sweater matched her modest stud earrings.

The prioress led the leadership team in prayer before their meeting. At the conclusion, Sister Lou added her "Amen" to the voices of the other team members before she made the sign of the cross, touching the tips of her right index and second fingers to her forehead, chest, and left and right shoulders.

Sister Barbara's warm gaze touched on each sister seated at the table. "I have two news items to share before we move to our agenda. First, Kathy and her talented team of scarf makers have raised almost eight thousand dollars for our orphanage in Haiti."

"That's wonderful." Sister Paula clasped her hands together in enthusiasm.

"Yes, it is." Sister Barbara smiled. "Please continue to spread the word about the scarves. They made wonderful Christmas presents. They'll make lovely gifts for all occasions."

"Perhaps we should update the website to include how much money we've raised for the orphanage." Sister Lou glanced from Sister Paula back to Sister Barbara. "Knowing their purchase supports such a worthy effort would encourage other people to buy the scarves as well."

Sister Barbara inclined her head. "That's a good idea, Lou."

Sister Lou made a note on her blue-lined writing tablet. "I'll speak with Kathy about it."

"Thank you." Sister Barbara turned her attention to the rest of the team. "Second, Mayor Heather Stanley will be our guest during this Lenten season. She'll be staying in one of our guest accommodations starting today."

A sense of surprise wove through the silence. Sister Lou noted the curiosity in Sister Paula's brown eyes.

Sister Angela's eyebrows knitted in question. But neither woman could match the burning inquisitiveness in Sister Marianna's gray gaze.

Sister Angela looked puzzled. "Will she be staying for the entire season?"

"I'm afraid I don't know how long she'll be with us." Sister Barbara waved her hands in a vague gesture. "She assures us that her presence will be unobtrusive. And she's committed to making a donation to cover her stay, which is very generous."

"Indeed." Sister Paula nodded. "Even if she only stays a few nights, it's a donation that we hadn't expected. Are there any special instructions, like don't talk to her?"

"Nothing so dramatic." Sister Barbara smiled. "We can certainly interact with her. All she asks is that we respect her privacy. She's asked for our discretion. Please don't let anyone know that the mayor is staying with us. I'd appreciate your help in conveying that message to all of our members."

"I don't understand, Barbara." Sister Marianna adjusted the silk scarf around her neck. "Why is the mayor staying with *us*? Why *can't* we tell people that she'll be here during Lent? Why *don't* we know how long she'll be here with us?"

Still smiling, Sister Barbara turned to Sister Marianna. "Those are the requests the mayor has made. They seem simple and innocent enough. In any event, this is an excellent opportunity to teach the mayor about our congregation and our mission. I believe I read somewhere that the mayor is a lapsed Catholic. Perhaps we can also bring her back to the Church."

Sister Marianna's expression grew more stubborn. She fiddled with her scarf again. "Yes, but *why* is her stay here a big secret?"

Sister Lou felt guilty for putting Sister Barbara in the direct path of Sister Marianna's interrogation. "This is by the mayor's request, Marianna."

Sister Marianna turned her probing gaze on Sister Lou. A light shifted in her gray eyes. Sister Lou knew the moment Sister Marianna identified her as the source of information.

The scarf slipped a bit from Sister Marianna's shoulders. "Do *you* know why the mayor's coming here?"

Now I've put my foot in it. "Barb and I assured Mayor Stanley that the congregation would be discreet about her staying here. Are you comfortable with that, Marianna, or should we ask the mayor to go elsewhere?"

Sister Marianna looked taken aback. Her scarf floated from her shoulders. "Of course, I'm comfortable with that. There's no need to ask the mayor to leave. I was simply asking a question."

More than one. Sister Marianna's curiosity conflicted with the mayor's need for privacy. Could her prying jeopardize Heather's safety?

"Welcome to the motherhouse." Late Wednesday morning, Sister Lou unlocked the guest room the congregation had offered to Heather. She pushed the door open and stepped aside to invite the mayor in. "You're welcome to stay for as long as you'd like. We hope you'll be comfortable here."

"I'm sure I will be. Thank you for allowing me to stay in your motherhouse." Heather wheeled her large, black cloth-and-metal suitcase across the threshold. She turned to face Sister Lou in the center of the room. Her vibrant emerald green pantsuit emphasized her slim, fit figure. Her matching green pumps added three inches to her above-average height.

Sister Lou ignored the quick, furtive glances Heather kept giving the cross that was drawn on her forehead with ashes in recognition of Ash Wednesday. She was used to the startled looks. "You'll be safe here. After the situation with one of our motherhouse tours, we increased our security awareness. In addition, private rooms aren't part of our tours."

"I forgot that today was Ash Wednesday." Heather blurted the admission.

"It's understandable. You've had a lot on your mind." Sister Lou spoke as she did a visual inspection of Heather's accommodations.

The room was bright, cozy, and clean. Its walls were painted powder blue. Its floor stretched wide beneath warm rose carpeting. The main area included a walnut wood dressing table on the left. A small, black television stood on the dressing table. The scent of peppermint teased the air from the bowl of potpourri beside the television. On the right were two single beds and a walk-in closet. Opposite the room's door, a writing table stood beneath a picture window framed by warm rose curtains. A full blue-and-white-tiled bathroom was tucked behind a partial wall.

"I wish I could blame my not knowing it was Ash Wednesday on my being busy, but the truth is I never thought about it." Heather stood her suitcase at the foot of the far single bed.

"That's all right. You know now." Sister Lou sensed Heather's agitation and frustration. *Why is Heather making such a big deal about her oversight?*

"I'd planned to take an early lunch break to move some additional things into your motherhouse."

Heather pulled her right hand through her hair. "I didn't realize I'd be disrupting your holy day."

"You're not disrupting us."

Heather didn't look convinced. "All right. Good." She planted her fists on the hip of her emerald pantsuit. Her shoulders were squared. She tilted her curved chin at a defiant angle. "You should probably know that I'm a lapsed Catholic."

"Only God is perfect." Sister Lou gave the public official a beatific smile.

Heather looked puzzled. "Does that mean that I can still hide out here?"

"Of course." It was Sister Lou's turn to be confused. "Our hospitality isn't based on a person's religious practices—or lack thereof." She smiled. "We welcome everyone. In fact, the Catholic Church has a long history of providing sanctuary to those in need. Pope Francis, our Holy Father, has emphasized the importance of the culture of relationships and the culture of encounters. That's how people meet Jesus Christ. Making that personal connection marks the beginning of your relationship."

"I see." Heather looked uncomfortable.

Sister Lou linked her fingers together in front of her. "We celebrate Mass at seven fifteen and ten o'clock Sunday mornings, and four thirty Saturday evenings. We also have daily Masses at seven fifteen and eleven o'clock in the morning, and five fifteen in the evening. You're always welcome to join us."

Heather's nervous gaze swept left, then right. "I don't think I can make any of those times during the week, but perhaps I can try a weekend Mass."

"You're not required to attend Mass while you're

here. I just want you to know that you're welcome to join us at the chapel."

"Thank you." Heather lowered herself onto the powder blue–cushioned seat at the writing table. She crossed her long legs and gestured toward the bed. "Do you have time to talk with me?"

Sister Lou checked her crimson Timex. It was just after ten o'clock. "I have a few minutes." She lowered herself onto a corner of the bed, smoothing her ivory polyester skirt over her lap. The thick mattress was firm beneath her thighs.

"Thank you." Heather drew her fingers through her hair. "I was relieved—and grateful—when Shari told me you'd agreed to investigate these ridiculous threats against me."

"I don't know whether I'll be able to identify the person behind the threats, but I'll do my best." Sister Lou knotted her fingers together on her lap. *Lord, I hope I'm not promising more than I can deliver.*

"I appreciate that." Heather sat straighter on the cushioned seat. "Where do we begin?"

We? "You're going to take part in the investigation?"

"Of course." Heather leaned forward on her seat. "These letters have been sent to *me*. These are threats against *me*."

"Yes, I know, but—"

"You don't expect me to hand the case over to you and meekly bow out, do you? I'm not going to just hang around knitting da— sweaters while you conduct an investigation about me without me."

Sister Lou saw the determination in the mayor's eyes. She also recognized the fear. "You have my word that we'll keep you completely informed of our progress."

Heather was shaking her head before Sister Lou finished speaking. "That's bu— not good enough. I want to help with the actual investigation."

"This could get dangerous."

"I'm already in danger, Sister Lou." Heather wasn't going to back down.

Sister Lou conceded to Heather's resolve. "All right, we'll work together on the investigation."

"Great." Heather smiled.

Sister Lou rose. "I'll leave you to settle in."

Heather stood with her. "Thank you again for your hospitality—and your help."

"You're welcome." Sister Lou turned to leave.

The arrangement may work to the mayor's satisfaction, but Sister Lou had her doubts. *Why do I have the sense that I've just put my team in jeopardy?*

Shari sat on the visitor's chair opposite Diego's desk late Wednesday morning and considered the black ash cross drawn on her editor's broad forehead. Before she'd left for work that morning, Shari had read a few pages of the booklet about Lent that Sister Lou had given her. She understood the significance of the ash cross. She didn't understand why it had to be on one's forehead, though.

"What're you giving up for Lent?" She was fascinated by the things people chose to sacrifice for the season.

"TV." Diego took a sip of coffee from his Toronto Raptors mug. The scent of caffeine was giving Shari cravings.

The idea of giving up television wasn't as horrifying

as Chris's decision to give up coffee, but still. "For forty days?"

Diego's coffee brown eyes gleamed with humor. "I can catch up on my reading."

"But what about the NBA." They were midway through the National Basketball Association's season. "Aren't you going to support your team?" Shari gestured teasingly toward Diego's mug. She knew he wasn't a Raptors fan. He only used that mug because he'd lost a bet—or so he claimed.

Diego drank more coffee. "I can get stats and scores from the Internet."

"That's not the same. And March Madness is around the corner. What were you thinking?" The National Collegiate Athletic Association's March Madness was an annual televised competition of the best women's and men's college basketball teams across the country.

Diego shrugged his broad shoulders under the snow-white cotton shirt he wore with a gold tie. "That's what makes the sacrifice meaningful."

Shari still didn't get it, but she was willing to move on. "I just spoke with Sister Lou. She said Heather's settling into the motherhouse."

"Thank you for arranging that."

Shari felt Diego's relief from the other side of his desk. "Thank Sister Lou. I just made a call. She's the one who arranged it with her congregation."

"Then I'd like to call her. What's her number?" Diego wrote the telephone number that Shari repeated from memory. It was the direct phone line to Sister Lou's office.

"The mayor means a lot to you, doesn't she?" Shari regarded her boss closely.

"We've known each other a long time." Diego put down his pen and settled back onto his chair.

"I remember that you knew each other fourteen years ago in El Paso, but were you friends?"

"Sort of."

Shari felt the defensive walls rising around Diego. The personal discussion was making him uncomfortable. She could understand. Diego was her boss, after all. He also was becoming a father figure to her. It was an awkward feeling, but one she was starting to enjoy. "I know you care about her, but are you sure you want to go there? Heather's pretty prickly."

Diego gave her a half smile. "People say the same about you."

"I know. That's why I'm warning you."

His smile faded. "I appreciate your concern, Shari."

"I just don't get the attraction."

"To prickly women?" Diego chuckled. "Ask Chris."

"Whatever." She hesitated before adding defiantly, "I want you to be happy."

"I appreciate that."

"You're welcome. And don't worry. I'll be your shoulder to cry on if things head south." Shari pushed herself from her chair. She turned toward Diego's office door. "Sister Lou's amateur sleuth team's meeting with Heather tonight."

"I'd like to join you."

Shari turned back to Diego. "You really do care about her. I'll have to check with Sister Lou. She's the one running the show. And we're meeting in her apartment, which is pretty small."

"I appreciate your checking with her."

"Sure." Shari paused in the doorway. "Sister Lou serves weird tea and homemade cookies during the meetings. The tea's growing on me and the cookies are delicious. We should serve snacks during our editorial meetings."

Diego looked dubious. "I'll take that under advisement."

"You should. It would make the meetings much more pleasant. Do you know what would make them even better, though?"

"What?"

"If Hal didn't attend." Shari left her editor's office, allowing Diego to digest her parting salvo in private.

Chapter 10

"I started reading the booklet you gave me on Lent." Later that afternoon, Shari followed Sister Lou and the scent of cream of mushroom soup to one of the few available tables in the Briar Coast Café.

The two were meeting for lunch on Ash Wednesday. Chris wasn't able to join them. In his role as vice president for college advancement, he was meeting with donors of the College of St. Hermione of Ephesus. Shari was a little disappointed. Finally, she had a date for Valentine's Day—and the occasion was being hijacked by college donors and Ash Wednesday.

The happy chatter and bursts of laughter surrounding her in the cozy café reminded Shari that she was still better off this Valentine's Day than she had been in the past. She wasn't spending this one alone. Instead she was having a relaxing and nutritious lunch with a caring friend. That was part of being normal, wasn't it?

Sister Lou took the seat on the far side of the table for two, leaving the closer chair for Shari. Sister Lou kept her coat on, apparently in deference to the chilled breeze seeping through the window beside them. Shari folded her emerald coat over the back of the honey wood chair.

Once she was settled at the table, Sister Lou bowed her head, making the sign of the cross and saying grace over their lunch. Shari echoed the "Amen" before lifting her head and dousing her colorful garden side salad with honey mustard dressing.

"The information in the booklet is very detailed and will help you to better understand and appreciate the Lenten season." Sister Lou spread the white paper napkin over her lap.

"I want to understand what you and Chris are experiencing and what you hope to gain from Lent."

Sister Lou looked up at Shari. "Do you have any questions about what you've read so far?"

"I have a lot." Shari lifted her fork in preparation for digging into her salad. "Like what's the big deal with penance? Why is there such an emphasis on that?"

Sister Lou swallowed a mouthful of lettuce and other vegetables from her salad. "Penance is the opportunity to recognize that we've sinned, how we've sinned, and to make amends for the wrongs that we've committed. The acts of penance help us to restore our harmony with God and to have a conversion of the heart."

"That's a big deal in the booklet." Shari started on her salad. The sweet honey mustard dressing made the raw vegetables more palatable.

Sister Lou took a drink of her ice water. "It's a big deal in real life, too. Acts of contrition encourage us to turn away from the darkness and what is wrong, and to turn toward the light and what is right. A true conversion allows us to focus on Jesus Christ, on goodness, on beauty, and on the truth. That's the purpose of penance and why it's encouraged, especially during Lent."

Shari was in awe of the message Sister Lou had shared with her. If Shari's fourth foster mother—the religious zealot—had taken the time to explain her faith beliefs, how different would Shari's life have been? If any of her foster parents had taken the time to see her and to care for her the way Sister Lou had in just the last six months, what impact would that have had on her life?

Shari drank deeply from her glass of water. The cold, refreshing drink eased her dry throat. "Some of my questions are about things I've wondered off and on over the years."

"What are they?" Sister Lou gathered some more of her salad with her fork.

"I've heard that most of Jesus's followers thought He was going to lead them in a revolution against Rome." Shari had a vague memory of a minister making that claim during a particularly impassioned speech. "Why didn't He?"

"Jesus was here for a bigger purpose. The revolution He led was the fight for our minds, our hearts, and our souls. He preached peace, love, and unity. That was a much more important and lasting message to share. And it also was very revolutionary. It still is today."

Shari wasn't certain she bought into that. Perhaps in time, she'd change her mind. But based on what she knew about history and the very little she'd read in the Bible, Jerusalem had needed a more traditional revolution to bring about change.

As she ate her salad, Shari's gaze roamed the café. Perhaps a handful of diners had ashes drawn in the shape of a cross on their foreheads. Was it that there weren't that many Catholics in Briar Coast or that there weren't that many *observant* Catholics?

Shari turned again to Sister Lou. "You've explained the importance of Ash Wednesday, but what about Good Friday?"

"What about it?" Sister Lou finished her salad and brought her vegetable soup to the center of her black plastic tray.

"What's good about the day Jesus Christ was crucified and died?"

Sister Lou offered another smile. "What's good is that He didn't stay dead. He rose again on the third day in fulfillment of His promise to defeat death."

The lightbulb came on in Shari's mind. "That's why I always see those 'He is risen' posters during Easter."

"That's right. His victory over death is the most important aspect of Easter and the reason we celebrate the season." Sister Lou ate a spoonful of the fragrant vegetable soup.

Shari started on her cream of mushroom soup. She usually chose one of the chicken soups, but in support of Sister Lou's Lenten observance, she chose one of the vegetable soups to abstain from meat on Ash Wednesday. It just so happened that today, the café offered a large variety of vegetable soups and meatless dishes. The owners must realize that at least some of their patrons were fasting.

Shari swallowed a spoonful of the cream of mushroom soup. Her taste buds enjoyed the rich flavors of butter, onions, garlic, and nutmeg. She didn't feel as though she was denying herself anything. "The sacrament of reconciliation involves you actually making your confession to a priest in an actual confessional."

"That's right." Sister Lou looked up from her soup. "It's another feature of the Lenten season that's encouraged although not required."

"Is there a statute of limitations on reconciliation?" Sister Lou looked amused. "Not at all."

"If I decided to confess, I've got a lot to repent."

Sister Lou seemed to hesitate. "May I ask the nature of some of these sins?"

Shari didn't detect judgment in Sister Lou's eyes or expression, just simple curiosity—and caring. Always caring. She dropped her gaze to track the wafts of steam drifting from her bowl of soup. She lowered her voice. "I've stolen things. School supplies. Food. I've broken into buildings to find a place to sleep. I'm not ashamed of what I've done, but I'm sorry that I couldn't figure out a different way to handle it. A better way."

Sister Lou reached across the table. She cupped her hand over the back of Shari's where it lay on her lunch tray. "You've survived difficult circumstances that many people simply can't relate to, but at the same time too many people have experienced. Don't be too hard on yourself. You didn't hurt anyone. You did what you needed to do at the time to survive."

As true as Sister Lou's words were, they didn't make the memories any easier to live with. "Speaking of warm, safe places to sleep, thanks for taking in Mayor Stanley."

"Of course." Sister Lou gave Shari's hand a final squeeze before accepting her abrupt change of topic.

"I'm glad that you and Chris are willing to help with this investigation as well. I couldn't do it without both of you."

"We just follow your lead, Sister Lou." Shari shook off the old memories and made the effort to lighten her tone. "Speaking of the investigation, my editor would like to come to the meeting tonight. I told him I needed to get your permission first since you're leading the team."

"His joining us would probably be a good idea." A thoughtful expression came over Sister Lou's serene features. The look in her eyes reminded Shari that this quiet, understated woman had earned a doctorate in philosophy and was reelected to an organization's leadership team. "You told me that Heather and Diego knew each other in El Paso. It's possible that he has some insights into the mayor based on their shared past."

"'Heather'?" Shari gave her friend a teasing look. "So that's how you roll? You're on a first-name basis with the mayor now?"

Sister Lou blinked. "She asked me to call her that."

Shari chuckled. "I'm teasing you. I'll let Diego know he can join us."

Sister Lou gave her a playful smile. "Who knows, by the end of this investigation, you could be on a first-name basis with the mayor, too."

Shari succumbed to another wave of amusement. "I doubt that. I don't think the mayor likes me."

Sister Lou seemed puzzled. "That's strange. The two of you share quite a few similarities."

"That comment was uncalled for, Sister Lou." Shari feigned offense although she'd noticed a few similarities herself. For example, neither woman could step away from a challenge, which was the reason they often butted heads. It also was the reason Shari understood Heather's need to hunt down this harasser herself.

The threads of their teasing faded and a comfortable silence settled over Shari and Sister Lou. Shari's attention drifted to the view outside their window. Pedestrians huddled deeper into their winter coats as they rushed between shops or from stores to their cars. A cynical smile tugged at her lips. These New Yorkers were so soft. They wouldn't last a week in a Chicago winter.

Sister Lou leaned into their table, drawing Shari's attention. She lowered her voice. "Shari, is it possible that Diego could be involved with these threats?"

Shari burst out laughing again, then she realized Sister Lou was serious. "No, Sister Lou. That's *not* possible. Diego really cares about the mayor. A lot."

Sister Lou sat back on her chair, but her look of concern didn't ease. "Still, if I remember what you said correctly, the two have a somewhat troubled past. We should look into it just to be sure."

Shari was still dubious, but perhaps Sister Lou had a point. "You're right. We shouldn't make assumptions or take anything for granted. The mayor's life is at stake. I'll speak with Diego."

She bit back another sigh. That was not going to be an easy conversation.

They were outnumbered.

Shari's gaze surreptitiously swept the small sitting area in Sister Lou's apartment at the motherhouse. The room was comfortably warm and fragrant with the scent of apples and cinnamon from the bowl of potpourri on the corner table beside Sister Lou's armchair.

The group had gathered after a meatless Ash Wednesday dinner. As usual, Sister Lou sat on the overstuffed sky blue armchair on the far side of the room. Shari and Chris shared the matching love seat to Sister Lou's left. Chris was so close to her, Shari could feel his body heat at her back. This wasn't the way she'd imagined a Valentine's Day date would play out. But she could admit, at least to herself, that the reality of it was even better.

Heather and Diego sat stiffly on the matching sofa to Sister Lou's right. Shari noted that she and the mayor were the only ones in the group who didn't have ashes on their foreheads. The other three—all devout Catholics—had worn their ashes all day. Not for the first time, Shari found herself in the minority. Well, at least she wasn't alone. She sent a grateful glance toward Heather.

The mayor didn't notice. Apparently, Heather had made a few observations of her own. "Why is the media here?"

Shari didn't like Heather's condescending tone. "To help with the investigation, of course."

Heather gave a long, silent considering look first to Shari seated on the other side of the small walnut wood coffee table and then Diego seated an arm's length from her. Her observations—whatever they were—didn't appear to reassure her. "I don't want either of you at this meeting."

Sister Lou's smile didn't warm her onyx eyes the way it usually did. "Shari is a valuable and critical member of my team. Diego is here at our request. We value his insights."

Shari warmed at the praise Sister Lou heaped on her. She masked a giddy smile behind her gold teacup, part of the set Sister Lou used to serve the tea and cookies for their meeting. Shari took a sip of the chai tea. She'd finally acquired a taste for the spicy brew. Its cinnamon scent wafted up from the mug. Hopefully, the snacks would impress Diego enough to spring for tea and cookies for their editorial meetings.

"Their only interest is in covering this event for the *Telegraph*." Heather's scowl deepened. "This isn't a news story. This is my life."

Behind her, Chris stiffened before facing Heather. "Shari has already proven on more than one occasion that she covers these news stories with great sensitivity."

Shari's cheeks heated with a blush. Now Chris was adding his praise, albeit in a voice tight with anger. Shari was overwhelmed. She could defend herself, of course. She was used to doing that. But this novel experience of having other people validate her work was nice.

Heather crossed her arms over her emerald green suit jacket. "I don't care if her articles come with a dozen roses, I don't want the press here."

Sister Lou spread her arms. "I'm afraid that's not your call, Heather. I can't perform an investigation without Shari's assistance. And I believe we would all benefit from Diego's input."

"Thank you, Sister Lou." Diego's expression of surprise was almost hilarious.

Shari turned to Heather before she gave in to the smile teasing the corners of her mouth. "I'll need this information to write the newspaper article later, but the article isn't our first priority. Your safety is."

Diego faced Heather. "No one in this room wants to hurt you. The reason we're here is to help you. However, you seem determined to hurt yourself."

Heather directed her temper toward Diego. "What does that mean?"

Diego gestured toward the mayor. "You helped yourself to Sister Lou's tea and cookies, then with almost the first statement out of your mouth reject two of the people who have volunteered to help save you. Do you want this investigation to fail?"

"Of course not." Heather lowered her glare to the vibrant scarlet and gold area rug beneath the coffee table. "Fine, I understand that Shari and Diego are critical to this investigation, but I need assurances that neither of you will write a word about these threats until *after* this criminal is caught."

Diego turned to Shari, appearing to leave the decision to her. Shari was grateful for that deference. "I'll give you that assurance provided I get the exclusive once the case is solved."

Heather looked confused. "The *Telegraph* is the only newspaper in town. Aren't all of your stories exclusives?"

Shari thought of Harold. She wasn't leaving this to chance. "*I* want to be the reporter to cover this story."

"Whatever." Heather shrugged. "I'll give you the exclusive interview."

Sister Lou helped herself to another chocolate chip cookie. "Now that we have that settled, shall we get started?"

Chapter 11

"I received the first note last Wednesday." Heather stood to pace Sister Lou's cozy sitting area. "You can't really call them letters. The first two were identical and only two sentences. The third note had four sentences."

Sister Lou studied the mayor's agitated movements as she crossed from the apartment's walnut wood door to the swinging door that led to Sister Lou's kitchenette. The heels of Heather's three-inch green pumps tapped smartly against the hardwood flooring. Her vibrant emerald green pantsuit projected understated authority. The outfit seemed as fresh and crisp this evening as it had when Sister Lou had met with the mayor almost twelve hours earlier.

Diego's eyes stretched wide. "You received three threats in a week and you didn't contact the sheriff's office?"

"How did you receive them?" Sister Lou crossed her ankles and cradled her mug in both hands. "Did they come in the mail or were they left where the stalker knew you'd find it?"

Heather tossed a glare toward Diego as she crossed back to the sofa. She reached into her purse and pulled out two plain white business envelopes.

"I don't have the first one, but I kept the last two." Heather reached over Diego to hand the envelopes to Sister Lou. Her gesture seemed deliberate. "The first two came to my office as though they were interoffice mail. The last one was left on my kitchen table. I found it when I got home from work."

"The evening you were attacked," Diego added.

Sister Lou's gaze shot up to Heather's. "Oh dear. Do you have any idea how the stalker got into your home?"

"My spare key is missing." The mayor rose to resume her pacing. "He must have used it to get into my house, then kept it."

"You didn't mention that," Diego said.

Heather shot him another quelling look. "There are a lot of things I haven't told you, Diego."

"We have to have your locks changed. Now." Diego was almost vibrating with tension.

Heather gave him a superior look. "Already taken care of. I'm not completely incompetent."

The newspaper editor was either a very good actor or Shari was right. Diego seemed genuinely agitated by the threat to the town's top executive. He cared too much about Heather to be involved in any way with these threats.

Sister Lou returned her attention to the notes. She removed a short piece of paper from the top envelope. Its message read, *Outsider, if you know what's good for you, don't run for reelection. Leave Briar Coast.* Its typed text was two lines long. That left a lot of empty space on the standard sheet of paper.

She reinserted the note into the first business envelope, then turned to the second mailer. The brief message in the second envelope read, *Outsider, Opal Lorrie wasn't supposed to die. That threat is just for you. I'd only wanted to scare her. But murder's even easier the second time around.*

The threat was clear and menacing. Sister Lou felt the hate behind the message. A chill raced down her spine.

Am I out of my depth?

Sister Lou refolded the second letter. Something seemed off. The top and bottom edges didn't align. Sister Lou set aside the second mailer and took the first note from its envelope. She trailed her right index finger across its bottom. To the naked eye, the edge seemed straight, but she was curious. She took her Sudoku puzzle book from the corner table beside her chair and laid the note on top of it.

"What are you doing?" Chris's question broke the silence that Sister Lou hadn't noticed.

She looked up and realized she'd become the center of attention. Keeping the note in place, Sister Lou turned the puzzle book around so that the others in the room could see her experiment. "The top and bottom edges of this note are crooked." She did the same thing with the second sheet of paper. "So is this one. Can you see it?"

Chris nodded. "Yes, I do. What do you think it means?"

"I'm not sure." Sister Lou returned the note to its envelope and gave both sets of mailings to Shari. "If I had to guess, I would say that the author of these threats didn't want us to identify his letterhead so he trimmed it."

Shari handed the mailers to Chris. "Why would someone print an anonymous letter on custom stationery in the first place?"

"Good question." Sister Lou looked up at Heather. "You received the first two messages in your office. At first, everything was going according to the stalker's plan. He somehow delivered his messages to Heather at her office. Opal's death, however, wasn't part of his plan, but he made the decision to take advantage of it to boost the fear factor. He took the risk of breaking into your home, which means that arranging the deliveries to your office must take more time and coordination."

"Shari's right." Diego reached forward to take the notes from Chris. "You're very observant."

Sister Lou's cheeks heated with embarrassment from the praise. "I wouldn't say that."

"I would," Chris said.

"So would I." Shari glanced at Heather. "Why does he call you 'Outsider'?"

"I'd only lived in Briar Coast for three years when I decided to run for mayor. Some people labeled me an outsider." Heather stopped pacing. "Still, I knew I could do a good job and I have."

"That took guts. And a lot of confidence." Shari gave the mayor a considering look.

"You mean arrogance, and maybe it did." Heather waved a hand toward Sister Lou. "How do these questions help us find the stalker?"

"They give us insight into the person we're looking for." Sister Lou sipped her tea. "The stalker is patient.

He found a way to get to your mail without anyone noticing. He's well organized. There aren't any superfluous marks on these messages. He's also an opportunist. Opal's death gave him an opening and he took it."

"All right." Heather seemed encouraged by Sister Lou's summation. "We're looking for a patient, well-organized opportunist. Who is that?"

Chris's dark eyebrows knitted. "It doesn't work that way. You have to help us come up with a list of suspects."

Sister Lou considered the Briar Coast mayor. She was arrogant, bordering on condescending; abrasive, bordering on rude; authoritative, bordering on bossy. "Who doesn't want you to run for reelection?"

Diego raised his left hand, palm out. "This isn't just about reelection. Someone wants Heather dead, and he's already killed Opal."

Sister Lou gestured toward the envelopes in Diego's hand. "Yes, he admitted his responsibility in the last message he left for Heather. But remember, when he had the opportunity to kill Heather while she was jogging, he didn't take it." She met Heather's wary eyes. "His primary goal is to get you out of the election and out of Briar Coast. Who doesn't want you to run for reelection?"

Heather gave a helpless shrug. "I have no idea. My job approval rating is good. I'm generally well liked."

"No, you're not." Shari's comment seemed spontaneous. "I agree that you're polling well as far as your job approval, but your popularity is pretty low. People don't like you as a person."

Heather gave Shari a dry look. "Don't sugarcoat it."

Shari looked surprised. "I didn't."

"As mayor of this town, I'm doing a good job." Heather braced her fists on her slim hips. "Our debt has gone down. Our schools are being modernized, and public services have improved."

"All of that's true." Shari inclined her head. "It's also true that taxes have increased, younger people are leaving Briar Coast in search of better-paying jobs, and we still have to drive ten miles outside of town for decent health care."

Sister Lou raised both hands to stop their exchange. "You've both shared very valid points. I understand the pros and cons as they would appear on paper. Thank you. Now I need to see for myself how other people react to and interact with Heather."

Heather frowned. "How will you do that?"

Sister Lou gave her a serene smile. "I'm going to accompany you to your office."

"Bring Your Sister to Work Day." Shari grinned. "I like it."

"How do I explain you?" Heather tossed the question over her shoulder as she crossed the Briar Coast Town Hall's second floor executive suite on her way to her office. It was just before eight o'clock Thursday morning.

The three-inch heels of her tall black boots were silent on the thin gray carpet. The boots matched the black faux leather belt around the waist of her brick red, ankle-length skirt suit.

"If anyone asks, why not tell them the truth?" Sister Lou followed the mayor into her office. "You're indulging my request to observe a typical day in the mayor's office."

"I don't have typical days, Sister Lou." Heather unfastened the big silver buttons on her winter coat as she crossed to her executive chair. She put her brief-case on her desk. "Make yourself comfortable at the conference table."

Sister Lou carried her computer bag and purse to the rectangular table. She considered its six matching chairs before choosing the one at the head of the table. The seat was closest to Heather and faced the door, giving her the best vantage point from which to observe Heather's visitors.

"Are you usually the first one in the office?" Sister Lou settled onto the comfortable thick cloth chair.

"I'm *often* the first one in." Heather stored her black faux leather handbag in her bottom desk drawer. "It depends on what's going on in the office. That's what I meant when I said that we don't have typical days."

"But your staff knows that you're usually in very early. That means that if someone wanted to slip something into your mail, they'd either have to arrive even earlier than you or leave very late."

"You're right." Heather circled her desk. "Would you like some coffee?"

Sister Lou tilted her head. "Do you have tea?"

The mayor's suite became increasingly crowded, active, and noisy as the eight o'clock hour drew nearer. Outside of the mayor's office, Sister Lou took a closer look at Heather's administrative assistant's work-station. On the counter above Kerry's desk, she counted six mail slots, one each for Heather; Kerry; Arneeka Laguda, her chief of staff; Yolanda Barnes, her chief legal counsel; Tian Liu, her communica-tions director; and Opal Lorrie, deceased finance and management director. Sister Lou recognized those names from articles in the *Telegraph*. Sister Lou again said a prayer for Opal. She also prayed for Penelope "Penny" del Castillo, who Sister Lou had read was the interim finance and management director.

Her visit to the executive suite's kitchen-cum-breakroom confirmed for Sister Lou that the mayor's office was a coffee lover's haven. The featured selection of teas failed to stir her interest. Sister Lou lowered her selected teabag into a cream porcelain mug, then poured hot water over it. She waited while Heather added cream and sweetener to her coffee. The scent of the strong, hot brew reminded Sister Lou of Chris's Lenten sacrifice. She smiled as she accompanied Heather back to her office. How was her nephew handling his second coffee-free day? If the past were any indication, not well.

A high-pitched peal of feminine, carefree laughter startled Sister Lou from her thoughts. She looked around to see a young couple enter the suite through the double glass doors.

"Good morning, Kerry." Heather's voice was warm but Sister Lou detected a hint of reserve in the words.

Kerry turned to her boss with a radiant smile. Her powder blue eyes shone and her round, milky cheeks glowed. "Oh, Mayor Stanley, good morning. Are you feeling okay?"

"Why wouldn't I be?" Heather stopped at the front of Kerry's workstation. Sister Lou waited beside her.

Kerry gestured toward her companion. "Jeff and I heard you fell while you were jogging last night, and that you spent the night in the hospital with a concussion."

"It's a small town, Mayor." Jeff nodded toward

Heather before shifting his curious gaze to Sister Lou. "You know, news travels fast."

"It appears that way." Heather gave the young man a quick look before turning back to Kerry. "I'm fine. Thank you for asking."

"I'm glad." Kerry pressed a small hand to her ample bosom. "Let me know if you need anything."

"Thank you, Kerry." Heather waved a hand between Kerry and her male friend. "Kerry Fletcher and Jefferson Manning, I'd like to introduce you to Sister Louise LaSalle. She's spending the day with us. Sister Lou, Kerry is my administrative assistant and Jeff is her friend. He's also the aide of a Buffalo city councilman, quite a distance away."

"It's not that far, Mayor Stanley." Jefferson's smile never faltered.

Sister Lou exchanged handshakes and greetings with the young couple. Kerry was a very pretty young woman who was obviously in love. Her doll-like face, framed by shoulder-length strawberry blond curls, glowed every time her wide eyes met Jefferson's. Her simple blue-green cotton sweater and woolen cherry red skirt showed off her curvy figure.

Jefferson's manner and appearance expressed an understated wealth. The handsome young man seemed well aware of his appeal. His perfect golden blond hair was professionally styled. It glowed beneath the fluorescent lights.

"Sister Louise LaSalle." Jefferson released Sister Lou's right hand. "Aren't you the sister, you know, who helped solve the last two Briar Coast murders?"

Sister Lou was disconcerted by Jefferson's question. It still surprised her when people referenced her participation in the murder investigations. "I did provide some insight to the sheriff's deputies on those cases."

"I thought I recognized your name." Jefferson glanced at his watch. "The Buffalo paper carried the *Telegraph*'s articles on those murder investigations, you know? Why are you spending the day with the mayor's office?"

Sister Lou gave the inquisitive young man a serene smile. "I'm interested in observing the day through the mayor's office." It wasn't a lie. It just wasn't the entire truth. Sister Lou was comfortable with that.

Jefferson glanced at Heather. "I thought no two days were, you know, the same at the mayor's office."

"They aren't." Kerry gave Sister Lou a dazzling smile. "But it's still nice to have you here with us, Sister Lou."

"Thank you." Sister Lou liked the young woman on sight. Still her amateur investigators would have to do a background check on Kerry as well as the rest of Heather's staff.

Sister Lou took in the hustle and bustle of the mayor's office. Was the stalker lurking among them or was he on the outside? She and her team would have to find a way to narrow their list of suspects, preferably before this threat hurt anyone else.

Chapter 12

"You and your executives have been together since the campaign." Sister Lou's words followed Heather into her office.

"That's right." Heather settled onto her chair and set her coffee mug within easy reach on her desk. "We've been through a lot together. It's made us very close, and before you ask, no one on my executive team would be involved in these threats nor would they have had anything to do with Opal's death."

Had Sister Lou heard the defensive note in her voice? Heather hadn't meant to sound combative, but it was important that Sister Lou understood that her executive team was off limits. They'd already lost Opal. Heather didn't want this investigation to affect them in any way.

Sister Lou seemed unruffled by either Heather's words or tone. "We should still check their backgrounds if only to rule them out."

Heather watched as her guest lifted a computer case onto the conference table. Sister Lou unpacked her laptop, then quickly and efficiently set up a makeshift workstation. The few gray strands of hair woven through the ebony bob that framed Sister Lou's gently rounded face glinted beneath the office's fluorescent lights. She smoothed the jacket of her slate gray polyester pantsuit before taking her seat at the head of the table. Heather's gaze dropped to Sister Lou's crossed ankles and her small black weatherproof boots. The sister must have chosen them for warmth rather than fashion.

Heather felt a twinge of guilt as she witnessed this example of the inconvenience Sister Lou had accepted to help a virtual stranger. "Thank you again for everything you're doing for me. I realize that it's a great imposition."

Sister Lou's almond-shaped onyx eyes stretched wide. "One member of our community was already killed. You were attacked. Although I think you should go to the deputies, in as much as you're reluctant to do that, I'm willing to help you. So are Chris, Shari, and Diego."

"Thank you." Heather was humbled by Sister Lou's response. "I still don't think you need to interview my team, though. It would be a waste of your time."

"It would give us peace of mind." Sister Lou returned Heather's steady stare. "They might also be able to shed some light on viable suspects."

Heather tried to shrug off her impatience. "All right, just as long as you don't reveal anything about these threats. I don't want them to be involved. What else?"

The knock on Heather's open office door interrupted their exchange. Arneeka stood framed in the doorway, her fisted hand against the walnut wood door. Her chocolate gaze swept first to Sister Lou before meeting Heather's. "Should I come back?"

Heather sat taller on her seat. "No, please come in. Arneeka Laguda, my chief of staff, I'd like to introduce you to Sister Lou LaSalle. She's here to see what it's like to be mayor."

Arneeka's black flats were silent on the office's wall-to-wall carpeting as she crossed to the conference table. Her bronze hijab covered her head and chest, and complemented her warm olive complexion. Her sapphire pantsuit was fitted to her slender figure.

"Sister Lou." Arneeka offered her right hand and a warm smile. "I've read all about you in the *Telegraph*. It's a pleasure to meet Briar Coast's Sleuthing Sister."

"It's nice to meet you, too, Arneeka." Sister Lou stood to shake Arneeka's hand. Her smile was puzzled. "'Sleuthing Sister'?"

Arneeka released Sister Lou's hand but her smile remained in place. "That's what some of us are calling you because of the alliteration, and because of your investigative skills. We're really impressed."

"Oh. Thank you." Sister Lou returned to her seat. Her disconcerted expression was amusing.

Arneeka sat on one of Heather's guest chairs. "Today's a good day to host Sister Lou. Your schedule's pretty quiet for a Thursday."

"It's quiet for now." Heather tossed Arneeka a skeptical glance. "Let's see how long that lasts."

"Oh, ye of little faith." Arneeka deadpanned her response. She handed a folder across the wide desk to Heather. "If the fates favor us, you should have plenty of time today to review the plans for the spring fund-raiser."

Heather took the proffered folder with a groan. "Do we *have* to do this event?"

"Yes. We do."

"Every year?"

"Every single one." Arneeka spoke in a singsong voice.

Heather sighed. "Have I told you how much I hate event planning?"

"I fail to understand how you can hate something you don't actually do." Arneeka made a note in her computer tablet. "This event is only once a year. Do you need me to remind you how important it is?"

"Do you need me to remind you that you're a bully?"

"Only because you need bullying."

Heather scanned the contents of the folder. She loved matching wits with Arneeka. These exchanges often were the only bright spots in her often stressful days. "I know how important the event is. This is a hoity-toity gala designed to shake loose future big dollars from the who's-who of Briar Coast for our non-profit community organizations."

"In the crudest terms." Arneeka sighed as though disappointed. "I prefer to think of it as a charity fund-raiser to support the missions of our community's public service agencies like the libraries, public schools, aging programs, shelters, and food banks."

"That's the only reason I opened this folder." Heather lifted a memo to study it more closely. "You and your team have made great progress on the planning. Thank you."

Arneeka lowered her gaze. A slight smile lifted her lips. "It's a start, but there's still a lot of work to do and less than three weeks in which to do it."

"You've pulled off miracles with less time and fewer resources than this." Heather reminded Arneeka of her recent successes, including Heather's election victory. "I'm glad you expanded the invitation list. The additional registration fees should help reach our fundraising goal for the proposed health clinic."

"I'm glad you made that suggestion." Arneeka looked to Sister Lou. "We've already received the paid registrations for your congregation, Sister Lou. Thank you."

Sister Lou looked up from her laptop and smiled. "Our leadership team always enjoys the gala, and this year, it's for an exceptionally good cause."

Heather's meeting with Arneeka continued for almost an hour. Finally, Arneeka reorganized her folders and rose from her chair. "I hope you enjoy your day with us, Sister Lou."

"Thank you. Good luck with the gala."

Arneeka nodded good-bye before leaving Heather's office.

"You have a good rapport with Arneeka." Sister Lou kept her attention on Heather's office door. "Do you have a similar rapport with all of your cabinet members?"

Heather made a final note on her writing tablet before spinning her chair to face Sister Lou. "I think so. As I mentioned, we became very close during the campaign. That's why I think you'd be wasting your time by interviewing them. They're not involved."

"We need to be sure, Heather, which means we not only have to rule people in. We also have to rule them out." Sister Lou tilted her head to one side. "Which brings me to another question. What's your relationship with Diego DeVarona?"

"Diego?" Heather's eyebrows lifted. The question amused her. "If I didn't know better, Sister Lou, I'd think you were using this investigation to get gossip."

Sister Lou returned Heather's skeptical look. "Luckily,

you do know better. I understand that you and Diego knew each other fourteen years ago in El Paso."

Uncomfortable with the direction of the conversation, Heather looked away. "You'd be wasting your time checking into his background, too. Diego isn't involved in these threats."

"How can you be so certain of that?"

Heather shrugged a shoulder. "What would he have to gain by my not running for reelection?"

"I understand that the two of you had a contentious relationship in El Paso." Sister Lou's tone grew pensive. "You certainly continue to butt heads now."

"Diego has nothing to do with these threats. He's a decent person." Heather turned back to Sister Lou. She managed to drag a smile to her lips. "Now if *Diego* was the one receiving these threats, I'd be the first to encourage you to add me to the suspect list."

Sister Lou's arched ebony eyebrows knitted. "Why would you do that?"

"Because I'd have a motive for the crime. Since Diego is the reason I had to leave El Paso, my motive would be revenge."

Chapter 13

Sister Lou wasn't certain how she should respond—
or even if she should respond. "Apparently, Diego
hasn't told us everything. What happened fourteen
years ago, Heather?"

Heather sat behind her desk, staring fixedly at her
dark wood bookcase across the room. She seemed
fourteen years and nineteen hundred miles away. "I
worked for the city's Department of Environmental
Services, but I had big dreams of becoming the mayor of
El Paso, the twentieth largest city in the United States."

"That dream may still come true."

"I think that ship has sailed, Sister Lou." The mayor
of Briar Coast's voice held no regrets. She settled back
on her chair and crossed her arms and legs. "Diego
was the city beat reporter for *The El Paso Crier*. I know;
it's a stupid name for a newspaper."

Sister Lou was startled. "I didn't say anything."

"But you're a smart woman. You were probably
thinking it." Heather shifted on her chair. "Diego was
smart, handsome, and charming."

"He's still all of those things."

Heather's violet eyes widened. "I didn't think sisters were allowed to notice things like that."

Sister Lou gave a dismissive sniff. "We're not blind."

Heather smiled. "No, you're not." She stretched her shoulders as though trying to relieve a knot in her muscles. "Our attraction was immediate and mutual. It wasn't just physical, though. I was impressed by his intelligence and I think he felt the same way. We had a mild flirtation, but it never went anywhere."

"Why not?" The question was out before Sister Lou realized she'd spoken.

"I suppose we were waiting for the right time. Too bad it never came." Heather's gaze strayed to her bookcase again. "The chief of staff for one of our city council members came to me for help. Graham Irsay. I'll never forget his name. He said the city had won the bid to have a national real estate developer open an office in El Paso. It was a highly sensitive move because of the competition. It required strict confidentiality, and he couldn't trust anyone in his office. I was so flattered. And so stupid. I agreed to relay messages and packages between them."

Sister Lou could see where this would end. "How did you find out he'd misled you?"

Heather's lips tightened with what appeared to be residual self-disgust. "Diego told me he'd learned about a corrupt land deal coming through my office. It involved this real estate developer. You see, Irsay wasn't helping the company open an office in El Paso. He was helping the developer bypass environmental laws. Diego said the information he'd been given on the corruption allegations implicated me."

"Oh no." Sister Lou's right hand pressed against

her chest. She studied the clean lines of Heather's profile. The mayor's features were taut and pale.

"Oh yes." Heather's voice was tight with anger even fourteen years later. "I told Diego that he'd been fed lies. I wasn't involved in anything corrupt, then I warned Irsay about the rumors."

The deception and betrayal made Sister Lou sick to her stomach. "How did he respond to what you'd told him?"

"Oh, he was reassuring." Heather shook her head in disgust. "He told me Diego was an ambulance chaser who worked for a disreputable rag, and that we were honorable public servants who had nothing to worry about." She gave Sister Lou a dry look. "Right."

Although this misfortune had happened almost a decade and a half ago to someone else, Sister Lou felt the tension in her neck and shoulders as though she was going through Heather's experience now. "How long did it take for the fallout to occur?"

"That was instantaneous, thanks to Diego. The *Crier* ran the article on its front page the next morning."

"Oh dear."

"My reaction was a little stronger." Heather paused, taking a deep breath. "I didn't keep the news clipping, but I can still remember the headline, ENVIRONMENTAL SERVICES INVOLVED IN PAY-TO-PLAY SCANDAL. Diego hadn't named me as a suspect, but the Ethics Office called me in the same day his article ran."

Sister Lou's eyes stretched wide with concern and shock. "How did they know to contact you if Diego hadn't included you in his article?"

"Someone else must have contacted them—and given them everything they needed to convict me on fraud: my phone number on the call logs with the developer, my e-mail address on the message exchanges, and my signature on the package delivery slips. If they'd charged me, my reputation would've been destroyed."

Sister Lou was puzzled—but relieved. "What stopped them from charging you?"

"Not what, who." Heather spun her chair back to face Sister Lou. "Diego linked the package deliveries to Irsay. The account for the courier service Irsay had used was in his name. And the courier's records showed that I signed for each package just minutes before I signed the visitors' log at the security desk at Irsay's office. When the city's Ethics Office confronted him, Irsay admitted that he'd been using me to throw suspicion off of him."

Sister Lou sniffed. "Well, I'm glad he did the right thing in the end by confessing his guilt."

"I wish he'd never involved me in the first place." Heather groaned, tugging both of her hands through her hair. "I wish I'd never involved myself."

"Your mistake is far away in the past, Heather." Sister Lou softened her voice as she expressed her understanding. "You've learned from it and moved on."

Heather wasn't as confident that she'd learned from her past. She heard Diego's voice in her head. *Do you remember El Paso?*

The newspaperman was reminding her of the Irsay incident and the way she'd worn blinders while the people around her made her their dupe.

Am I still wearing blinders?

Heather turned to Sister Lou. "Let's do the background check on the members of my team—just so we can exclude them from the suspect list."

"We will." Sister Lou's expression didn't reveal her reaction to Heather's change of heart. *Good.* "We're also developing a list of other more viable suspects like our former mayor, Owen Rodney."

"I've been thinking about him as well. The guy's such an as— totally unpleasant person." Heather's face heated. That slip would have been mortifying, and she'd been doing so well in cleaning up her language while she was with the congregation.

Sister Lou's eyes twinkled as though Heather's dilemma amused her. The other woman's reaction allowed Heather to relax.

"Mr. Rodney did refer to you as the Outsider throughout the campaign," Sister Lou pointed out. Heather remembered the incumbent's childish name-calling. "I've read that he's considering another run for the mayor's office, but how would he get the messages into your in-box?"

Heather's attention moved to her open doorway. Her mind rebelled at the stray thoughts forcing their way in. "It's possible that the stalker has an accomplice, which is another angle that implicates the people in my office."

Sister Lou shifted on her seat, turning back to her laptop. "I should let you get to work. We can talk more about this later."

Heather opened the manila project folder Arneeka had left behind for the Mayor's Charity Spring-Raiser. She refocused on her work. She wouldn't let some deranged control freak affect her job performance.

Several hours later, a knock at her open door shattered Heather's concentration. Ian Greer stood just outside her office. The town council president looked startled to find that Heather wasn't alone. Heather noticed Sister Lou regarding Ian with curiosity and her customary warmth.

"Come in, President Greer." Heather waved a hand between Ian and Sister Lou. "Allow me to introduce Sister Lou LaSalle. She's a member of the leadership team of the Congregation of the Sisters of Saint Hermione of Ephesus. Sister Lou, this is Town Council President Ian Greer, but I'm sure you recognize him from the many council meetings you've attended."

"Yes, I do. It's nice to formally meet you, President Greer." Sister Lou rose to her feet.

Ian crossed the room to accept Sister Lou's outstretched hand. His clean-shaven brown pate and salt-and-pepper goatee gave him a regal bearing. He was of average height. His long legs crossed the room with a grace that almost masked his slight limp. His dark brown suit fell fashionably over his slender form.

"The pleasure is mine, Sister Lou." Ian inclined his head. "I've read about you in the *Telegraph*. You've helped our law enforcement solve the last two murders in our town. Thank you."

"You're welcome, President Greer." Sister Lou returned to her seat.

Heather sensed her companion's discomfort. She glanced at her rose gold wristwatch. It was nearly noon. The morning had almost disappeared.

"What can I do for you, Ian?" Heather gestured toward the guest chairs. She noticed Ian's hesitant glance toward her guest. "You can speak freely in front of Sister Lou. She's the essence of discretion as you can tell from her work with our sheriff's office."

"I heard about your accident the other night." Ian settled onto the seat closest to the conference table. "How are you?"

"News travels fast in a small town." The muscles in Heather's back stiffened. She didn't like the implication that she was somehow frail and vulnerable. She especially didn't like that implication coming from one of her critics. "I sometimes wonder if we really need the *Telegraph*. The residents of our town do a fine job getting the news out on their own."

"There's no need to be defensive. I'm just concerned." Ian crossed his legs and rested his elbows on the arms of the guest chair.

"I'm sure you are, Ian. You're probably wondering how you can work my fall to your advantage when you challenge me for the mayor's office."

"Now you're sounding paranoid, which means you must be fine." Ian's smooth reply had the rough edge of irritation. *Good.* "We need to reschedule the finance meeting with the rest of the council. Is Penny up to speed?"

A weight pressed on Heather's shoulders. She thought of Penelope del Castillo, the finance manager and interim finance and management director, struggling to keep up with her work and Opal's. Earlier this morning, she'd discussed with Arneeka the need to promote Penelope to director and bring in a consultant to serve as a temporary finance manager until they could hire a manager full-time.

"Yes, Penny's ready to address the town's budget." Heather gave Ian a challenging stare. "But regardless of what you do, Ian, you won't be able to get the numbers to support a tax abatement for new businesses."

"The numbers add up when you factor in the revenues the new businesses will bring in to Briar Coast."

"The revenue that you're assuming the abatement

will generate amounts to paper money. We need *real* money to support Briar Coast."

"Heather, will you see reason?" Ian pushed himself up on his seat and leaned forward as though to emphasize his argument. "We need to grow Briar Coast. Young people are leaving. If we don't do something to attract jobs and entertainment, we're going to become a ghost town."

"If we do the wrong thing, we're going to go bankrupt." Heather leaned into her desk and folded her hands on its surface. "I'm not going to change my mind about opposing the tax abatement, Ian. Briar Coast needs those corporate taxes."

"You're going to make the party look fractured if you oppose the abatement while the majority of us support it."

Heather unclenched her teeth. "My priority is not representing the party. It's representing my constituents, the majority of whom do not need a business tax abatement. They need a solid education, medical facilities, and emergency services."

Ian was silent for a time, considering Heather. She could sense him looking for additional points to bolster his position, searching for weak spots in her argument to challenge her decision. Finally, Ian nodded. "Fair enough, Heather. I won't change my mind, either. I'm supporting the tax abatement."

"I can see that." Heather inclined her head.

"The difference is you don't have the votes in council to block the abatement." Ian sat back on his seat. "Two of the other four council members have a more rational perspective of the abatement. With my vote, this gives us the majority."

"We'll see." Heather sat back as well. "Is there

anything else I can do for you, Ian? Sister Lou and I have a lunch date."

"No, there's nothing else." Ian stood. "I'll look for you and Penny to reschedule our finance meeting."

"Of course. We'll look forward to reviewing the budget numbers with you. Have a good day."

"You, too." Ian found a smile for Sister Lou. "It was a pleasure to meet you, Sister Lou."

"You as well, President Greer."

Heather watched as Ian disappeared beyond her door. "I have to find a way to stop his insane abatement idea. It's fiscally irresponsible."

"I don't think you'll have any trouble stopping his plan." Sister Lou sounded pensive.

Heather turned to the older woman. "What makes you say that?"

Sister Lou folded her arms on the conference table in front of her laptop. "If he has the votes now to pass the abatement bill, why is he so anxious to reschedule the finance meeting with you?"

Heather's eyes widened with realization. "That's true."

"If the budget doesn't support a business tax abatement, you'll have another opportunity to make that argument to the council during your rescheduled meeting." Sister Lou glanced toward the doorway. "Is President Greer really after your office?"

Heather shrugged restlessly. "I'm not positive. It's more of a feeling I get from him and some of his devotees. There are rumors that his fans want him to run."

"We should add him to our list of suspects." Sister Lou turned back to Heather. "Is there anyone else?"

"The list seems to grow by the hour." Heather's tone was wry. It was depressing to realize how many people disliked her. "There's one donor in particular who supported Owen during the campaign. He was pretty aggravated when I was elected."

"We'll have to investigate him as well."

Heather frowned. "If this list gets any longer, I'll have to reconsider running for reelection. Perhaps I should go into the witness protection program instead."

Chapter 14

"How's that Lenten sacrifice working out for you?"

"I'm fine. Thanks for asking." Chris detected a touch of gloating in Shari's voice as she slurped her coffee.

His darling skeptic didn't believe he was serious about giving up caffeine for forty days and forty nights. Did she think having lunch at the Briar Coast Café on the second day of Lent would break him? The little café was a den of temptation. The aroma of rich, robust coffee was strong beneath the competing scents of chocolate, confectioners' sugar, fresh-baked bread, and made-from-scratch soup.

"I'm only asking because I'm concerned." Shari swept her spoon through her bowl of chicken-and-rice soup. "I want you to have a good Lenten season."

"Are you sure?" Chris jerked his chin toward a white porcelain mug overflowing with coffee. It sat on Shari's black plastic lunch tray beside her soup bowl. "I don't recall you ever requesting coffee with your soup-and-salad lunch before."

Shari lowered her soupspoon to her tray. She lifted

her white porcelain coffee mug and cradled it in both palms. "*I* didn't give up coffee for Lent."

Chris grinned, shaking his head at her antics. "The Bible is full of quotes about temptation."

"I'm sure it is." Shari took a deeper drink of java. "There are a lot of other, less painful sacrifices you could have made."

"They wouldn't have been as meaningful."

"Chris." Another woman's voice called for his attention.

Chris looked up to find Lorna Alexander, the vice president for finance with the College of St. Hermione of Ephesus, beside their table. Curiosity gleamed in her dark eyes. Bone-straight, dark brown hair in a pixie cut framed her diamond-shaped brown face. Her fur-lined black leather winter coat hung open over her fire engine red pantsuit.

"Hello, Lorna." Chris rose, straining to exhibit a civility he didn't feel. His efforts didn't extend to inviting his coworker to join them for lunch, though. He'd rather not match wits with her career ambitions during his meal.

"I dropped by this little café to pick up something for lunch." Lorna gripped her black leather clutch in both hands. Her nail polish matched her suit to perfection. "There's always so much to do at the college, isn't there, between meetings and projects. I'm surprised you were able to get away."

Chris sent Shari an apologetic look before turning back to Lorna. "I've found that getting away for lunch makes my afternoons more productive." He glanced at his watch for emphasis.

"Oh. Well." Lorna used her long, red nails to brush back her bangs. "I'm sorry to interrupt your lunch, though I have to admit that I was surprised to see you here." Her inquiring eyes finally landed on Shari.

Chris frowned. "Why is that?"

Lorna wrinkled her nose and tapped Chris's bicep above his tan long-sleeved shirt. Her red lips parted in the attempt of a teasing smile. "The Briar Coast Café doesn't seem like the kind of place for you to bring potential donors."

"This isn't a business lunch." Chris swept a hand from Shari to Lorna. "Sharelle Henson, Lorna Alexander."

Shari's cocoa eyes were suspicious. "Hello."

"Lorna is the college's vice president for finance." Chris smiled, proud to be able to say, "Shari is an investigative reporter with the *Telegraph* and my girlfriend."

Lorna's dark eyes seemed even more curious. "So you *do* have a personal life." She tapped Chris's bicep again. This time, her touch lingered. "I'll let you get back to lunch, then. Nice to have met you, Cheryl."

Shari's grin seemed predatory. "You, too, Lena."

Lorna gave Shari a startled look before turning on her black Burberry suede boots to find a place in the café's customer order line.

"Should I be worried?" Shari tracked Lorna's progress to the front of the café.

"I'm not romantically interested in Lorna, if that's what you're asking." Chris readjusted his winter coat on the back of his chair before reclaiming his seat.

Shari leaned toward him, lowering her voice. "Should *you* be worried?"

"Everyone who works with Lorna should be worried." Chris didn't believe he was exaggerating. "Her top priority is making other executives look bad in front of the president."

"Oh." Shari returned to her soup. "Why did you introduce me as your girlfriend?"

Chris lowered his steak-and-cheddar-on-whole-grain sandwich and gave Shari a puzzled look. Her tone was casual, perhaps too casual. "We've been dating for three months. How should I introduce you?"

Shari shrugged her slender shoulders under her silver turtleneck sweater. "I don't know."

Chris stared at her. Her response was worse than unhelpful. It only added to his confusion. Shari was outspoken to a fault, so why wasn't she speaking out now?

"I realize you're not a girl." He tried to read her reactions, but her expression was carefully closed. "You're a grown woman, but I'm not familiar with any other titles for our relationship."

"Neither am I."

"Then until you come up with something better, I'll stick with 'girlfriend.'"

Shari's gaze wavered before falling back to her tray. A block of ice squeezed into Chris's chest. Was Shari searching for a way out of their relationship? Why? What had he done wrong?

Sister Lou packed her laptop back into its case Thursday afternoon as she watched the young man who'd delivered the mayor's cabinet members' lunch order from the Briar Coast Café. "Are you certain that you want me to join you? You said this was a working lunch for your team."

"We're not discussing state secrets." Heather paid the deliveryman. She must have added a generous tip, judging by the surprised grin he shared with her before bouncing out of her office. "This will give you a chance to observe our interactions. You'll see for yourself why I'm sure no one on my staff would participate in these threats."

"I appreciate your intent, but I don't want to be in the way." Sister Lou joined Heather in unpacking the meal containers and eating utensils from the Briar Coast Café bags.

"You won't be in the way and my team knows you're joining us." Heather identified each container she lifted from the carrier before placing them in front of a chair.

Apparently, each member of Heather's cabinet took the same seat for every meeting. Noting this, Sister Lou decided to wait before choosing a chair for herself. There would be an extra seat since Kerry was having lunch with Jefferson.

She looked up as the executives walked into the office, silent but unified. Arneeka took the seat to the left of the head of the table. Penelope sat across from Arneeka. Tian was beside Arneeka, and Yolanda settled onto the chair at the foot of the table. Sister Lou carried her soup and sandwich to the empty chair on Yolanda's left. It was the closest to the door.

Sister Lou looked to Heather. "May I say grace?"

Heather turned to Arneeka. "Well, I—"

"It's all right, Mayor Stanley." Arneeka interrupted her boss. "Please go ahead, Sister Lou." She bowed her head and waited.

Sister Lou made the sign of the cross, touching her index and second fingers to her forehead, chest, and left and right shoulders. "For what we are about to receive let us truly be thankful. Amen." Sister Lou lifted her eyes as she made the sign of the cross again. The others were smiling at her.

Heather broke the silence. "Thank you, Sister Lou. I should've known you'd say the right thing."

"Of course. Catholics respect all faiths." Sister Lou moved her fork around her garden salad, mixing the tomatoes, cucumbers, carrots, lettuce, and blue cheese with her vinaigrette and oil dressing.

Aromas from the various dishes tempted Sister Lou: Heather's tangy salmon salad, Arneeka's spicy blackened chicken salad, Tian's cheesy baked ziti, Yolanda's well-seasoned chicken-and-sausage gumbo, and Penelope's tomato-based tortilla soup.

Despite these mouth-watering scents, Sister Lou's companions seemed disinterested in their meals. Their silence and body language spoke volumes. Their grief blanketed the table and made the air in the room seem heavy and stale.

Sister Lou considered Arneeka. When she'd first met Heather's chief of staff that morning, the other woman had seemed thoughtful and friendly. Her interaction with Heather had been entertaining. Now Arneeka's almond-shaped dark chocolate eyes were shadowed.

Seated beside Arneeka, Tian's stylish gray suit jacket was buttoned over a matching gray turtleneck sweater. The slim communications director also appeared to be lost in thoughts that were burdened by regrets.

To Sister Lou's right, Yolanda had the seat at the foot of the table. The senior legal counsel was petite with short, wavy dark brown hair framing an attractive diamond-shaped face. The expression of loss in Yolanda's eyes nearly broke Sister Lou's heart. On Sister Lou's left, Penelope appeared to be the youngest member of the group. The interim finance director seemed devastated.

The loss Heather's team had suffered had left them shattered and unsure of how to handle their grief. Sister Lou made the decision for them. They would face it in the open. "Tell me about Opal."

Her five companions couldn't have appeared more stunned if Sister Lou had announced that their beloved Buffalo Bills professional football franchise was relocating to San Diego, California.

Heather lowered her plastic fork. She wiped the corners of her mouth with the paper napkin she'd spread across her lap. "She earned her undergraduate—"

Sister Lou held up her left hand, palm out. "Tell me something personal about her."

Heather and her team exchanged puzzled expressions. They appeared confused as to the motivation for Sister Lou's question.

Finally, into the silence Yolanda called out. "She was afraid of ladybugs." After another pause, the room erupted into childish giggles.

"I'd forgotten about that." Heather covered her mouth and tossed back her head as she was overcome by hilarity.

"How could you forget?" Tian squealed through her laughter.

Heather looked to Sister Lou. "Once my campaign picked up momentum, I rented office space near the Briar Coast Café. I think it's an ice cream parlor now."

"That's right." Yolanda chuckled as she picked up the story. "In the summer, the side door was a magnet for ladybugs. Dozens of them."

"Scores of them." Arneeka sounded almost gleeful.

"Opal *hated* them." Tian held Sister Lou's gaze as

though to impress upon Sister Lou how uncomfortable her deceased friend had been around the bugs. "She'd scream whenever she saw one, and she'd freak out every time she had to go through the door." Then Tian fell back against her chair with peals of laughter. Her associates and Sister Lou joined in the hilarity.

Arneeka caught her breath. "Then one day, Heather had the brilliant idea to put a big plastic ladybug in Opal's desk drawer on top of her calculator."

"The shriek was ear piercing." Heather's tone was dry as she struggled with a smile. "But it was so worth it. At least it was until Opal paid me back."

Sister Lou wiped tears of laughter from her eyes. "How did she do that?"

"She reset all of Heather's clocks. *All* of them." Tian screamed with laughter.

"I was an hour early to all of my appointments that day." Heather's tone was dry, but her eyes twinkled with humor.

The happy reminiscences seemed to help improve their appetites. They approached their soups, salads, and sandwiches with much more enthusiasm.

Sister Lou sent her gaze around the table again. "What else?"

"She was one tough cookie." Yolanda made the observation with pride. "Opal told me once that she *hated* math."

"What?" The chorus circled the room in shocked tones.

"But she's such a brilliant accountant." Heather's eyes were wide with amazement. "Her work was impeccable. How could she hate math?"

Yolanda's eyes twinkled as though she was sharing an exciting secret. "She said all through primary school and into high school, she struggled with math, but she was determined to conquer it before she'd let it crush her. Majoring in accounting and then getting her M.B.A. was her way of proving that she wouldn't let math beat her."

Sister Lou was impressed. "You're right. She was one tough cookie."

"I admired Opal's intellectual curiosity." A smile hovered around Arneeka's full lips. "She said after she'd met me, she started reading books and articles about Islam because she wanted to understand my religion. She asked questions because she wanted to learn, not because she wanted to judge."

That touched Sister Lou's heart. "She was a caring person."

Arneeka nodded. "Very much so."

"That's what I remember most as well." Penelope's voice was muffled. "My mother died from cancer two years ago."

"I'm so sorry for your loss," Sister Lou murmured.

"Thank you." Penelope inclined her head. "Opal came to the hospital several times to sit with me while I visited my mother. We'd talk or watch TV while my mother rested. She'd come by straight from work, stay for an hour or so, make sure I had something to eat, then she'd go home. I really appreciated that."

Sister Lou reached over and squeezed the young woman's hand as it rested on her lap.

Tian's voice eased the sudden silence. "Every Tuesday of the campaign, we'd go to the shopping center's discount bookstore during lunch."

Sister Lou released Penelope's hand. "What types of books did Opal prefer?"

"Autobiographies." Tian shook her head with a smile. "Everything from legendary historical figures to scandal-plagued celebrities. She loved them all. She said she wanted to *know* people in their own words."

Heather sighed. "Thank you for letting us share these memories with you, Sister Lou. I hadn't realized this was what we needed."

"Thank *you* for sharing these memories with me." Sister Lou cast her gaze around the table again. "I wish I'd known Opal as well as you did."

"Opal can never be replaced." Heather smiled at Penelope. "But I know we're in good hands with Penny, which takes me to one of our agenda items. President Greer wants to reschedule the finance meeting with the town council members."

Arneeka frowned. "Why? I thought he had the votes to pass the abatement."

"Sister Lou had a suggestion." Heather slid a glance toward Sister Lou. "Maybe his voting block isn't as secure as he wants us to believe. We may have another chance to defeat this bill."

Yolanda looked from Sister Lou to Heather. Her lips curved in a grin. "What's the plan?"

Chapter 15

"Shari." A light, feminine voice hailed Shari as she strode back to her desk Thursday afternoon.

Taking two steps backward, Shari landed outside the cubicle of the *Telegraph*'s education reporter, Poppy Flowers. The woman's parents had an unfortunate sense of humor. The tall, shapely blonde crossed to her cubicle's entrance. Her chin-length bob framed round pink cheeks. She'd coupled a cream knit sweater with powder blue, taper-legged pants.

Shari looked up to meet the taller woman's big blue-green eyes. If she had to guess, Shari would say the education reporter was in her early thirties. But that was a rough guestimate. The other woman's youthful features made it hard to pinpoint her age.

"Yes, Poppy?"

"Do you have a few minutes?" Poppy waved a hand in the general direction of the guest chair behind her.

Shari checked the time on her silver smartphone. It was just after two o'clock. "Sure. I've already filed my story."

"I noticed your victory lap." Poppy stepped back, clearing Shari's path to the guest chair.

Shari settled onto the thick cream tweed seat. "Victory lap?"

Poppy returned to her gray cushioned desk chair. "That's what I call the bathroom break I finally allow myself after filing my story. I took my victory lap right before you did."

Shari tilted her head. "I don't know whether to feel exposed or amused that you pay such close attention to my bladder."

The education reporter's eyes twinkled with mischief. Her fine honey blond bob swung as she shrugged. "That's what happens when your cubicle's right next to the bathrooms. You get to see everyone's victory laps."

"You have a point." Shari gave in to amusement.

A few of their coworkers found Poppy to be abrasive, bordering on obnoxious. Shari thought the other woman was hilarious. She considered the knickknacks on display in Poppy's cubicle. What would Sister Lou deduce about Poppy based on these trinkets?

Today, a red-haired troll doll stood on the gray metal shelf above Poppy's desk, clutching a big red heart. It was a holdover from yesterday's Valentine's Day greeting. The Christmas greeting had come from a purple-hair troll in a red Santa Claus suit. A few of their scrooge-like coworkers had not seen the humor.

A creepy, little wind-up toy in the shape of a bloodshot blue eye on oversized orange feet paced next to her beige telephone. A large coffee mug with the phrase I SEE STUPID PEOPLE stenciled on it made its statement beside her computer monitor.

Shari turned her attention back to Poppy. It was several degrees warmer inside the reporter's cubicle than out. She identified the source of the extra heat as the space warmer beneath Poppy's desk. Shari was convinced human resources would have an objection or two about that. "What did you want to ask me?"

"It's about Hal."

Shari flashed a grin. "You know he doesn't like to be called that, don't you?"

"Who cares?"

That's why she liked Poppy. "What's your question?"

"What's Hal's problem with you?"

That wasn't even on the list of things Shari had expected her coworker to ask. Her defensive walls—never far away—rose. "What do you mean?"

"Oh, come on." Poppy crossed her right leg over her left. She wore comfortable-looking but unremarkable tan ankle-high boots. "We've all noticed it. He's been trying to get information from us about your partnership with Sister Lou."

Shari made an effort to contain her stirring temper. "He's questioned *all* of you? What have you told him?"

Poppy gave her a wry look. "We don't have anything *to* tell him. Besides we don't like him so we tell him to ask you."

"Thanks for that." According to Poppy, their Anti-Hal Contingent was in the majority, so what had Perry seen in him—and why had Diego kept him on staff?

"Yeah, well, he just complains that you aren't forthcoming with information." Poppy snorted. "As though you owe it to him to tell him anything. The kid has a misplaced sense of entitlement."

"I've noticed." Shari exhaled. She caught the scent of tomato sauce, garlic, and oregano. Poppy must have had pasta for lunch. "I've told Hal to worry about his own beat, but he won't listen."

"Be careful around him, Shari. That kid is bad news."

"I agree." Shari considered Poppy. "I'm curious. Why are you all so concerned for my professional safety?"

"You're so blunt. I love that." Poppy chuckled. "We know how hard you work and how much time you've put into helping to raise the *Telegraph*'s profile in the community. Our subscription rates are up, even in the neighboring areas."

"That's because of all of us."

Poppy shook her head, setting her honey-blond bob in motion again. "You and Diego stuck your necks out to get the *Telegraph* back on track. Now this rookie thinks he can show up and take over your beat. That's not right."

Shari flexed her shoulders with a mixture of irritation and impatience. "Does he think I'm just going to hand over my sources and let him take my bylines?"

"He thinks your beat's easy because you make it seem that way." Poppy rolled her eyes. "He doesn't have a clue."

"I don't know what Perry was thinking when he gave Hal a full-time job here." Shari scowled at the thin gray carpeting. The sounds of an impending deadline—shouting, cursing, running—echoed just outside of Shari's awareness. "Hal never did any work as an intern. What made Perry think he'd be any more productive as a reporter?"

"I've got a better question." Poppy spread her arms. "Why is Diego keeping Hal around?"

Shari wished she had an answer. Instead she felt

compelled to defend the editor. "Diego's only been in charge for four months."

"What's he waiting for?" Poppy shrugged. "All I'm saying is that Diego was the news editor before he became editor-in-chief. He knows what Hal's like."

"I can't explain it, either." Shari stared at the thin gray carpeting, trying to fit together imaginary puzzle pieces that didn't have anything to do with each other. "At the very least, Hal needs a work performance plan."

"As long as Hal's with the paper, we'd all better watch our backs, especially you." Poppy crossed her arms. "I've seen this kind of thing before. Hal has a hard-on for *your* news stories, but I don't think any of us is immune from his backstabbing."

"Thanks for the head's up, Poppy."

Shari rose and walked out of the education reporter's cubicle. Firing someone was easier said than done, but why wasn't Diego doing something—anything— to hold Harold accountable for his work? And why was Harold so determined to find out what Shari and Sister Lou were working on? If he wanted to cover crime stories, why didn't he hound the sheriff's deputies? Why was he fixating on Sister Lou's amateur sleuth team?

Heather froze in the doorway to her office. She sensed Sister Lou come to an abrupt stop beside her.

"What are you doing in my office?" Heather gritted the question through clenched teeth. A quick breath drew the strong scent of her third and final coffee for the day. She clutched the hot mug between her palms.

"I'm glad I caught you, Mayor Stanley." Wesley Vyne

circled her desk. He hesitated when he spotted Sister Lou with Heather. "Who are you?"

Heather bristled at his tone. She crossed into her office, ready to teach Wesley some manners, but Sister Lou spoke first.

"Wesley Vyne, isn't it?" Sister Lou stepped forward with a polite smile. "You're the president and chief executive officer of the Briar Coast Insurance Corporation."

Sister Lou managed to sound at the same time gracious and chiding. How did one accomplish that? It was as though she was gently taking their uninvited guest to task for his rudeness.

And it worked. Wesley appeared disconcerted. He stood in front of Heather's desk, a tall, middle-aged white man with a sad salt-and-pepper comb-over. The cut of his expensive Italian navy suit only masked so much of his beer belly.

Wesley sent Heather an uncertain look before addressing Sister Lou. "You have me at a disadvantage."

"Most people do." Heather marched past Wesley, ignoring the flash of irritation in his brown eyes, and stood behind her desk. "This is Sister Lou LaSalle. She's a member of the Congregation of the Sisters of Saint Hermione of Ephesus."

Wesley tossed a brief look toward Sister Lou before focusing again on Heather. "I need to speak with you. Alone."

Heather scowled toward the source of her disappointment. "You can speak freely in front of Sister Lou. She's a member of a religious order, for pity's sake."

"Thank you, Mayor Stanley, but I'm happy to give you some privacy." Sister Lou turned back toward the door. "It will give me a chance to stretch my legs."

Translation: Sister Lou needed a bathroom break. Heather could use one as well before she and Sister Lou drove back to the motherhouse. Heather watched the older woman stride past Wesley on her way out of the office. Sister Lou had left behind a very definite chill. The older woman didn't appear to think much of Wesley. Heather gave her points for good judgment.

The area outside of Heather's office was much quieter now. Most of her staff had gone home for the day. Heather would leave as soon as she'd packed the documents she needed to review tonight, Sister Lou returned—and Wesley left.

She shifted her attention to the unwelcome visitor. "What can I do for you, Wesley?"

Wesley made himself comfortable on a guest chair. He steepled his fingertips in front of his mouth and gave Heather a considering look. "One of the state senators is willing to retire her seat for you."

Heather schooled her features to mask her emotions, chief among them anger and surprise. "Did this come up in conversation?"

"I promised to support her campaign for state's attorney general." Wesley drilled his gaze into hers as though trying to read her mind. If he succeeded, what he found would hurt his feelings.

Heather folded her arms and locked her knees as her body began to tremble with anger. "I appreciate your thinking of me, Wes, but I'm not interested in running for a state office."

"Why not?" Wesley lowered his hands as his voice rose in surprise. "It's a much higher profile position, and you'll have the power to make decisions that affect the entire state."

Heather narrowed her eyes. "You want me to run

for state office because you don't think I'd win. You're hoping that if I lose at the state level, I won't return to politics."

"You sound paranoid, Heather." Wesley gave her a curious look. "Don't you have any ambition beyond my little town?"

Heather didn't miss the implication that she was the outsider in *his* little town. "I'm quite happy serving the residents of *our* little town. I'm sorry that you wish that someone else was in this office."

"This town needs fresh ideas."

"Like the tax abatement?"

Wesley frowned. "That policy is too shortsighted. What about the businesses that have been here the whole time? Don't we also need tax relief?"

"What about the residents who depend on the revenue from those business taxes to support their public services? They're your neighbors as well as your customers."

Wesley stood. "If I were you, Heather, I'd consider running for the state senate seat. I have a feeling the mayoral race will be too challenging for you."

"What makes you think that, Mister Vyne?" Sister Lou's question came from the doorway.

It was Wesley's turn to be startled. He spun to face Sister Lou. "It doesn't take a great intellect to realize that Heather's dismal popularity rating will make things difficult for her campaign." He held Heather's gaze over his shoulders. "Think about my offer."

Heather watched the businessman leave her office. "My popularity isn't *great*, but it's not *dismal*," she muttered. "I resent that."

"This has been a very long day." Sister Lou crossed

to Heather's conference table. "How many of your days are as bad as this one?"

Heather chuckled without humor. She rose to pack several of her manila folders into her briefcase. "A lot of my days in this office are as bad as this one and quite a few are worse."

Sister Lou paused in the process of packing up her notes and her laptop. "You have days that are worse than this? I can't imagine that."

Heather's laughter was more natural this time. "It's true."

"Then why do you do it?" Sister Lou turned to face her. "What makes you so willing to take on this stress and conflict to be mayor of Briar Coast?"

Heather considered Sister Lou's question. She took her time, trying to make sense of what motivated her. "At first, I got into politics for the power, the influence, and the prestige. I wanted to work with people to affect policy. It was exciting." She continued packing her briefcase. "But the thing is, once you start talking with the people who'll be impacted by those policy decisions, you realize what it means to be a public servant."

Sister Lou nodded as though in approval. "Is that the reason you're so adamant to remain in the mayor's office?"

"Yes, it is." Heather crossed to the silver-and-black coat tree to collect her coat. "I've found that the real excitement is taking on the people who have the power, influence, and prestige in an effort to help those who don't."

"I sense that you love what you're doing, but is it worth your life?"

Heather held the older woman's gaze. "I won't be intimidated."

"That's your ego talking. Are you running for re-election for your ego or for the community?"

"Today wasn't exactly conducive to my ego, so I must be running for the community." Heather led the way out of her office. She was keenly aware of the target on her back. Someone in the community she loved wanted her out—dead or alive.

Chapter 16

Who made this pot of coffee?

Shari stared into her porcelain mug, barely suppressing a tremor of disgust. Its contents looked like coffee. It smelled like coffee. But despite the four packets of sweetener and generous helping of almond creamer she'd stirred into the brew, it tasted like diesel fluid. Even so, she couldn't imagine giving up coffee for *forty days* . . .

"Do we need to talk?"

Diego's puzzling question drew Shari's thoughts away from the coffee impostor. She turned to find him standing with his right shoulder braced against her cubicle threshold.

It was the end of a long Thursday. Yet, as usual, Diego looked as fresh and crisp as a new morning. His dark gold crewneck knit sweater and chocolate brown pants were casual elegance. In lieu of his usual coffee mug, Diego was carrying a transparent, teal, thirty-two-ounce water bottle, a signal that he was wrapping up his day.

"You must think so, otherwise you wouldn't ask."

Shari set down her mug. She hit a couple of keys on her keyboard to save the notes for her latest story, then turned to Diego. "What's on your mind?"

"Direct as always." Diego's brown eyes twinkled with humor. He crossed into Shari's cubicle and settled onto the guest chair at her small conversation table. "Harold has been asking about your investigations with Sister Lou."

Shari hoped she masked her surprise. "How do you know that?"

Diego's full lips curved into a half smile. "I can't reveal my sources."

Shari was more puzzled now than she'd been when Diego had asked if they needed to talk. "Why are you asking about Harold? Are you concerned that I'll tell him about our latest case?"

"I know you wouldn't do that." His tone was chiding as though he was disappointed that she'd think he would doubt her discretion. Diego took a deep drink from his water bottle.

"Then what is it?"

"I'm concerned about you." He spread his arms. "I'd considered speaking with Harold on your behalf, but I didn't think you'd want my interference."

"I can handle Harold." Shari crossed her arms. "I'm glad other people have noticed his obsession with my partnership with Sister Lou. I was starting to feel paranoid."

"You're not paranoid. He's asked several reporters and a couple of copy editors about your working with Sister Lou. He's even asked me."

"You?" Shari's eyebrows shot up her forehead. "That's pretty ballsy. What did you tell him?"

"Apparently, we all said the same thing . . . that he should ask you."

Happiness wrapped around Shari like a warm blanket. She'd never before experienced this level of support from coworkers. She was used to fighting her own battles.

"Thank you." The words didn't feel like enough, but they were all she had.

"I don't want to lose one of the best reporters on my staff."

The blanket got a little warmer. "Thanks."

Diego swallowed another deep drink from his water bottle. "Harold's supposed to be covering the election. He shouldn't have time to nose around your beat or anyone else's. He's supposed to be writing about the election issues, the candidates, and the candidates' positions on the issues."

"I know." Shari arched an eyebrow. "How's that working out for you?"

"Not well." Diego scowled at the thin gray carpeting. "He's had to rewrite every story he's submitted at least once."

"That explains why I haven't seen many of his bylines."

Diego sighed. His expression was as tense as Shari had ever seen it. "He definitely has a problem with deadlines, which is one of the reasons I can't trust him with time-sensitive news."

"A *newspaper* reporter who can't make a deadline?"

"I don't know what persuaded Perry to hire Harold for the paper." Diego's voice crackled with irritation.

"Harold was a lazy intern. Now he's one of the laziest reporters I've ever worked with."

"I agree."

Shari's thoughts scattered. "Then why is he still here? Perry's not in charge anymore. You are."

"I don't want to give up on him." Diego's tone was simple.

Shari thought of all the people who'd given up on her, foster families, teachers, and employers. "I wish I'd had an employer like you when I first started out in the business."

"If you had, you may not be the excellent reporter you are today." Diego stood. "Are you sure you don't need me to talk with Harold?"

Shari shook her head. "I've got this. If I can't warn Hal off of my beat, he'll always see me as a target."

"Let me know if you change your mind." Diego turned to leave. "I'll see you later tonight when the team meets to discuss the case."

"Diego." Shari stopped him with her voice. "Is there any reason you wouldn't want Heather to run for re-election?"

Surprise swept across Diego's features to be replaced by his customary amusement. "Am I a suspect?"

"I'm just doing my due diligence." Shari's skin heated uncomfortably with embarrassment.

Diego once again propped his shoulder against the entrance to her cubicle. "I agree that I'm a viable suspect. Heather and I do have a volatile past."

"But you're not holding a grudge against her. *She's* angry with *you*."

Diego shrugged his eyebrows. "I did ask you to spy on her."

"But if you had deplorable reasons for spying on her, you wouldn't involve me in your plans."

"Probably not." Diego cocked his head. "I knew about the finance meeting."

"So did everyone who reads the *Telegraph*."

"Then maybe I just want her to leave Briar Coast."

"But you don't." Shari was as certain of that as she was of her name.

"What makes you so sure?"

She held Diego's curious gaze. "Because you're still a little in love with her."

Surprise flared in his eyes before he masked their expression. "Direct as always."

Shari watched him walk away. That was one less suspect on their list.

"What are you doing here?" Heather watched Diego settle onto Sister Lou's sofa Thursday evening. He was barely an arm's length from her. Was he going to sit there for the whole meeting?

She'd been surprised when the newsman had joined her, Sister Lou, Chris, Shari, and Sister Carmen for dinner, but she'd thought he'd come for the meal. She hadn't considered that he'd follow them afterward to Sister Lou's quarters on the third floor of the motherhouse.

"I want to help." Diego held her gaze as though daring her to turn him away.

She wouldn't dream of it. After mulling over Sister Lou's observations today, Heather had come to the realization that she could use all the help she could get.

"Thank you." Heather smiled at Diego's failed attempt to mask his surprise at her rapid acquiescence. The woman she'd been when they'd first known each other wouldn't have accepted his help. Actually, the woman she'd been last week wouldn't have accepted his help, either.

"You're welcome." Diego frowned. "I'll also take you to work in the morning, then bring you back here at the end of the day."

"Don't push it, Diego. That won't be necessary." Heather started to turn away, but Diego's warm hand on her shoulder stopped her.

"You should have a protective detail. You're a public figure who's been threatened."

"I've already been chased out of my home." Heather shifted to face him, a little disappointed when his touch fell away. "I'm not going to walk around with armed guards as though I can't take care of myself."

"If you aren't going to tell the deputies about this stalker, then I'll—*we'll*—have to protect you."

Heather noted the glint of determination in Diego's eyes and the bullheaded angle of his squared jaw. What was the appeal he had for her? She could feel him trying to lure her in just as he'd done almost fifteen years before.

"I don't need babysitters." Did her objection sound as weak to Diego as it sounded to her?

"We don't have time for false pride." Diego's expression became even more determined. "Someone's trying to kill you."

"I don't think so." Sister Lou's comment startled Heather from her disagreement with Diego. She'd forgotten that she and the newspaperman weren't alone.

She flinched, jerking her head to look behind her. Sister Lou looked comfortable on her overstuffed armchair. Her gaze dropped to the blue, gold, and white cross pinned to the older woman's taupe knit sweater. She'd noticed that all of the sisters wore the same pin.

"What do you mean? He's already killed Opal." Despite Diego's measured question, the flush on his sharp cheekbones indicated he'd also forgotten that he and Heather weren't alone.

"That's true and I'm very sorry about Opal's death." Sister Lou crossed her legs at her ankles and leaned them to the side. The hem of the powder pink skirt she'd worn to Heather's office that morning fell over her knees. "But the stalker admitted that he hadn't planned to kill her."

"He also said killing a second time would be easier for him." Diego's voice held a barely perceptible trace of . . . fear. "I'd rather not take that risk, Sister Lou."

"Of course not." Sister Lou looked at him with empathy. "I don't want to risk Heather's safety, either. I'm only pointing out that, after Heather was attacked during her evening jog two days ago, I realized that these threats aren't about killing her, despite what the stalker implies. If he'd wanted to kill her, he would have done so Tuesday night. He could have waited for her in her home and caught her by surprise."

"Aunt Lou's right." Chris joined the discussion in somber tones. He and Shari looked cozy together on the love seat across from Heather and Diego. "If this stalker wanted to harm the mayor, he wouldn't send her a series of letters about it. He'd just do it."

Heather struggled to suppress a shiver. "You probably think you're all being very reassuring and comforting, but you're not. This is actually disconcerting and . . . creepy."

Shari regarded Heather as though puzzled. "Do you *want* to leave Briar Coast?"

Heather scowled. "No, of course I don't want that. This has become my home."

"Then buckle up, princess. This is going to get real." Shari crossed her long, slender legs and folded her arms, which were covered by the long sleeves of her turquoise cotton sweater. "Your anonymous pen pal is obsessed with the mayoral race."

Heather had opened her mouth to protest the "princess," label, but Sister Lou's nephew spoke first.

"The election is the key." Chris nodded his agreement. "This stalker implies that he'll do something drastic—unless you declare that you *won't* run for reelection."

"The fact that he wants you out of the race makes me think he wants to run on your party's platform." Diego seemed deep in thought.

How could she feel both frozen with fear and on fire with outrage at the same time? Heather wrapped her arms around her torso in an effort to pull herself together. She watched Sister Lou reach for a notepad on the small walnut table beside her chair.

Shari's voice stopped her. "I'll take the notes, Sister Lou. I'll need them when I eventually write this story."

Heather frowned at Shari's pointed look. "You're not going to write that story anytime soon, are you?"

Shari's gaze shifted to her editor. "Diego and I will let you know when we're ready to publish it."

Heather's scowl deepened. That wasn't the response

she'd wanted, but she'd let the matter drop. For now. She followed the investigative reporter's movements as Shari dug into the large purple tote bag beside her feet and pull out a reporter's notebook and a ballpoint pen. Heather took a moment to admire Shari's navy stilettos, which exactly matched the other woman's narrow-legged slacks.

Sister Lou smiled at Shari. "Our suspect is someone who opposes Heather's administration. He has access to her office and her schedule, and knew about her spare key."

Heather spoke to keep from gaping. "How can you sound so certain that those are the exact characteristics of the person we're looking for?"

Sister Lou shook her head. "These aren't the aspects of your stalker. They're just some of the puzzle pieces that fit the bigger picture."

"That's right. This is a start." Chris caught Heather's attention. "This person is obviously someone who opposes your administration; otherwise he wouldn't want you to leave. And he must have access to your office to deliver his messages."

Heather turned her attention back to Sister Lou. "You haven't actually narrowed down the list of suspects. A lot of people oppose my administration. My margin of victory over Owen Rodney was very small, not even twenty percent. Everyone has access to my office. My door's always open when I'm in the building. Anyone can walk in."

"How many people knew about the spare key to your home?" Shari sounded defensive. It was as though she took Heather's comments as criticism against Sister Lou and wasn't happy about it.

"Not many," Heather conceded.

"Sister Lou's observations are important." Diego added his support for Sister Lou's preliminary assessment of their suspect. "Every detail that we can identify puts us a step closer to this guy."

"All right." Heather squared her shoulders and faced Sister Lou. "What's next?"

"We'll put together our initial list of suspects." Sister Lou gestured toward the sofa on her left. "Then Chris, Shari, and I will meet with them."

"I'll help with those interviews, too." Diego sat forward.

"What will I do?" Heather glanced at the others around the room.

"Wait for us to contact you." There was a look of satisfaction in Shari's reckless cocoa eyes as she gave Heather that order. "If you don't want to give your stalker the satisfaction of telling the deputies about his threats, you certainly don't want him to know you're chasing around Briar Coast looking for him."

"We'll need your help to put together the suspect list." Sister Lou's tone was conciliatory. "We've already agreed to include your executive staff."

Heather sighed in frustration. "I know we discussed that, but I think the stalker is a man. He lifted me while I was jogging. The members of my executive team are all women, and I'm pretty sure none of them could do that."

Shari shrugged as though dismissing Heather's concern. "They could be working with someone else."

Heather threw up her arms. "Fine, but I feel as though I'm betraying them." Heather jumped a bit when Diego wrapped his long, warms fingers around her right forearm.

Diego guided her arm back to the sofa cushion. "Wouldn't it be worth your peace of mind to officially remove your team from the suspect list?"

"Your staff will probably also be able to provide us with insight that could help us identify your stalker." Chris shifted as though making himself more comfortable on the love seat. His movements brought him closer to Shari.

Heather was marginally appeased by Chris's statement. "That's true. All right."

Shari's hand rushed over the top page of her reporter's notebook as she documented their list. "We should add Owen Rodney to the list since everyone knows he wants his office back and he hates you."

Heather arched an eyebrow at the reporter's delighted observation about the former mayor's feelings for her. "In that case, add Wesley Vyne. He hates me, too."

"Oh yeah." Shari seemed almost gleeful as she added the campaign donor's name to the list.

Sister Lou leaned forward, returning her mug of chai tea to the serving tray. "Shari, could you also add Ian Greer's name, please? Heather, you'd mentioned rumors that Town Council President Greer was considering running against you."

"I've heard those rumors, too." Shari didn't look up as she continued with the list.

Heather frowned at the reporter's notebook. "How many names do you have on the list?"

"Eight," Shari answered cheerfully. "Arneeka, your chief of staff; Kerry, your admin; Yolanda, your legal counsel; Tian, your communications director; Penelope, your acting finance director—"

Heather interrupted. "We've just made Penelope permanent."

Shari nodded as though in approval before continuing the count. "Ian, Owen, and Wesley."

Heather's eyes widened. "Wow, those are a lot of people."

Sister Lou nodded. "And we're just getting started."

Chapter 17

"This is stupid." Heather glared at Diego from across the roof of his seven-year-old black Honda SUV early Friday morning.

Diego found Heather's irritation amusing. He circled his vehicle to open the passenger door for her. "It's good to see you, too." Diego's grin broke free when Heather rolled her eyes.

"You know what I mean."

They were standing in the motherhouse parking lot shortly before seven o'clock Friday morning. Heather had been waiting when he'd pulled up in front of the residence, but Diego wasn't deluding himself that the mayor had given up her objections to being chauffeured around Briar Coast. His experiences with Heather during the past three years had shown him that she was just as stubborn today as she'd been fourteen years ago when they'd known each other in El Paso.

As he circled his SUV, Diego noted the chill in the moist early morning breeze. The local meteorologist hadn't predicted snow, but the gray sky, swollen with clouds, didn't appear to be in agreement. Spring was less than two months away, but the scent and feel of winter was still heavy in air. Despite his three-year residency in Briar Coast, Diego's El Paso, Texas, blood recognized the Mid-Atlantic weather as a danger to his system. Much to his relief, as soon as he opened his vehicle's front passenger door, Heather slipped onto the seat without further complaint. Maybe she was cold, too. Diego got back behind his steering wheel and put the car in gear.

Heather turned to him. "I could have opened my own door."

"Why didn't you?" Diego gave her a brief glance as he turned his Honda toward the parking lot's exit. Her deep blue winter coat made her violet eyes appear even more striking.

"You caught me off guard. I was hoping you'd forgotten about your offer to drive me to work."

Diego heard the disappointment in her voice. It bothered him. "I wouldn't forget. You should know me better than that."

"We haven't known each other in almost fourteen years."

"More like eleven years. I moved to Briar Coast three years ago."

The swooshing sound from the passenger side of his car indicated that Heather had shifted on her seat to face him. "Are you going to cart me to work every morning until we catch this jerk?"

"Yes, and I'm going to bring you back to the mother-house every evening." Diego activated the right turn signal. He kept his eyes on the traffic, waiting for an opportunity to merge onto the main road from the motherhouse's long and winding driveway.

"We don't even know how long the investigation will take."

"What are friends for?" Diego shrugged, making an effort to appear confident and carefree as he rejoined the traffic. But he was growing impatient. Each year for the past three years, Heather seemed more determined to keep him at a distance.

"We aren't friends, Diego."

"We were once." He at least wanted to return to that.

More swooshing sounds. In his peripheral vision, Diego saw that Heather was once again staring out of the windshield. In the brittle silence that engulfed the car, her powdery perfume taunted him.

Diego stopped at a red light. The businesses that populated Main Street's sidewalks had packed away their Valentine's Day decorations for next year. Although Easter was more than a month away, images of laughing bunnies, smiling chicks, and colored eggs covered the store windows. Even in this sleepy community, capitalism was king.

He considered what passed for rush-hour traffic in a town of less than one thousand residents. The cars driving north with him were most likely going to work at places like the sheriff's department, post office, fire department, Board of Education, or town hall. The largest employer for those in the southbound vehicles was the College of St. Hermione of Ephesus.

Finally, Heather spoke. "Thank you for taking me to work—although I don't understand why I can't drive myself." She was nothing if not predictable.

"And I don't understand why you're being so stubborn about this." *And about our friendship.* "Someone killed Opal and physically assaulted you. You shouldn't be left alone."

This time, the silence was even longer before Heather spoke again. "I don't want people to see you taking me to work." Her words were matter-of-fact.

"You'll have to get over that." Diego checked his rear and side mirrors before easing into the left lane. "It's a small town. Everyone sees everything."

Heather grunted. "Don't I know it."

Diego passed a slower-moving vehicle on his right before returning to that lane. "If anyone asks—and they undoubtedly will—just tell them we're dating."

Heather snorted. "As if." She blew out a deep, heavy sigh. "I'd rather tell them to mind their own business."

"Suit yourself, but my response is a lot friendlier." Diego turned right onto Town Street. "Frankly, your image can do with some warming up." *A lot of warming up.*

"Thanks for the tip." Heather collected the black handbag she'd settled on her lap and reached for her black briefcase at her feet. "Oh, look. We've arrived at town hall. You can let me out here."

Diego glanced at the familiar federal colonial style building through the windshield. The redbrick, two-story structure presided over a concrete courtyard that offered weathered wooden benches, small evergreen bushes, and young maple trees.

"I'm not going to put you out on the curb." Diego turned into the visitor/staff parking lot behind the town hall. Heather was opening the door before he brought the vehicle to a stop near the rear entrance. He caught her left arm to detain her. "What I did in El Paso . . . I was trying to be a friend."

Heather didn't close her door, but she relaxed onto the seat. "I know."

Diego released her. "Then why were you so angry with me? Why are you *still* angry?"

Heather let the silence lengthen. "I don't know." She gathered her purse and briefcase, then stepped from the car.

Diego watched her climb the steps to the town hall. He wasn't satisfied with her answer, but he wouldn't press her this morning. He'd have other opportunities while she was a captive audience during their carpool.

"What is going on, Louise?" Sister Marianna marched right up to Sister Lou's desk Friday morning. It was barely eight o'clock.

Sister Lou looked away from her personal computer monitor and up at her uninvited guest. She resisted the urge to roll her executive chair out of harm's way. Instead, she forced a bright smile to her lips and a cheerful lilt to her words. "Good morning, Marianna. How are you enjoying this beautiful day?"

Sister Marianna's thin shoulders bunched under the jacket of her navy blue skirt suit. Her navy-red-and-white-patterned silk scarf, another original creation from Sister Kathy's team, slipped a little more from its position around her neck. "Really, Louise? Must we *always* play this game?"

This time, Sister Lou's smile was genuine. "I do enjoy it so."

Sister Marianna settled onto one of the guest chairs. She sighed gustily as she gave Sister Lou a flat stare. "My day's just fine, Louise. How is your day progressing?"

"It's going well so far, Marianna. Thank you so much for asking." Sister Lou gestured toward her computer monitor. "It's going to be very hectic, though. There are several projects I need to wrap up before the weekend."

"Fine." Sister Marianna's cool gray gaze was more demanding than curious. "Now that we've exchanged these perfectly unnecessary pleasantries, tell me why the mayor has moved into our motherhouse."

Sister Lou blinked. *Was I too subtle in describing how very busy my day was going to be? More than likely, Marianna is more focused on her personal mission.*

Sister Lou leaned into her desk, surrendering to Sister Marianna's takeover. "The mayor needs to clear her head, Marianna. As I'm sure you can understand she was devastated by her finance and management director's very recent and unexpected death. Opal Lorrie wasn't only Mayor Stanley's finance director. She was also a very good friend."

Sister Marianna waved her hands in a dismissive manner. "Yes, yes, I realize that Mayor Stanley needs time to grieve, but she could have stayed in her own home to do that."

"She chose not to." Sister Lou tried a casual shrug. *Did it work?*

"I believe there's more to it than that, Louise." Sister Marianna's skepticism was palpable.

Sister Lou folded her hands together and forced herself not to squirm under Sister Marianna's penetrating scrutiny. She didn't want to mislead the other woman, but neither did she want to violate Heather's privacy or the confidences the mayor had shared with her.

"There also are a lot of critical issues that the mayor must decide on very soon." Sister Lou gripped her hands more tightly together. She could feel the sweat starting to pool in her palms. "She needs to focus. Fortunately, the mayor has a very competent staff, but I'm certain she misses Opal's experience and input. The change of venue will help—"

"Was it *your* idea for the mayor to stay here?" Sister Marianna pounced.

"No, it wasn't, but I'm glad she's here." Sister Lou swallowed a sweet sigh of relief. Thank goodness she didn't have to lie.

"Why doesn't Mayor Stanley know how long she'll be here?"

"We can't put the grieving process on a timer, Marianna." Sister Lou unclenched her hands and wiped her sweaty palms on the hips of her brown polyester pants. A rhythmic tapping caught her attention. She followed the sound to Sister Marianna where the other woman was drumming her fingertips on the wooden arms of her cushioned chair.

Sister Marianna's gaze continued to scan Sister Lou's features for clues. "Louise, does the mayor's sudden decision to stay with us have anything more to do with her finance and management director's death beyond her grief?"

The muscles in Sister Lou's neck stiffened. *Time to go on offense.* "Marianna, why are you asking so many questions? Why can't you accept that the mayor has called upon our hospitality as a calm oasis in the midst of her very personal grief?"

"I want to know what's going on, Louise. After all, I live in the motherhouse, too. Don't I have a right to know why our mayor has moved in?"

"We take in guests all the time. Heather's staying here isn't unusual."

Sister Marianna's thin silver eyebrows came together. "Are you on a first-name basis with the mayor?"

Sister Lou drew a deep breath, catching the fragrance of the white tea potpourri she kept in a bowl on top of her bookcase. "I've told you all that I can, Marianna. Please try to understand that Hea— the mayor doesn't want us to make a fuss about her staying here during this difficult time."

Sister Marianna sniffed. She sat back on her chair as though mortally offended by Sister Lou's implication that she couldn't be discreet. "I certainly *can* keep a secret, Louise."

"I'm aware of that. Thank you."

"Does Barbara know why the mayor has chosen to stay with us at the motherhouse for an unspecified amount of time?"

"Yes, I believe Barb spoke with Mayor Stanley shortly after the mayor arrived." Sister Lou stopped short of suggesting that Sister Marianna should harass the prioress instead and leave her in peace.

Sister Marianna's gaze narrowed. "Tell me, Louise, are you investigating something for the mayor? Does Mayor Stanley's stay with us have anything to do with your sleuthing hobby?"

Sleuthing hobby? Sister Marianna made it sound as though Sister Lou collected very rare stamps or vintage autographed baseball cards.

Sister Lou considered how to best—and diplomatically—respond to Sister Marianna's distressingly insightful question: "Come now, Marianna, if Mayor Stanley needed investigative services, don't you think she would go to the sheriff's office?"

"That would be the sensible plan of action." Sister Marianna rose from the guest chair and smoothed the skirt of her navy suit. "But people aren't always sensible when they're under duress, are they? And your sleuthing skills have garnered very well deserved praise. You're a talented investigator, Louise."

Sister Lou watched in stunned silence as Sister Marianna left her office. Considering the opposition the other woman had given Sister Lou when she'd investigated Dr. Maurice Jordan's murder and even as she'd worked to clear Sister Marianna by investigating Autumn Tassler's murder, Sister Lou had never expected Sister Marianna's praise. She was shocked— and uneasy. Could she live up to the accolades?

Chapter 18

Running late. Sorry. On my way.

Sister Lou read Shari's text on her cellular phone while standing just inside the Briar Coast Café Friday afternoon.

That's fine. Drive safely. Sister Lou sent her four-word reply to Shari, then slipped her phone back into her large purse.

Her mind wandered as she waited for her friend to join her for lunch. As usual, the customer order line moved at a brisk pace. Sister Lou enjoyed the café's tempting aromas of hearty soups, fresh breads, well-seasoned meats, and sweet pastries. Her stomach grumbled in a low but long protest, chastising her for waiting so long between meals.

"You're Sister Lou, right?" The male voice beside her held more than a hint of urgency.

Sister Lou interrupted her contemplation of the café's baked goods display. Giving up the treats for Lent didn't mean she couldn't look at them.

The young man at her side focused on her with

intense brown eyes from a height about half a foot above her. He seemed young, perhaps in his mid-twenties, but his manner seemed even younger. His black Burberry cashmere winter coat and gold Movado wristwatch were signs of an attentive and well-to-do family. He'd made every effort to hair-gel his unruly brown curls into conformity, but a few strands had reasserted themselves.

"May I help you?" Sister Lou gave him her complete attention and a curious smile.

The stranger offered Sister Lou his right hand. It was soft to the touch and swallowed her fingers like a mitten. "I'm Harold Beckett. I'm a reporter with the *Telegraph.*"

Shari wasn't very chatty about her coworkers, but Sister Lou made a point of noting their bylines. Harold's name wasn't familiar. Perhaps he was new to the paper. "How do you do, Mister Beckett?"

"Call me Harold, and you're Lou?"

Sister Lou's smile remained intact. "It's Sister Lou."

Harold seemed startled by Sister Lou's response, but he rallied. "What a coincidence running into you here, right?" He shot a quick glance at the window behind her, which offered a view of the café's parking lot. "I mean, I've read a lot about you and your investigations."

"Have you?" Sister Lou wasn't comfortable with the attention given to her amateur investigations. *I'll ask Shari to keep my name out of future articles.*

"I have a proposal for you." Harold stepped around to stand in front of Sister Lou. He looked behind her before meeting her gaze again. "You work with Shari on the murder investigations, and you can continue that."

"Thank you." Sister Lou regarded Harold with amusement. *He probably doesn't realize how obnoxious he sounds.*

"Sure. Sure. Briar Coast doesn't have that many murders anyway. But you can help me with other investigations like robberies or assaults." Harold's attention bounced from Sister Lou to the window and back. "What do you think?"

Sister Lou turned to scan the parking lot through the café's side window. She had a pretty good idea of who Harold had been looking for. She turned back, sensing the young man's growing discomfort. "Are you expecting someone?"

"What? No!" His denial was too vehement. "No! So what do you say? Are you going to chase some bad guys with me?"

"Why would we do that when Briar Coast already has a very competent sheriff's department?"

"Well, we would come from a more biblical approach." Harold's gaze bounced over Sister Lou's shoulder and back again. "You know, quote a few lines from the Bible, like the Ten Commandments, 'Thou shalt not steal.' Whaddaya think?"

Sister Lou tried to school her features to mask her horror but feared she may have failed. "I'm not going to do that."

"Why not?" Harold looked surprised. "It's a great idea."

"It's the worst idea I've ever heard."

"I think people in this town would—" Harold cut himself off as his attention was once again drawn over Sister Lou's shoulder. "I've got to go, Sister. I'll follow up with you later. Let's just keep this meeting between us. Okay?"

"No, it's not okay." Sister Lou looked over her shoulder and caught sight of Shari stepping out of her car. She returned her attention to Harold. "I don't keep secrets from my friends. In the future, if you want to discuss something with me, please don't play games. I much prefer the direct approach."

"I still don't know what you mean." Harold didn't wait for Sister Lou to respond. He spun on the heels of his black imported wingtips and maneuvered past the café's tables intent on escaping through the rear exit. *Interesting.*

"I'm so sorry to keep you waiting, Sister Lou." Shari's voice greeted Sister Lou moments later.

Her young friend was a pleasant distraction from the recent unpleasant encounter. "I haven't been waiting long, dear."

Shari stepped behind Sister Lou as the older woman moved to the end of the café's long lunch line. She was thankful that the customer order line was moving quickly. She was hungry enough to start eating her shoes.

After ordering their usual soups and salads, Shari followed Sister Lou to an empty table for two toward the front of the dining area. Shari bowed her head and waited for Sister Lou to say the grace over their meal.

"How was your morning?" Sister Lou spread a paper napkin over her lap.

Shari sighed, exhaling a small bit of the exasperation that lingered in her shoulders. She ripped open her packet of honey mustard dressing. "It was fine until I tried to leave my desk. I knew I shouldn't have answered the phone. The call was from some city council member's office in *Buffalo*. Weird. Why do they care about our small town's election?"

"A Buffalo councilman?"

Shari wondered at Sister Lou's odd reaction. "Yes, Brice Founder. Is something wrong?"

Sister Lou lowered her packet of olive oil and vinaigrette salad dressing. "Was the caller Jefferson Manning?"

Surprised, Shari paused in the act of dousing her bowl of spring vegetables with salad dressing. "How do you know him?"

"I met him yesterday." Sister Lou emptied half the packet of dressing over her salad. "He's a friend of Kerry Fletcher."

"The mayor's admin?" Shari picked up her silver fork. The metal was cool in her hand. "That's bizarre. He asked a bunch of questions about our election issues. Why didn't he just ask Kerry?"

Sister Lou's attention shifted toward the rear of the café before she met Shari's gaze again. "Is that call the reason you were delayed?"

Shari shrugged as she forked up bits of lettuce, carrots, and celery. "I told good old Jeffie that he should contact the reporter assigned to the elections. He must be hard of hearing because I had to repeat myself twice before he finally agreed to take my advice."

"And the reporter assigned to the elections is Harold Beckett." Sister Lou spoke as though she knew she was right.

Shari lowered her hands to the table and gave her friend an incredulous look. "Are you clairvoyant? How did you know Hal was assigned to the election? None of his articles have run yet."

"He was just here." Sister Lou inclined her head toward the rear of the café as she picked up her fork.

"Somehow he knew that I would be at the Briar Coast Café. He stopped by to introduce himself to me."

"That little creep." Shock ran through Shari's system like an icy river. Her thoughts raced as she tried to solve this latest puzzle. "He must have heard me on the phone with Chris this morning, telling him that I was meeting you for lunch. What else has he heard me talking about?" Shari felt sick. "Did Hal ask about our investigations?"

"No, but he did have a proposition for me."

"Oh boy." Shari's appetite dwindled. "What was it?"

"He said you and I can continue our *murder* investigations. He wants to work with me on *robbery* cases." Sister Lou seemed to be enjoying her lunch. She pressed her fork with great precision into her salad bowl, selecting her vegetables with care.

"What did you say?" Shari regarded her meal with measurably less enthusiasm.

The look Sister Lou gave her questioned Shari's common sense. "I told him that Briar Coast has very competent law enforcement officers. There's no need for me to investigate the town's robberies. You and Chris of all people know that I'm not enthusiastic about these investigations, but it seems that I've been called to them."

"Hal can be persistent."

"I've given him my answer." Sister Lou's tone was matter-of-fact. She returned to her salad, underscoring her position that the subject was closed.

A reluctant smile curved Shari's lips. Her friend could be stubborn. She'd proven that time and again. Shari envied Sister Lou her confidence.

They ate in silence, each apparently lost in their thoughts. Shari's salad, covered in sweet honey mustard dressing, usually tasted too good to be healthy, but today it was like bitter dust. With each passing moment, a bubbling resentment rose ever higher in her throat until she couldn't force her salad past it.

"Every time I think I've found the place where I'm supposed to be—a foster home, a school, a job—someone tries to chase me out." Shari froze. The words had spewed out of her without warning. Her eyes flew up to meet the concern in Sister Lou's onyx gaze. "I hadn't meant to say that out loud."

"Why not?" Sister Lou's voice was soft, gentle. "You've never guarded your words before."

"All right." Shari couldn't help the defensive note in her words. She tightened her right fist around the warm silver fork. "You've met Hal. He's . . . normal. Granted, he's arrogant, irresponsible, and completely without boundaries—obviously—but other than that, he's normal, isn't he?"

"I suppose he did seem so." Sister Lou sounded confused.

"That's right." Shari struggled to express feelings she'd never before verbalized. She'd never had anyone to share those words with. "I'm tired of *pretending* to be normal. I want to just *be* normal."

"What's your definition of normal? Perhaps we should start there."

Shari could sense her friend struggling to understand her feelings. "*You* are. *You're* my definition of normal. You grew up with stability. You know what that looks like and what it feels like. You know who your parents were. You know who your siblings were. You have some sense of your ancestral past. 'Having roots' isn't some nebulous concept for you, but it is for me. I don't know who I came from, where I came from, or whether I belong *anywhere*."

"You belong *here*, Shari. You belong in Briar Coast."

Shari was shaking her head even before Sister Lou stopped speaking. She swallowed the sour, burning lump of emotion in her throat and lowered her voice, hoping the occupants of the other tables couldn't hear her. "Suppose people realize I'm a fraud? Suppose Diego realizes that Hal is normal and I'm not, that Hal is better than me?"

"Wait!" The word shot from Sister Lou. Her tone was firm and determined. "Just stop right there. You and Harold have different backgrounds, but he's *not* better than you and you're *not* less than he is."

Shari's shrug was a stiff movement of muscle. "I'd rather move on myself than have someone show me to the door while Hal gets my beat."

"This doesn't sound like you, Shari." Sister Lou's dark eyes seemed to reach inside Shari's mind and search through the cobwebs of her thoughts. "I can't imagine you backing away from a challenge."

Shari pushed her half-eaten salad aside and feigned an interest in her cooling lentil soup. These meatless Fridays during Lent were like mini booby traps. Without thinking about it, she could slip up and find herself biting into a burger.

She shifted on her seat. "I'm not backing away. I'm looking for other opportunities."

"That sounds like a very creative way of saying that you're quitting."

Shari flinched. She frowned at Sister Lou. "That's harsh."

"Help me to understand what you're afraid of." Sister Lou searched Shari's eyes. "I want to understand. You have a job that you enjoy, a new apartment that you're happy with, and friends who love you like family. Yet you're willing to give that up because someone else is interested in your beat?"

"What *is* 'home'? Tell me because I don't know." Shari's frustration itched just beneath her skin, a burning irritant that she couldn't scratch. It was driving her to distraction. "What makes a home?"

"You do."

Shari was temporarily rendered speechless. It was a first. "How?"

"Shari, you had a difficult childhood. I'm not trivializing that, but you're not the only person who has moments of self-doubt. We all do. No one's *normal*. Normalcy's a myth."

"But how do I make a home?"

"You make a home by fighting for what you want and where you want it. Don't let anyone or anything stop you from going after what you want, not Harold, not doubts, not even yourself."

Shari took a long drink of her lemonade. The condensation around the hard plastic container was cold and slippery to her touch. "Sister Lou, that's very encouraging and inspirational, but in my experience, the reality is different. There's always someone or something hanging around, waiting to tear the rug out from under you."

Sister Lou shook her head. "Perhaps that's been your experience because that's what you're expecting. You've allowed your expectations to dissuade you from going after what you want. You can change that, but first you have to believe in yourself and your ability to do so."

Shari considered Sister Lou's theory. She drew her

silver metal spoon through her lentil soup. The tantalizing scent of vegetables and spices wafted up to her. It didn't reawaken her appetite, though. "You might have a point."

"I think that I do. Let's try an experiment. Instead of waiting for someone to steal your rug, work on silencing your self-doubts and going after your goal."

This time, Shari took a little longer to consider Sister Lou's proposal. "All right. Why not? What do I have to lose?"

"Nothing." Sister Lou shrugged. "In fact, you have everything to gain, including that home you've been looking for."

Shari ignored an uncharacteristic surge of optimism. There were no guarantees that she wouldn't still trip over that rug.

Why do I feel as though I'm kicking a puppy?

Sister Lou sat with Shari and Kerry late Monday morning. They were huddled in the executive kitchen-cum-breakroom of the mayor's suite in the Briar Coast Town Hall. She tried to imagine Kerry as the villain behind the threats against the mayor.

She failed horribly.

With her vibrant, shoulder-length, curly strawberry blond hair framing her round, kewpie-like features; wide-and-ready smile; and big, powder blue, innocent eyes, the twenty-something-year-old woman looked more like a baby doll than a menacing stalker. However, one of the things Sister Lou had learned from her past investigations was that people aren't always what they seemed.

Sister Lou stiffened her resolve to get to the truth regardless of where the path might lead her. "Mayor Stanley's executive team seems like a close-knit group."

Both Shari and Kerry were drinking coffee. The hot, dark roast aroma drifted across the small, rectangular faux wood table where Sister Lou sat facing the two young women. She glanced into her cardboard cup of tea. The container was warm within her palm, but the drink was tasteless.

Kerry swallowed a mouthful of coffee. She nodded, causing her glossy curls to bounce against her round, pink cheeks. "They've all known each other for years, ever since the start of Mayor Stanley's election campaign almost six years ago."

Sister Lou smiled at Kerry's misunderstanding. She tried to clarify what she'd meant. "Mayor Stanley includes you as part of her executive team."

Kerry gaped at Sister Lou. Her bright red lips parted and formed a near perfect circle. Her baby blue sweater made her eyes appear even wider and bluer.

"*I'm* a member of the exec team?" Kerry paused. Her eyes moved around the breakroom, seeming to take in the pale yellow walls, nearby matching chairs and tables, and the worn silver appliances. "I've never considered myself to be part of the *exec* team."

"You attend the meetings." Shari lowered her disposable cup of coffee. She'd added her customary three packets of sweetener and a generous amount of cream to the drink. The reporter seemed content with her coffee, giving Sister Lou further reason to second-guess her choice of tea.

Kerry giggled. "But I just take the notes."

"Don't minimize your contributions, Kerry." Shari

leaned closer to the younger woman. "Heather said you've offered a lot of good ideas during those meetings."

Footsteps tapped against the tile behind Sister Lou as a member of the mayor's staff entered the breakroom. Sister Lou caught Shari's attention. Their silent exchange was an agreement to wait until they were alone with Kerry before continuing the conversation. Sister Lou sipped her tea as she watched the middle-aged man cross to the coffeepot, fill his mug, then turn to leave the room. She returned his nod of greeting with a smile.

Switching her attention back to their table, Sister Lou contemplated Kerry's guileless demeanor, casual tone, and innocent words. Those characteristics created a conflict with the image of Kerry as Heather's harasser. Kerry had the means and opportunities with which to stalk Heather. The assistant had access to Heather's calendar, mail, e-mail account, voice mail system, and file cabinets. She also had a spare key to Heather's home.

But did she have motive?

Sister Lou set aside her half-full cup of tea. "Do you enjoy working for the mayor?"

Kerry's sigh was deep and weighty. "I love what I *do*, I just wish it wasn't in politics."

Sister Lou glanced at Shari. The reporter looked just as confused as Sister Lou felt. She turned back to Kerry. "What do you mean?"

"Some people treat politics like a game." Kerry sounded disgusted. "People come to the mayor's office because they're in trouble. They've lost their job or they're afraid they're going to lose their health care. They're having trouble caring for their elderly parents or they can't afford their utility bills. Does that sound like fun and games?"

"No, not at all." Sister Lou could feel Kerry's passion for helping people. She could use someone like Kerry on her outreach committee.

"Exactly!" Kerry threw her arms up. "People's lives are not games."

The tap of heels against the tile announced another staff member's presence. Sister Lou paused their exchange until the trio was alone again. It only took a few moments for the older woman to get her coffee and leave.

No one was getting tea.

Sister Lou's eyebrows knitted. "Isn't Jefferson in politics?"

"That's his only drawback." Kerry sighed. "He's so smart and charming. And handsome. He'll probably have a very successful career. I asked him once what his political goals were. He said he wanted to go as far as he could."

Kerry didn't seem very enthusiastic about Jefferson's ambitions.

"What kind of boss is Heather?" Shari asked.

Kerry appeared to collect her thoughts before answering. "She's tough. She really likes having her own way."

Shari grunted. "Who doesn't?"

Kerry giggled again. "And she's very opinionated."

"Do you know of anyone who has trouble with her, either someone on the staff or outside of it?" Shari asked.

Kerry's full lips curved into a reluctant smile. "*Most* people have trouble with her. Like I said, Heather can be difficult." She glanced at her watch as she stood. "I should get back to work. There are a few things I need to do before lunch."

"Of course." Sister Lou remained seated as she watched Kerry leave. "Thank you for talking with us."

There had been affection in Kerry's voice even as she admitted that Heather could be hard to deal with. It was clear that she cared about the difficult, opinionated, stubborn person she worked for. She couldn't fake that emotion.

The question was who could?

Chapter 19

"Remind me to recommend Heather stock a better brand of tea." Sister Lou poured the bitter brew down the sink, then dropped the cardboard cup into the recycle bin.

Shari gave her friend a smug smile. "It's hard to ruin a cup of coffee."

"Is that what you call what you were drinking?" Sister Lou led the way from the breakroom. "I couldn't tell with all that cream and sugar."

Shari grunted. "You wouldn't be so grouchy if you'd had the coffee."

It wasn't quite eleven thirty. In addition to Kerry, Shari and Sister Lou had hoped to speak with Arneeka Laguda, Heather's chief of staff, before lunch. They followed the narrow gray-carpeted hallway from the kitchen-cum-breakroom to Arneeka's office. Sister Lou knocked on the open door.

Arneeka looked up from the binders and folders spread across her Maplewood desk. Her orange hijab lent a warm undertone to her olive skin and deepened her brown eyes.

Despite her welcoming smile, the chief of staff appeared distracted. "Sister Lou. Shari. Please come in. Have a seat."

Sister Lou took one of the black cloth guest chairs in front of Arneeka's desk. "Thank you, Arneeka. We appreciate your time."

"We wanted to ask you a few questions about working for Mayor Stanley." Shari took the matching chair beside Sister Lou, hooking her emerald green wool coat over its back.

Arneeka shifted her attention from Sister Lou to Shari. "Are you doing a story about the mayor? Does she know?"

Shari crossed her left leg over her right. Her nose tickled from the faint scent of sage in the room. "If I didn't know you better, Arneeka, I'd think you were stalling."

Arneeka sat back on her black executive seat and crossed her arms. That quickly, the quiet, studious public official became a tough-as-nails executive defender. "But since you do know me, Shari, you realize that I won't allow my boss to be blindsided."

Shari raised her hands in a gesture of surrender. "Sister Lou and I told the mayor we were going to ask her team a couple of questions about working for her. She doesn't mind. We just finished talking to Kerry. It was painless. Ask her." She gestured toward Arneeka's beige desk phone.

Although she was a better liar than Sister Lou, Shari was relieved to be able to tell Heather's staff the truth. She liked them.

"That won't be necessary." Arneeka relaxed her arms. "How can I help you?"

Seated beside her, Shari sensed Sister Lou's intense

scrutiny of their hostess. What were Sister Lou's powers of observation telling her? Shari was impatient to find out.

Just like Kerry, Heather's chief of staff had access to Heather's schedule, voice mail system, e-mail account, and files. She didn't have a copy of Heather's house key, though. But the theory was that the stalker had gained access to Heather's home by using the spare key that the mayor had kept hidden under a flowerpot on her porch.

Sister Lou smoothed her brown wool winter coat across her lap. "How would you describe working for Mayor Stanley?"

Arneeka seemed to pull her gaze from one of the folders on her desk. She took another moment to answer the question. "The mayor is extremely smart and very empathetic. She's also incredibly strong willed."

Shari had been in Arneeka's office several times over the past two and a half months or so. Still today she tried looking at the other woman's surroundings from Sister Lou's perspective. Arneeka was almost obsessively well organized. She had two pen-and-pencil holders on her desk. One was for pens and the other for pencils. Her stapler, tape dispenser, and notepad were lined up beside the holders.

On the walnut wood bookcase to the left of her desk, the books were arranged by category, with neatly printed labels designating each section. A candleholder sat on top of the gray metal five-drawer file cabinet behind Arneeka's desk. A still-smoking incense stick was propped inside of it. That was the source of the sage scent that circulated the room. The only disarray was Arneeka's desk, and the books and folders spread across its surface. What would that tell Sister Lou?

"Do you enjoy working for Mayor Stanley?" Sister Lou's questioning continued.

"Yes, of course." Arneeka sounded preoccupied as though she was only giving the conversation half of her attention. "Why else would I work for her for more than six years?"

"I don't know." Shari shrugged. "Maybe because you need the job."

Arneeka's startled gaze flew to Shari. "I don't *need* this job. I *want* this job. I enjoy working for Heath—for Mayor Stanley."

Shari wasn't sure she believed the chief of staff, but Arneeka had always been difficult to read. "Rumor has it that she's hard to work for."

"That's not true." Arneeka shook her head with a brief chuckle. "Mayor Stanley isn't *hard* to work for. She's *impossible* to work for."

Sister Lou blinked. "But . . . you just said you enjoy working for her."

"I do." Arneeka held Sister Lou's gaze. "Heath—Mayor Stanley is a great boss and she's an even better mentor. She's also a wonderful friend. I've learned so much from her. But she's a machine and she assumes that everyone else is, too."

"Do you find Mayor Stanley's demands unreasonable?" Sister Lou pinned Arneeka with a probing gaze.

"Not at all." Arneeka's brown eyes sparkled. Her voice was gleeful. "It's a challenge, and so far I've never lost. I don't intend to, either. Several people, especially people outside of our office, have had problems meeting her expectations. But I never have—and I never will."

Sister Lou gave Shari an amused look before turning back to Arneeka. "How does the mayor react to missed deadlines?"

"She's disappointed, of course." Arneeka spread her arms. Her tone sobered. "If the time frame is unreasonable, she expects to be told in advance. I think that's perfectly fair."

"Yes, it is." Sister Lou inclined her head toward the far corner of Arneeka's desk. "Arneeka, please forgive me, but I couldn't help but notice the résumé on your desk. Are you looking for another job?"

Shari's wide-eyed stare shot to the corner of the desk that Sister Lou had indicated. Sure enough, the top of a résumé peeked out from under one of the file folders. How had she missed that? She waited for Arneeka's response to Sister Lou's question.

Arneeka tucked her résumé farther under the folder with quick, jerky motions. She looked at Sister Lou, then Shari, and back. "Yes, I am looking for another job."

Shari's eyebrows jumped in dismay. "Does the mayor know?"

"I haven't told her yet." Arneeka sighed. "I do enjoy my job here. And I enjoy working with Heather, but it's time for me to move on."

"Move on to what?" Shari asked.

"I want to focus more on education policy." Excitement and enthusiasm had returned to Arneeka's voice.

Sister Lou smiled. "Then I wish you every happiness and success."

Shari nodded. "So do I, but the mayor's office won't be the same without you."

Arneeka flashed a grin. "Thank you."

Sister Lou glanced at her crimson Timex wristwatch as she stood. "We should let you go. Thank you again for your time."

Shari stood as well. "And don't worry. We won't say anything to the mayor."

Arneeka rose from behind her desk. "I'm going to tell Heather about my plans soon. I'm just not ready yet."

Shari shrugged into her winter coat as she followed Sister Lou down the wide marbled staircase. She sensed that her friend was deep in thought. Shari crossed the bright white-and-silver-tiled lobby beside Sister Lou. She reached forward to push open the white wooden exit door and held it for her friend.

"Do you think Arneeka's involved?" Shari matched her steps to Sister Lou's brisk pace as they walked toward the other woman's bright orange, four-door Toyota Corolla.

"No, and I don't think Kerry's involved, either." Sister Lou tossed Shari a quick look. "What do you think?"

"You're right about Kerry." Shari shrugged deeper into her coat. "She seems devoted to Heather, but with Arneeka looking for another job, maybe she's the one who doesn't want Heather to run for reelection."

Sister Lou stopped beside her driver's side door. "Do you think sending threatening letters and committing murder seem a bit excessive just to quit a job?"

"I do. It sounded like a stretch as soon as I said it." Shari glanced over her shoulder. Her car was parked two spaces away. She turned back to Sister Lou. "Promise me that you'll obey the rules of the road on your way back to the congregational office."

Sister Lou gave Shari a dry look. "I'll be fine." She

pressed the button on her keyless entry remote to unlock her car. "Try not to dawdle. Chris said he's meeting you for lunch. You don't want it to become dinner."

Shari chuckled and turned away. She waved at Sister Lou over her shoulder as she walked to her own car. She lowered her arm, suddenly uneasy, and rubbed the back of her neck. She had the eerie feeling that she was being watched. Shari flexed her shoulder muscles as she cast a surreptitious look across the lot. Was all of this talk of stalkers and threats making her paranoid?

"What are you and the sister investigating at town hall?"

Harold threw the belligerent question at Shari from the doorway of the *Telegraph*'s breakroom after lunch Monday afternoon. She turned to Hal with a scowl. The rookie slouched against the threshold. His arms were crossed over his chest. He wore a thick gold cashmere sweater, skinny black pants, and his usual arrogance.

Shari braced her hips against the breakroom's counter and sipped her coffee while she counted to ten. The wood-paneled cabinet felt cold and hard despite her thick violet sweater. "Have you been following me, Hal?"

An irritated expression planted itself on Harold's pale, thin features. He lowered his arms. "I've asked you repeatedly *not* to call me Hal."

"And I've asked you to stop creeping around my beat." Shari shrugged. "I guess neither of us is getting what we want. Yet."

She took another sip of coffee. The dark roast bit back as it traveled past her taste buds. Shari had had a mug of coffee at town hall and another during her lunch with Chris. That didn't take into account the two mugs she'd had earlier in the morning. Maybe she should consider cutting back on the caffeine.

"What's going on at town hall?" Harold's question reminded Shari of their most recent contention.

"Do you mean you *don't* know?" Shari tsked between sips of coffee. "If you'd been working your election beat, you probably would."

Harold left the doorway and approached Shari. "Since you and the sister were there for more than an hour, why don't you just tell me?"

The heels of Harold's wingtips clapped against the faded linoleum flooring. Several yards from his target, Harold came to an abrupt stop. Had he finally noticed the vexation in Shari's eyes?

Shari swallowed another sip of java. She was battling her temper with deep breaths that drew in the scent of the strong, hot brew. "How're your election articles going? Think any of them will be published before Election Day?"

"What were you doing at town hall?"

"Why were you following me?"

"Are you and the sister investigating Opal Lorrie's death?"

"Stop calling her 'the sister.'" Shari glared at him. "Her name is Sister Lou. And stop following me, eavesdropping on my conversations, and nosing around my beat."

Harold braced his legs and crossed his arms again. "Your beat is a lot more interesting than mine."

A movement in the doorway distracted Shari.

Poppy Flowers, the education reporter, entered the breakroom. Her smile of greeting faded. Poppy seemed to sense the tension in the room. She turned and left without comment.

Shari returned her attention to Harold. "How would you know whether your beat's interesting?" She gave Harold a dismissive look as she straightened away from the cabinet. She walked toward him with long strides stiff with anger. "You haven't spent any time on it."

"I don't want to write about the election." Harold jumped out of Shari's way as she advanced on him. "It's boring."

"It's up to you to make it interesting and relevant to our readers—while sticking to the truth. Make them care about the issues on the ballot. After all, those issues only affect their *very lives.*" Shari took her sarcasm and brushed past the rookie on her way to the door.

"Tell me about your investigation into Opal Lorrie's murder." Harold's question flew after her as she strode toward the breakroom door. "The deputies said her death was an accident. Were they wrong?"

Shari froze. She took two calming breaths. Neither one worked. She turned to walk back to Harold. "You've been asking the other reporters and the copy editors for information about my partnership with Sister Lou." She stopped less than an arm's length from the rookie reporter. "If you want to know about my work, come to me. Don't slither around behind my back."

"I *have* come to you." Harold took a cautious step back. "You won't tell me anything."

"That's because it's my beat, so back off." Shari's cheeks were growing warm with temper.

"Or what?" Harold's smile was shaky. "You'll go running to Diego?"

Shari took a moment to indulge in her fantasy of punching Harold in the nose. She imagined the satisfying cracking sound it might make. Shari shook her head. She shouldn't have thoughts like this, especially during the Lenten season.

"I don't have to go to Diego. I can handle you myself." Shari turned and marched back to her cubicle.

She strode right to her desk and braced her palms against its surface. Anger made her skin burn and her heart thunder in her ears. She struggled to control her breathing. Shari hadn't felt this upset and out of control since her years in foster care. That was when she'd first learned to fight for herself, and to stand up for what she wanted, for what was hers.

Sister Lou was right. This wasn't the time to stop fighting. She wanted to be an investigative reporter with the *Telegraph*. She wanted to make her home in Briar Coast. She wanted to continue her friendship with Sister Lou, and she wanted to be with Chris. Those things were all worth fighting for.

Shari's attention dropped to her telephone. Still, it wouldn't hurt to have a backup plan.

Chapter 20

"It was kind of you to agree to meet with us on such short notice, Mr. Rodney." Sister Lou followed Owen Rodney, the town's former mayor, down the hallway to his office at the Rodney Real Estate Agency early Tuesday morning.

Sister Lou rubbed her nose. The suite smelled moldy. The structure must be older than it looked.

"Yes, thanks for your time." Shari walked beside Sister Lou. The thick blue-gray carpet that ran the length of the wide hallway muffled the sound of her cranberry stilettos.

"Of course. I always have time for the media." Owen tossed a broad grin over his shoulder and split it between Sister Lou and Shari. It looked forced.

The former mayor's voice was confident and boisterous, bringing back Sister Lou's memories of that voice on the last mayoral campaign trail.

"We in the media appreciate your taking the time to give us an interview." Shari's response was dry.

Owen didn't seem to notice the reporter's tone.

His forced grin remained in place as he allowed Sister Lou and Shari to precede him into his office.

Sister Lou's first impression of the office rocked her back on her heels. Shari's hand on the center of her back both steadied her and propelled her forward. Sister Lou was grateful for the former, not so much for the latter.

Owen's office looked like the eye of a storm. Everything felt like they were on top of her, pushing against her. And the air was pregnant with the stench of clutter. Binders and books were stacked on every flat surface. Papers, folders, and circulars spilled from all the drawers in Owen's office.

To get from the doorway to the gray cloth guest chairs, Sister Lou bravely followed the path formed by the directories and manuals piled across the dark blue Berber carpet. She tried not to think of what could be buried alive under the stacks. Sister Lou removed the folders from the far left chair, leaving the seat on the right—and its folders—for Shari to deal with.

"Let me take those from you." Owen hustled to Sister Lou and relieved her and Shari of the folders. He dropped them to the floor behind his desk before collapsing onto his gray faux leather executive chair. "So what questions do you have for me?"

"Rumors have it that you're running for mayor of Briar Coast again." Shari hung her winter coat on the back of her guest chair and pulled her reporter's notebook from her oversized green purse. "When will you make your official announcement?"

Owen looked pleased by Shari's question. He straightened on his chair and cleared his throat. "The people of Briar Coast deserve strong, capable leadership from an experienced political leader who knows the residents and this great town in which we live."

Sister Lou winced at Owen's planned impromptu campaign speech. Her gaze was drawn to Owen's desk. Her eyes widened in horror. How deep were his piles of papers? Somehow Sister Lou managed to tear her gaze from the disturbing sight. She forced herself to scan Owen's office, even knowing she'd never be able to unsee the manmade disaster.

Beside her, Shari transcribed their interview. The reporter's pen moved quickly across her notebook. "Yes, but when will you announce that you're running?"

"I'm going to announce my candidacy and officially launch my campaign any day now, perhaps as soon as the first day of March."

Sister Lou frowned in bewilderment. This was the twentieth day of February. March first was more than a week away. "Why are you delaying your announcement for so long, Mr. Rodney?"

Owen's confused gaze moved from Shari to Sister Lou. "If you don't mind my asking, Sister, why are you here? I thought this was a newspaper interview."

"I have my own questions," Sister Lou answered in a gentle tone. "For example, when did you decide to run again? Was this a fairly recent decision?"

"No." Owen's voice was noticeably cooler. "I've always known that I would run against the Outsider again."

Sister Lou was even more puzzled. "Then why are you delaying your announcement? Is it that, although you're anxious to run again, potential donors aren't as interested in your candidacy?"

Owen angled his chin in an obstinate direction. "My

supporters are very enthusiastic about my campaign. They know that I offer them a mature, experienced alternative to our current, struggling mayor."

"Heather Stanley isn't struggling." Shari's words were firm and abrupt. "In fact, she's reduced the town's deficit by almost a third of the red ink you left her. And she's secured government funding for infrastructure improvements. Longtime residents have told me that the streets are in much better condition than they were when you were mayor."

Owen turned his now cold eyes on the well-informed reporter. "You weren't here during my administration, were you?"

"You know that I wasn't." Shari didn't even blink in the face of Owen's tangible temper. "But people who were here during your time in office have been willing to fill me in on how you lost to an outsider. Think about that. Exactly how bad would you have to be to lose a mayoral race to someone who's brand spanking new not just to the town but to the entire state?"

Anger flickered across Owen's broad features. "It seems that they *didn't* tell you that I'd inherited a lot of that debt. I needed to deal with it before I could fix the potholes."

Sister Lou heard the antagonism in Owen's voice. His grudge against his former election opponent sounded as strong as ever. And he'd referred to Heather as the "Outsider." Interesting. Sister Lou waited for Shari's next move.

The reporter was taking notes of Owen's responses. "Mayor Stanley found a way to deal with both the debt and the potholes simultaneously."

Sister Lou watched the uncertainty flicker in Owen's eyes. "I *was* here during your administration, Mr.

Rodney. Mayor Stanley is much more effective in her management of Briar Coast. Does that cause you any concern for your campaign?"

Shari lips twitched in a smile. "What's your campaign slogan? *I Want a Mulligan*?"

Sister Lou rubbed her mouth in an effort to cover her smile. Shari had used the gulfing terminology that referred to permitting an extra stroke after a poor shot.

Owen leaned back on his chair and crossed his thick arms. He wore a teal cable sweater over a white collared shirt. "I'm surprised anyone lets you interview them. You have a very unpleasant attitude."

Shari shrugged, unconcerned. "I'm not here to make friends."

Owen grunted. "That's obvious. Listen, I'm not afraid to go head-to-head with Heather Stanley and run against her record. She's got plenty of weak spots."

"Name one." Shari's eyes glinted with challenge.

The way the reporter defended and praised the mayor to her future election challenger wasn't lost on Sister Lou. Perhaps Shari wasn't as disapproving of Heather as she pretended to be.

Owen counted off his examples, starting with his left index finger. "She's underfunded our emergency services—"

Shari interrupted him. "Isn't that because the deficit left over from your administration doesn't allow for increased funding?"

Owen ignored Shari's comment. He tapped the second finger on his left hand. "Her policies are punitive to the business community and are crippling Briar Coast's job growth."

Shari nodded. "You may have a point there."

Owen's smile was smug. "I'm not afraid of challenging Stanley's record. In fact, I'm looking forward to it."

Sister Lou wasn't convinced that Owen's confidence was warranted. "Mayor Stanley's job approval rating is very strong. People are much more confident of the town's future now than they were under your administration. What makes you so confident that you'll be elected this time?"

Owen snorted. "After more than four years of Stanley's policies, voters will welcome me back. You'll see. Especially after our debate, they'll see there's no comparison. I'm a shoo-in."

"We've taken enough of your time." Sister Lou had heard enough. She stood to leave. "Thank you again for meeting with us. We can show ourselves out."

"Thank you for the interview. It's been quite illuminating." Shari pushed herself from the real estate agent's guest chair.

Sister Lou led the way out of Owen's office. Back in the parking lot behind the Rodney Real Estate Agency, she used her keyless entry to let her and Shari into her Corolla.

Shari fastened her seat belt before turning to Sister Lou. "What do your Spidey Sleuth Senses tell you? Is the Sore Loser Heather's stalker?"

"I don't think so." Sister Lou put her car in gear and maneuvered out of the agency's parking lot. "He doesn't seem to fit our profile."

"We have a profile?" Shari sounded skeptical.

Sister Lou gave her friend a dry look before returning her attention to the street. She glimpsed an opportunity to merge her compact car into the first lane of traffic if she moved quickly. Sister Lou pressed on the gas pedal and spun the steering wheel, squeezing her car into the lane.

A gasp from the passenger seat broke her concentration. She shot a quick glance at Shari before returning her attention to the road. "Are you all right?"

"Yes." Shari spoke on a sigh. "I just wasn't expecting that quick turn—although I should've been."

"Oh, come on. It wasn't that bad." The silence was heavy and spoke volumes. "All right. I apologize. I won't do that again."

Shari chuckled. "Yes, you will, but tell me about our suspect profile."

Sister Lou shrugged off her guilt and focused on the profile. She was somewhat disconcerted that she'd been able to create it so quickly and without conscious thought. "Heather's stalker is well organized. He planned the letters and how to get them to Heather anonymously."

"You don't think Owen's capable of figuring out how to get the letters to Heather?" Shari sounded skeptical. "He worked in that office suite for five years."

Sister Lou slid Shari another look. Her tone was dry. "Does Owen's office look like it belongs to a well-organized person?"

"Good point." Shari inclined her head. "The whole time we were in Owen's office, I was waiting for the rest of his staff to dig themselves out from under his piles of paper. How do we *know* there aren't people under there?"

Sister Lou grinned. "Now that you mention it, I could see that happening."

"What else?"

Sister Lou grew somber again. "The stalker doesn't want to campaign against Heather. That's why he's trying to get her to leave Briar Coast before the election, but Owen says that he *wants* the opportunity to attack Heather's record. And I believe him."

Shari heaved a sigh. "You're right. I believe him, too."

"Although I think he's fooling himself if he thinks he can win against Heather."

"She'll eat him for breakfast."

"I thought you didn't like our mayor." Sister Lou tossed her friend a smile. "You sound almost proud of her."

Shari shrugged a shoulder. "Heather has her redeeming qualities, like her ability to make grown men cry."

"Did you give up coffee for Lent after all?" Chris's expression revealed a blend of curiosity, confusion, and concern.

His question over lunch Tuesday afternoon surprised Shari. She gave him a baffled stare from the other side of the small blond wood table in the Briar Coast Café's dining area. "No, why are you asking?"

Chris paused with his spoon hovering just above his beef and vegetable soup. "You've been quiet and distant all week. I was hoping that it was just caffeine withdrawal and not . . . something else."

Shari played with her chicken and rice soup. Each sweep of the warm metal spoon through the bowl released a flavorful waft of vegetables, seasoned meat, and soup stock. "If I had to go without coffee for even a day, I wouldn't be quiet and distant. I'd be catatonic."

Shari was serious, but Chris seemed amused. "Then what's on your mind? Why have you been acting so strangely lately?"

The muscles in Shari's neck and back stiffened.

"I'm not acting strangely. You're imagining things."
She sensed Chris's probing gaze, but couldn't bring
herself to meet his eyes.

"That's the other thing that's changed." His tone
was quiet but no less compelling. "You don't seem to
trust me anymore."

Shari's gaze flew up to meet Chris's. "What are you
talking about?"

"During the three months that we've been dating,
you were starting to confide in me. Suddenly, for
some unknown reason, you've stopped. What's happened?"

Shari lowered her eyes to scowl at her soup. "It's
nothing. I can handle it on my own."

"Handle what?" Chris reached across the table to
cup his large, warm hand over hers. His palm was
rough against her skin. "Come on, Shari, tell me
what's going on."

Shari sensed herself weakening under Chris's touch
and persuasive tone. She tightened her lips against
her disintegrating resolve. She could take care of herself. She'd been doing so for years through every
foster home she'd been bounced in and out of. This
situation with the *Telegraph* wasn't any different. "I can
handle this. Really. I don't need anyone's help."

"I'm not just anyone. We're dating, remember?
You're not alone."

"There's a problem at work, but it's nothing that I
can't manage on my own."

Chris sighed. "Shari, if you can't trust me with a
problem at your job, when will you ever be able to
confide in me?"

"Of course I trust you. What makes you think I

don't?" Shari had heard the impatience in Chris's tone. She was beginning to lose her patience as well.

"If you trusted me, we wouldn't be having this conversation." Chris's thick, black eyebrows knitted. "You'd confide in me of your own free will. I wouldn't have to beg you to tell me why you've been preoccupied and distant."

Shari felt her scowl deepen. "I don't want to bring my work into our relationship. I spend my whole day at the newspaper. When I'm with you, I want it to be separate."

"That's not working out quite the way you'd hoped, is it?" Chris gave her a dubious look. "You've been so preoccupied lately. I thought you were trying to find a way to break up with me."

Shari's jaw dropped. For a moment, her mind went blank. "That's ridiculous. Why would you think that?"

"For one thing, you weren't talking to me." Chris shoved aside his soup and leaned into the table. "But your surprised reaction is reassuring. So is the fact that we've had lunch together two days in a row this week."

Shari allowed her gaze to roam the café, using the time to collect her thoughts. After six months at Briar Coast, the patrons were becoming recognizable. A few of her coworkers from the *Telegraph*, including Poppy Flowers, were absorbed in an animated conversation a few tables away. At another table, several faculty members from the College of St. Hermione of Ephesus were laughing and smiling through their lunch. In contrast, at a nearby table, a group of college students were more subdued. Shari surmised their moodiness was due to their upcoming midterms. Once the midterms were over, the students would be the ones laughing through lunch while the professors fretted over entering the test grades.

She returned her attention to Chris. "I'm sorry I gave you the impression that I wanted to break up with you. Nothing could be further from my mind."

"I'm relieved to hear that." Chris didn't seem appeased, though. "Why don't you tell me what *has* been on your mind? What's this problem at work? I may not be able to fix it, but at least I can be your sounding board."

Shari parted her lips to repeat her assertion that she could "handle it on my own." That's the line she'd been feeding herself and everyone else her entire life. But something—the look in Chris's eyes, the little voice in her head—warned her that he wasn't going to drop this particular line of questioning. She might as well confess.

She sighed in defeat. "One of the other reporters, a rookie, has been trying to insert himself into my work with your aunt. Yesterday, he followed us to town hall."

"What?" Chris's brow furrowed in temper. He straightened on his seat.

Shari sensed Chris was in full protective mode. "Maybe I should've left out the part about Hal following your aunt and me."

"No, you shouldn't have." Chris's tone was firm. "Is he dangerous?"

She shrugged. "Only if you consider arrogant, lazy, twentysomethings with delusions of entitlement to be dangerous."

Chris didn't look satisfied or amused. "Did you tell Diego that Hal has been harassing you?"

"No, I haven't, but one of the other reporters must

have. Diego offered to talk to Hal, but I told him I didn't need his help."

Chris's eyes stretched wide in apparent disbelief. "Shari, if this guy is following you—and my aunt—around Briar Coast, he's taken his obsession to another level. You should have Diego talk to him. Maybe a reprimand from his boss will give him a wake-up call."

Shari was shaking her head through Chris's entire speech. "I'm not going to have Diego fight my battles for me."

"I don't understand you and Heather." Chris dragged a large hand over his close-cropped hair. "Asking for help isn't an admission of weakness."

"If I let someone else deal with Hal, he won't respect my claim on my beat. He'll think all he has to do is bide his time until he can find a way to take it from me."

"All right, but how will you keep him off of your beat?"

Shari shrugged again. "I'll ignore him and keep working my beat. Hopefully, he'll give up. Soon."

"And if he doesn't?"

Shari locked eyes with Chris. She could tell that he knew what she was thinking. If Hal didn't leave, she'd have to. That possibility scared them both.

Chapter 21

"Shari's considering leaving Briar Coast." Chris pulled his bronze Toyota Camry into a space in the parking lot in front of the Briar Coast Insurance Corporation after lunch Tuesday.

Wesley Vyne, a prominent donor of both the college and the congregation, owned the corporation. This was the first time either Sister Lou or Chris had been to his headquarters.

"I know." Sister Lou got out of Chris's car. He—and Sister Carmen—were opposed to letting her drive them. Anywhere.

A sharp winter breeze stole Sister Lou's breath as she turned from the car. She shrugged deeper into her brown wool coat. Sister Lou walked with Chris to the two-story, brown stone building that housed the insurance company. The silence between them was thick, pensive, and a little depressed.

"I don't want her to go." Chris's voice was low as they approached the five-step stone entrance. The business's name was engraved in a simple black font on its wooden front door. The same logo had appeared on the sign at the parking lot's entrance.

"Neither do I." Sister Lou adjusted the strap of her purse and mounted the stone steps. "But this is her decision."

"I know that it is, but I care too much about her. I have to at least try to convince her to stay." Chris climbed the steps beside her.

Sister Lou stopped on the top step and turned to face her nephew. The hurt and confusion in his eyes caused her pain. She took a breath to ease her own heartache. "'If you love someone set them free. If they return to you, they're yours. If they don't, it wasn't meant to be.'"

Chris returned her gaze in silence for a beat. "I don't like that quote."

"Neither do I." Sister Lou turned to open the door to Wesley's agency.

The company's interior screamed, *Opulence!* The furnishings seemed to be crafted from real cherry-wood and upholstered with sapphire satin fabric. Crystal-and-pewter chandeliers dotted the high ceiling.

A baby-faced young man with tired gray eyes looked up from what appeared to be the receptionist's desk. "May I help you?"

Sister Lou glanced at Chris before preceding him to the desk. Her low-heeled black boots sank into the plush sapphire carpeting. The office smelled like pine needles on a snowy day. She didn't see any potpourri, scented candles, or air wicks. Was the scent coming from the air vents?

Chris unfastened the buttons on his tan wool over-coat. "I'm Chris LaSalle and this is Sister Louise LaSalle. We have a two p.m. appointment with Mr. Vyne."

"Just a minute." The receptionist seemed to smother a yawn. The nameplate on his desk identified him as Otto Smith. Otto positioned a wireless headset over lank brown hair, then stabbed four of the buttons on his sapphire desk phone. The color was a perfect match to the fabric featured on the office's furniture. Otto stared past them as he waited for the call to connect. A vacant expression settled onto his doughy face. Suddenly, he jerked as though waking. "Your two o'clock appointment is here. Of course." He disconnected the call, removed his headset, and stood. "This way, please."

Sister Lou walked beside Chris. Otto may seem fatigued, but he set a brisk pace down the wide aisle. His brown suit was baggy and worn. The hem of his pants was frayed. Briar Coast Insurance Corporation was a loyal and generous supporter of both the college and the congregation. However, Wesley seemed to spend more money on his company's appearance than he invested in his employees. Did Otto have to work a second job to pay his expenses? Was that the reason for his fatigue? The questions made Sister Lou both sad and angry.

She followed Otto's lead as he turned the corner. At the end of the short, wide hallway was a door that opened onto a spacious, extravagantly decorated office. The furnishings inside—including the wood, satin cloth, and chandeliers—mirrored the reception area.

"May I take your coats?" Otto collected Sister Lou's and Chris's coats. "Excuse me, Mr. Vyne." He knocked on the open door, then walked to a closet hidden in the far right wall. It was in there that Otto hung Sister Lou's and Chris's outerwear.

"Chris, Sister Lou, it's good to see both of you."
Wesley Vyne stood and circled his desk to cross to
them. He shook their hands.

Chris stood a head above the older man. "Thanks
for agreeing to meet with us."

"Don't mention it." Wesley gestured toward his guest
chairs. "Please, come in. Have a seat. Thanks, Otto."

The young receptionist disappeared from the office
without a sound. Sister Lou wondered whether the
brisk walk across the office would help him stay awake
for the rest of the afternoon.

She settled onto one of the four cherrywood-and-
sapphire-satin visitor's seats. It felt as comfortable as a
bed. Chris sat on the matching chair beside her.

Sister Lou watched Wesley amble back to his sapphire leather executive chair. His steps were silent
against the plush carpeting. The pine scent that had
teased her in the reception area drifted into Wesley's
office as well.

She wasn't an expert on men's fashion, but the
metallic gray Italian-styled wool suit Wesley wore with
a navy silk tie probably cost ten times as much as
Otto's suit.

"What can I do for you?" Wesley freed the buttons
of his suit coat, which was snug around his midsection.
He gave the appearance of relaxing back onto his
chair, but he'd asked his question with the air of time-
is-money.

"We wanted to share with you some updates on
both the congregation and the college." Chris's tone
was warm and relaxed.

Wesley's office was almost as impeccable as Sister
Marianna's. He must automatically file all of his documents in his desk drawers or the matching cabinet

behind him. No loose papers were allowed anywhere near his desktop. Industry books and journals were shelved on the bookcase to the right of his office. A small rectangular conference table stood on the left side of the room. Four fabric chairs were tucked under it. The sapphire speakerphone looked lonely on its glass-and-steel surface. If his office reflected his personality, Wesley was very well organized.

Organized enough to plan a campaign of intimidation against the town's mayor?

Sister Lou turned her attention to Wesley. "Will you be attending the Mayor's Charity Spring-Raiser on March first?"

"Yes, that's in less than two weeks, isn't it?" Wesley smoothed his comb-over. There was more gray than brown in his thinning hair. "Don't get me wrong. I don't support that outsider's policies, but the event is good face time with the community's movers and shakers."

Sister Lou worked hard to mask her surprise. Wesley's reference to Heather as an outsider was a chilling and unnecessary reminder of the threatening letters to the mayor.

Chris must have had a similar reaction. "Whether we agree with her policies or not, Heather Stanley isn't an outsider anymore. She's been Briar Coast's mayor for four years."

Wesley snorted. "That wasn't my fault. I voted against her in that election, and I plan to vote against her again."

"Who do you plan to support?" Chris asked.

"Anyone but Heather Stanley!" Wesley slashed his hand through the air above his desk. His diamond pinkie ring seemed too small even for that finger.

"I voted for Owen Rodney last time. If he decides to run again, I'll vote for him again—and this time, he'll wipe the floor with that outsider."

Bile rose in the back of Sister Lou's throat as she listened to Wesley's vehement opposition to Heather. His anger seemed out of proportion considering Heather's positive impact on their community. "What is your greatest concern about her administration?"

"Her cabinet!" Wesley's narrow, brown eyes widened. He seemed surprised by Sister Lou's question. "It's a bunch of *women*."

Sister Lou was stunned. "What does that have to do with her policies?"

"It has *everything* to do with her policies!" Wesley spread his arms. His gold cuff links twinkled under the chandelier's lights. "Women don't have what it takes to make the hard decisions necessary to run an organization, much less a town."

Sister Lou thought about the Hermionean order of which her congregation was a member, and the thousands of other orders of religious women whose missions had established the foundations of communities all over the world, including hospitals, businesses, farms, ranches, educational institutions for all age groups, and the list continued. These institutions served the public in a myriad of ways, including providing a tax base that helped spur the growth of the communities they served.

And the congregations were all led by women.

"I'm sorry that you feel that way, Wes." Chris stood. "We'll see ourselves out."

Sister Lou was relieved that Chris was ready to leave, too.

"Is that it?" Wesley's surprised words stopped them.

Sister Lou turned back to the businessman, who'd risen to his feet behind his desk. Her muscles trembled with anger and resentment, but she made the effort to appear calm. "Mr. Vyne, my congregation has appreciated your support over the years. Unfortunately, we can't accept your patronage in the future. The fact that you can so easily and unjustly dismiss the contributions of more than fifty percent of the community shows that our mission of social justice and equality obviously conflicts with your views."

Wesley looked as though she'd slapped him. He turned to Chris. "What about you? Do you agree with her?"

Chris inclined his head. "Of course, I do. The college was founded by the strong, courageous women of the Congregation of Saint Hermione of Ephesus. Its mission is to help prepare men—*and women*—for leadership roles to help advance their communities. By your own words, you don't support that goal."

Wesley stuffed his pudgy hands into the front pockets of his pants and rocked back on his heels. "I guess I'll just have to find somewhere else to spend my money."

Sister Lou considered the real cherrywood furnishings, the crystal-and-pewter chandeliers, his diamond pinkie ring, gold cuff links, and Italian suit. "Might I suggest you reinvest in your employees? Either way, I'm sure you'll be fine. The college and the congregation will be, too."

Sister Lou led Chris from Wesley's office. She nodded in farewell to poor, sleepy Otto as she and Chris exited the building on their way back to the parking lot.

"He's got to be Heather's stalker." Chris pressed the keyless remote entry to unlock his car.

Sister Lou buckled her passenger seat belt in preparation for the world's most sedate drive back to the congregational offices. "What makes you think that?"

"Are you kidding?" Chris reversed out of the parking space and pointed the car toward the lot's exit. "He calls Heather the Outsider. He hates her, her administration, and her policies."

Sister Lou counted at least three opportunities for Chris to merge onto the main street. Granted these openings were a little snug, but he could have made it by applying just a touch of muscle to the gas pedal. "But why would Wesley try to scare Heather into leaving Briar Coast?"

"So that Owen would have a better chance of winning the election." Chris finally crawled forward to join the traffic flow.

Sister Lou prayed they'd make it back to the congregational offices before Good Friday. She loved her nephew, but she could have knitted a sweater in the time it took him to get into the traffic lane—despite the fact that she didn't know how to knit.

"Wesley sounded confident that Owen would win this time." The insurance agent's exact words—*wipe the floor with Stanley*—still galled Sister Lou. "I could be wrong, but I don't think Wesley is Heather's stalker. We're looking for someone who believes that Heather *will* win reelection."

Chris glanced at Sister Lou before moving forward with the traffic. "Like who?"

"Everyone else on our suspect list."

* * *

"I'm sorry that we won't be able to meet for lunch." Chris spoke into the beige receiver of his office telephone. He was sorry—but not surprised—that Shari had called to cancel their lunch plans. She was pulling further and further away from him. Her call to break their lunch date felt like more evidence that she was thinking of leaving Briar Coast—or at least thinking of leaving him.

If you love someone, let her go. If she returns to you, she's yours. If she doesn't, it was never meant to be.

He still didn't like that saying.

Shari's sigh traveled across the telephone line and traced down his spine. "I just have a lot to do."

Chris's gaze dropped to the photos on his desk. There was one of his parents and one of his aunt. He still hadn't convinced Shari to give him her picture. She claimed that she didn't like having her picture taken. Was that the truth or a sign that she wasn't fully committed to their relationship?

He tightened his hold on the receiver. Chris wasn't certain whether it was with disappointment—or fear. "I understand. We can get together for dinner instead."

"I'm covering the town council meeting tonight, remember?" Shari sounded almost relieved to have the excuse.

"Now I do." This time, Chris couldn't mask his disappointment. "All right, we'll try again tomorrow. Have you changed your mind yet about attending the Mayor's Charity Spring-Raiser with me?"

"No, I haven't changed my mind, and I'm not going to." Shari's chuckle sounded natural. It lifted

Chris's spirits, breathing new life into his hopes for their future.

"Oh, come on, Shari." He tried a cajoling tone, hoping it would prove more effective than his efforts with logic. "Do you really want me to attend this formal community event by myself?"

"You won't be alone. Sister Lou's going to be there."

"You know I'm just going to keep asking until you change your mind."

"You'd only be wasting your time. Do I seem like the kind of person who enjoys formal events? Unless I have to cover it for the paper, I'm not going." Shouted conversations in the background almost drowned Shari's response. It was only nine o'clock on Wednesday morning, but already the *Telegraph* sounded to be in full deadline panic mode.

"Exactly how many formal events have you attended?" Chris's mind raced for persuasive arguments.

"None."

His lips curved into a reluctant smile. That was Shari all over. She personified the term *stubborn.* "Then how do you know you don't enjoy formal events if you've never attended one?"

"I just know." There was a shrug in her voice. "I don't have to staple my tongue to the roof of my mouth to know that I wouldn't enjoy that experience, either."

Although Chris could sense his defeat, he had to make one last effort. "Why don't you attend this one before making your final decision? You might surprise yourself and enjoy it."

"I doubt that, but I hope you and Sister Lou have a nice time."

"All right. You win. I won't bring it up again."

"Thank you." She sounded relieved. "I'll call you after the council meeting tonight."

"I'd like that." Chris rang off, barely convincing himself not to ask Shari for the hundredth time why she was becoming so distant. Instead he cradled the receiver and prepared himself to "set her free."

Chapter 22

Wednesday evening, Shari scanned the crowded auditorium in which the Briar Coast Town Council held its meetings. She'd practically inhaled her dinner to arrive early and still the place was packed. No one could accuse Briar Coast residents of lacking a sense of civic duty. Was there even one unclaimed seat?

Shari noticed a few empty chairs in the front of the audience section near the walnut wood gate. She'd heard it was the same way in church. Most unclaimed spots were in the front of the sanctuary closest to the Mass's celebrant.

She moved forward down the center aisle with its threadbare raspberry carpet. The air was musty with age as though the building was even older than the town. The smell made her nose itch. What she wouldn't do for one of Sister Lou's bowls of potpourri. Maybe she'd recommend that to the council.

As Shari made her way to the front of the auditorium's public section, she exchanged nods of greeting with several Briar Coast residents with whom she was familiar. This included Owen Rodney who was sitting with Wesley Vyne. Was their joint appearance an attempt at a show of force to intimidate Heather? If so, they were already underestimating their opposition.

The mayor's executive team was in attendance also: Arneeka, Yolanda, Tian, and Penelope. Where was Kerry?

"Shari." Someone called to her as she marched past the rows of raspberry upholstered theater seats.

Shari turned to find the source of the greeting. Speak of the devil. Kerry had settled onto the aisle seat in a fully occupied row toward the center of the room.

Shari walked back toward Heather's administrative assistant. "Hi, Kerry. I was wondering where you were."

"Here I am." The younger woman giggled. Her eyes sparkled and her face glowed. "This is my boyfriend, Jefferson Manning. Jeff, this is Sharelle Henson. She's a reporter with the *Telegraph*."

Shari took in Jefferson's golden good looks and expensive clothing. She offered him her hand. His skin was rough and cool. His grip was limp and loose. "It's nice to meet you. We've spoken on the phone."

"Have we? I don't recall." His smile was charming at first glance, but there was a coolness in his manner that gave Shari pause.

Shari released his hand. "Yes, you called the *Telegraph*'s offices five days ago to ask about our election ballot issues."

"Sorry." Jefferson shrugged. "I make so many calls like that to other jurisdictions. I can't remember all of them."

It hadn't even been a week. Jefferson couldn't have forgotten that call. Why was he pretending that he had? He and Hal had planned that caper to give

Harold time to speak with Sister Lou without Shari being present. Why?

Shari gave Kerry's boyfriend a measuring look. "What made you decide to attend our town council meeting?"

Jefferson's smile remained in place. "I wanted to spend time with Kerry, of course."

At Jefferson's words, Kerry gave her boyfriend a look of pure adoration. It was sweet, but it also was a little disconcerting. Shari was happy for the younger woman, but she couldn't shake her unease. She wished the couple a good evening before continuing her search for a seat.

Shari settled onto a chair three rows behind the wooden bar railing that separated the residents of Briar Coast from their public servants. A microphone stood in front of the railing for the public to use for comments and questions.

From the corner of her eye, Shari saw someone following behind her into the row. She looked up to find Harold taking the seat beside her.

"Are you going to tell me what you and Sister Lou are working on?" Harold's question was low as though he was afraid of being overheard.

"Why did you have Jefferson Manning call me?" Shari sensed Harold stiffen beside her. She could smell his fear.

"I don't know what you're talking about."

"Really? Then there's nothing more to say." By denying their roles in the subterfuge, Harold and Jefferson had confirmed Shari's suspicions. The two obviously were friends, and Jefferson was doing Harold a favor. Shari filed her knowledge of the duo's connection for future reference.

Beyond the bar railing, members of the town council and the mayor entered the room through the secured side doors. Ian Greer, the town council president, entered first. Heather and the remaining four council members followed him.

Ian walked briskly to his chair at the top of the horseshoe-style seating arrangement. Each seat had a nameplate. Three council members sat with their nameplates to the left of Ian. The remaining member, the mayor, and the committee's administrative assistant sat behind their nameplates to the right of the council president. After a few opening remarks to the residents in attendance, the meeting began.

Shari observed Ian even as she took notes on the meeting. Could she detect a clue to the council president being Heather's stalker in the way he moved or his tone of voice, or perhaps in the way he interacted with Heather? Shari would bet good money that Sister Lou could. Shari flexed her right hand before returning to her notes.

The council concluded the formal part of the meeting in a little more than an hour. Shari flexed her hand again as they invited questions and comments from the public. Harold popped off of his seat and stepped over to the microphone. His prompt reaction made Shari think he'd been waiting all night for the invitation to address the council. This couldn't be good.

"What are you doing?" She hissed the question.

Harold waved her off. "Harold Beckett, *The Briar Coast Telegraph*. This question is for Mayor Stanley."

Heather's curious eyes moved from Shari to Harold. "What can I do for you, Mr. Beckett?"

Harold's expression became smug. "You can tell

me why our town's super murder sleuth, Sister Louise LaSalle, has been spending so much time with you at town hall. The public has a right to know."

Shari's blood boiled. Her heart pounded in her ears. She wanted to snatch Harold away from the microphone and smack some sense—any amount of sense—into him. Repeatedly. Instead, she knotted her hands together and waited with great trepidation to see how the mayor would get out of this one.

Heather's finely arched dark eyebrows knitted in seeming confusion. She tilted her head in question. "Have you been following Sister Lou? Do you have so little to do, Mr. Beckett, or is spying on pillars of our community part of your assigned beat?"

A smattering of chuckles came from the audience. Several of the council members fought losing battles with their own amused smiles.

Harold's smugness evaporated. His face filled with ruddy color. He seemed both startled and embarrassed. "I—I've . . . seen Sister Lou a few times at town hall," he mumbled into the mic before shuffling back to his seat.

Heather nodded in understanding. "Those must have been the few times she came to discuss the Mayor's Charity Spring-Raiser. The Congregation of the Sisters of Saint Hermione of Ephesus sponsors many of the causes the town's residents support."

Shari leaned toward him and lowered her voice to a whisper. "Satisfied now?"

Harold was unresponsive as he slumped farther down his seat.

The rest of the public questions were uneventful. After the meeting, Harold hustled out of the auditorium as though he had a full bladder. He left without a look or a word to Shari. Shari smiled cynically as she tucked her notepad into her tote bag. She stepped out of her row and turned to follow the rest of the attendees from the room.

Heather's voice stopped her. "Shari, can you give me a few minutes?"

Shari stepped out of the moving crowd and back into the row. She took the same seat she'd just vacated and waited while Heather settled onto the seat Harold had claimed earlier. "I didn't tell Hal anything about our project."

Heather shook her head. "I know. That's not what I want to talk with you about. I saw the look on your face when Hal stepped up to the mic."

Shari frowned. "What look?"

"Panic and insecurity. I often saw that look in my mirror when I was about your age."

Shari stared at Heather. Once again the mayor had caught her off guard. Denial tripped easily off her tongue. "I don't know what you're talking about."

Heather gave her a knowing look. "All right, but I'll give you a piece of advice. You're a da— darn good reporter. Don't let anyone tell you otherwise or make you feel as though you aren't as good if not better than them. Diego's lucky to have you. Any newspaper would be."

Shari's mind was swimming in confusion. She could have sworn the mayor didn't like her. "Thank you. I appreciate your saying that."

"I'm only speaking the truth." Heather squeezed her shoulder. "Harold Beckett is trying to get into your head. I know the type. Don't let him. Stand your ground."

Shari frowned. "How do I know whether it's my ground to stand on?"

"The better question is why would you doubt it?" Heather held Shari's gaze. "If you stake your claim, then that ground is absolutely yours."

She watched Heather walk away. Everyone at the *Telegraph* knew that the mayor wasn't a fan of the fourth estate. Nevertheless, she'd just encouraged Shari to stake her claim and continue her reporting.

When she got back to the newsroom, Shari would check the headlines. The end times must be near.

Chris's phone rang shortly before ten o'clock Thursday morning. The caller identification displayed Shari's phone number at the *Telegraph*. Was she going to back out of another lunch date? Between his donor luncheons and her civic meetings, it was getting harder for them to find time together.

Chris took a deep breath and answered her call. "Please don't tell me you're canceling lunch again."

A startled pause greeted him. "Hi, honey. How are *you* today?" Strangely enough Shari's flippant sarcasm was comforting.

Chris smiled into the phone. "All right. I'll play along. I'm fine, honey. How are you?"

"I'm great." Shari sounded less pressured than she'd sounded in some time.

But Chris was still suspicious. "Then why are you calling me now when I'm going to see you in two hours?"

Shari laughed. "Actually, I was anxious to tell you that I've changed my mind about the Mayor's Charity Spring Raiser. I'd like to go with you."

"Really? That's great." Chris loosened his grip on the receiver. "I'm glad to hear that, but what made you change your mind?"

"I decided not to look at it from the perspective of attending some stuffy formal event with a bunch of strangers. Instead I'm going to consider it an opportunity to spend more time with you."

She'd scrambled his brain. Chris exhaled, closing his eyes in gratitude before trying to bring his thoughts back together. "I agree. Thinking of the fund-raiser as an evening with you is a lot more appealing than the idea of being stuck in a room full of stuffy strangers."

"Great. I'll see you in two hours."

"Shari, wait!" Chris tried, but still couldn't shake the sense that there was something—probably a lot of somethings—that she was keeping from him. "Is there anything else you want to tell me?"

"Like what?"

Tread carefully. "I have the feeling that you've been trying to avoid me."

"No, I haven't." Shari's voice rose at the end as though she was asking a question. That was less than encouraging.

"I waited for your call last night."

"I'm sorry, Chris. I needed to go back to the paper to file my story last night, then it was so late when I got done . . ."

"I understand." No, he didn't. "I'm glad you changed your mind about the fund-raiser. I'll see you in a couple of hours."

Chris cradled his receiver and stared blindly at the phone. He couldn't fix their relationship if he didn't know what was wrong with it—and he desperately needed to fix this. If he didn't, he'd lose her.

"Let's go to my office." Ian Greer spoke over his shoulder.

Sister Lou followed the Briar Coast town council president to his office at Greer Accounting Group Inc., the accounting firm he'd founded. Shari walked beside her. It was only eight thirty on Friday morning. Ian's firm had been officially open for business for only half an hour, but the activity among his small staff was feverish. The sounds of ringing phones and clacking keyboards trailed Sister Lou down the wide, blue carpeted hallway. When had Ian's team started their day?

At the doorway to his office, Ian stepped aside and gestured for Sister Lou and Shari to precede him across the blond wood threshold. He smoothed his old gold tie, which was held in place by a sterling silver clip.

As Sister Lou stepped across Ian's office threshold, a wall of cold air almost pressed her back into the hallway. She shrugged deeper into her brown wool winter coat. There was no way she was taking off the garment.

"Wow, it's freezing in here." Shari paused just inside the office. She tightened her emerald green winter coat around her. Was her friend shivering?

"It keeps me alert." Ian maneuvered around Shari. He strode to a two-drawer walnut wood lateral file cabinet on which stood a small coffeemaker. "Would you like a mug of coffee?"

"Yes, please." Sister Lou joined him at the coffee station.

"Definitely." Shari followed them, tugging back on

her emerald knit gloves and buttoning her coat. "Maybe it will help to unthaw me."

"It's not that cold." Ian regarded the reporter with mild concern as he handed Sister Lou her coffee.

Yes, it is.

While she and Shari were shivering in their winter coats, Ian stood calmly beside them in his shirtsleeves. His crisp pine green shirt complemented his dark brown skin. His gray suit jacket was hanging over the back of his red faux leather executive chair.

Sister Lou cupped the full mug, letting its heat reactivate the blood flow in her palms. The steam floating up from the cream coffee mug carried the strong aroma of the dark brew and warmed Sister Lou's face. She ignored the creamer powder, but used a plastic stirrer to mix in one of the mini packets of sugar.

She stepped back so that Ian could offer Shari her mug. She watched in amusement as Shari added three packets of sugar and covered the surface of her coffee with the powdered creamer. She avoided eye contact with Ian, but sensed his surprise as he refilled his own mug. The council president took his coffee plain.

Sister Lou settled onto one of the two red cloth–upholstered visitor's chairs in front of Ian's white modular desk. Her gaze dropped to the top of the desk. Several files were labeled with a canary yellow sticky note and arranged in a horizontal row across its surface. It seemed an organized—if obsessive—way to approach his day.

"Thank you for meeting with us." Sister Lou sipped her coffee. The hot brew helped to chase away the chill.

Shari collapsed onto the matching chair. "And thanks for the coffee."

Sister Lou watched Ian cross to his desk. Despite a slight limp, he moved with a loose-limbed grace that reminded her of a modern dancer. His easy gait, smooth skin, and clean-shaven head made his age difficult to determine. Based on his salt-and-pepper goatee, however, Sister Lou estimated Ian to be in his mid to late sixties.

"You're welcome. What can I do for you?" A look of satisfaction settled over Ian's distinguished features as he took his first sip of coffee.

The words were barely out of the council president's mouth before Shari answered him. "Rumor has it that you're going to primary Mayor Stanley. Since you're in the same party, won't a challenge to her re-election hurt both of you?"

"Your sources are wrong." Irritation replaced Ian's satisfaction. "I've told the mayor that I'm not going to primary her. You can quote me on that. Is that all?"

"Far from it." Shari's smile was pure challenge.

Sister Lou searched Ian's dark gaze as she swallowed another sip of the hot, strong coffee. "Is it true that you want to be mayor of Briar Coast?"

Ian's expression morphed from irritation to exasperation. "Mayor Stanley and I disagree. Frequently. Our governing philosophies are very different. She wants to spend money we don't have and I want to be fiscally responsible."

Sister Lou gave Ian an impish smile. "Is that the reason you're pushing for tax abatements for businesses?"

"*New* businesses." Ian lowered his mug to his desk an arm's length from his manila folders. "Mayor Stanley can't understand the concept or the greater vision of the plan, either, which is the reason she's so bull-headed about it."

Shari's winged eyebrows flew up her forehead. "Do you often refer to the mayor as being bullheaded?"

Ian was irritated again. "Everything I'm saying to you now, I've said directly to Mayor Stanley. I don't talk about people behind their backs. They always find out. Things become very awkward when that happens. It makes it hard for people to trust each other enough to work together again."

Sister Lou stood. She had the information she needed. "Thank you for meeting with us, President Greer."

Ian rose to his feet. "Call me Ian."

"Thanks." Shari smiled at the council president. Ian gave her a dry look, which only made Shari smile wider. She took Sister Lou's half-filled coffee mug and carried it with her own back to Ian's coffee station.

Sister Lou waited for Shari to rejoin her before bidding Ian a good day and leaving his office. They hurried through the chill late-February air across the parking lot behind Ian's company to Sister Lou's Corolla.

Shari leaped onto the passenger seat and turned up the car's heater. "As cold as it is outside, it's still warmer than Ian's office. What is he trying to prove?"

Sister Lou blew into her hands to warm them before she put her car in gear and navigated out of the lot. "I don't know whether he was trying to prove anything with his freezing office, but I do know he's not who we're looking for."

Shari gave her a startled look. "How do we know

that? I think he's the perfect suspect. Did you see his desk? Talk about being well organized."

"Yes, but—"

"And he didn't deny wanting to be mayor of Briar Coast."

"That's true, but—"

"Since he and Heather are in the same party, short of primarying her, if Ian wanted to run for office during this election, he'd have to scare her out of Briar Coast."

Stopping the car, Sister Lou raised her hand, palm out, to catch Shari's attention. "Those are all good points, Shari, but Ian isn't who we're looking for. He's too direct and confrontational to send Heather anonymous threats."

Shari seemed to take a moment to process that. While she was processing, Sister Lou eased up to the parking lot's exit. A quick check of the road showed a fleeting opportunity to merge into the traffic. Sister Lou took it.

A startled squeak came from the passenger side of the car. Sister Lou shot a quick glance in Shari's direction. "Are you okay?"

Shari released the grab handle above the passenger-side window. "Yes. Sure. I just wasn't expecting you to do that. Again."

"That's what you said last time. I would think that you'd be prepared for it by now." Sister Lou could feel Shari's gaze on her.

"And I'd think a sister would know that patience is a virtue. Would it really be so hard to wait for a break in traffic that was less risky before making your move?"

It was Sister Lou's turn to process Shari's information. The young reporter was the only person who would let her drive. She could make the effort to operate the car more sedately. "I promise to try."

"That's all I can ask." Shari gave a satisfied sigh. "So we're looking for someone who's well organized and nonconfrontational. Where do those clues lead us?"

Sister Lou paused. "Back to our suspect list."

Chapter 23

Late Friday morning, Sister Lou stood with Shari outside the partially open door of Yolanda's office. The mayor's senior legal counsel was meeting with Tian, the communications director. Their animated voices carried beyond the room.

Sister Lou hesitated. *Should I come back later or interrupt them now?*

The decision was snatched from Sister Lou when Shari reached around her to knock on the door. Her action pushed the door open wider.

"Hey, you two. Do you have a few minutes for us?" Shari's tone hailed the other women with joviality as she gently nudged Sister Lou across the threshold.

The two senior members of Heather's administration rose to greet their guests. The warmth of Yolanda's smile and bright eyes belied her coolly professional appearance in her ice blue skirt suit. She'd accessorized with thin gold jewelry. Although equally professional, Tian's black pantsuit, worn with a scarlet sweater and chunky silver accessories, displayed more drama.

Yolanda gestured toward the empty guest chairs

beside Tian in front of her desk. "Please come in. We were just talking about both of you."

"It was all good, I'm sure." Shari tossed her winter coat over one of the black cloth chairs at the small rectangular walnut wood conversation table.

"Of course it was." Yolanda lowered herself to her black faux leather seat.

"We're sorry to interrupt your meeting." Sister Lou was relieved that the lawyer's office was warm enough to shed her coat. She shifted her visitor's chair closer to Tian to offer Shari more room before sitting on the padded seat. Sister Lou noticed a faint powder soft fragrance. Was it from Tian or Yolanda?

"We're finished with our meeting. We were just chatting." Tian's dark brown hair was gathered away from her face and fashioned into a bun at the nape of her neck. The style emphasized her large almond-shaped ebony eyes. "We were talking about Shari's colleague, Harold Beckett."

Sister Lou glanced at Shari before returning her attention to the mayor's staff. "Shari told me that Harold had caused a stir during the town council meeting Wednesday night."

Yolanda sat back on her seat and folded her hands together on her desk. Her long nails were polished with a neutral color. "What was he implying when he asked about Mayor Stanley's meetings with Sister Lou?"

Shari shrugged her narrow shoulders beneath her scarlet sweater. "Hal's assigned to cover the election issues. I don't know why he asked his question, and I have no idea why he chose to do so during the council meeting."

Yolanda turned her sharp eyes to Sister Lou. "Do *you* have any ideas, Sister Lou? I'd prefer to get ahead of any possible issues that may affect Mayor Stanley's policies or agenda."

Sister Lou made a quick decision. She would step out on faith and pray that the truth would deliver a much-needed lead. "Perhaps he's hoping to cover a story more controversial than our upcoming election."

Tian's tone reflected her confusion. "What do you mean?"

Sister Lou spoke gently. "Forgive me, but it seemed that Harold was implying that Opal's death wasn't an accident."

Beside her, Sister Lou felt Shari's tension. She also sensed her trust.

"But it *was* an accident." Yolanda's tone made it clear that she didn't tolerate shenanigans.

Tian's gaze moved from Sister Lou to Shari and back. "The deputies said she fell." Her trust in Briar Coast's law enforcement sounded unshakable.

"We know." Shari's voice was low and easy. "But Hal's looking for a scandal, and everyone knows the mayor's administration has its detractors."

Sister Lou smiled on the inside. Shari had recognized her strategy and was backing her up. In the five months that they'd been sleuthing together, they'd developed a silent communication.

"Ah, yes. The old boy's network." Irritation flickered in Tian's eyes. She shifted on her seat as though trying to find a more comfortable position. "You haven't been here long, Shari, but I'm certain Sister Lou remembers the town's previous administration. Their style of governing was the definition of insanity. They listened to the same people and did the same things year in and year out, but expected different results."

"Tian is blunt. She's also right." Yolanda smiled.

The warmth between the two friends was as visible as Sister Lou believed the affection between her and Shari to be. "For the most part, Mayor Stanley's detractors are angry that she turned away from what was familiar to them to try something new. She didn't bring in old white men for her administration's cabinet. Instead she brought in a cabinet of relatively young, very diverse women."

Tian scowled. "They call us Heather's Harpies."

Yolanda winced. "That's one of the nicer labels that they use. They also call us the coven."

"I've heard that one." Shari wrinkled her nose in disgust.

"Our congregation also is comprised of a diverse group of women who get things done." Sister Lou felt a stirring of anger. "We're active in the town, helping to raise awareness of vulnerable members of our community. It's beyond me why in this day and age people would still oppose having female representatives in government."

"I don't understand that attitude, either." Yolanda shook her head in what seemed to be part bemusement and part regret. "It's the twenty-first century, and the fact is women are the majority demographic in Briar Coast."

"The mayor's political rivals aren't the only ones who criticize her, though, are they?" Shari's question brought the conversation back to their investigation. "Isn't it true that people have a problem with her management style?"

"Look around the office." Yolanda gestured toward her office door. "Most of us on her executive team have been with her since the campaign. That's more than five years. The newest members of her staff have served for an entire term."

Tian nodded with enough enthusiasm to shake free several strands of hair. "People who are applying for other jobs aren't leaving because they don't like working for Mayor Stanley. They're leaving because they want to advance their careers."

Shari was persistent. "But people have complained about her. I've heard the criticisms. They say she's hard to work for."

"She is." Tian laughed. "Mayor Stanley is demanding, relentless, and tireless. She's a perfectionist, but she gets the job done. Working for her is a rewarding experience because at the end of the day, you can point to what you've done to make a positive impact on the town."

"The proof is in the numbers." Yolanda spread her arms. "Under Mayor Stanley's administration, Briar Coast's budget deficit has shrunk by more than thirty-three percent. When Mayor Stanley is reelected for a second term, we should be able to balance the budget. This will allow us to return normal funding to our schools, increase our emergency services staff, and do more infrastructure repair."

Yolanda's and Tian's belief in and dedication to Heather were contagious. Sister Lou wanted to grab the mayor's campaign flyers and knock on residents' doors. "It seems safe to say that you're looking forward to campaigning for her again."

"Absolutely." Tian nodded decisively. More strands of hair slipped free. "We need Mayor Stanley to be reelected."

Yolanda leaned into her desk as though for emphasis. "*Briar Coast* needs Mayor Stanley for a second term."

Perhaps Heather was right. Kerry, Arneeka, Yolanda, and Tian were far too devoted to their work and to the mayor to try to intimidate Heather into leaving Briar Coast. She still wanted to interview Penelope. Leave no stone unturned, but she was almost certain that the stalker they were looking for wasn't in this office.

"Thank you for speaking with us." Sister Lou adjusted her hold on her coat and rose from her chair.

Yolanda looked puzzled. "I thought there was something you wanted to ask me."

Sister Lou froze. She was hoping to make a smooth escape. She couldn't lie, but neither could she come up with a plausible answer to Yolanda's question.

Is our cover blown?

"No." Shari leaped into the silence, walking backward out of Yolanda's office. "We're going to talk with Penelope. Like you said, the numbers are the proof of Mayor Stanley's successful administration and she's the numbers person."

"We should try to catch up with her before lunch." Sister Lou hurried after Shari. She waited until they were several strides away from Yolanda's office before speaking. "Well done, Shari."

"We're going to have to work on your acting skills, Sister Lou." Shari stopped in front of an empty office. "Penelope's not here."

Sister Lou checked her crimson Timex. It wasn't quite noon. "Perhaps she's in the breakroom."

As they passed Kerry's empty desk, Jefferson pushed through the glass doors to enter the office suite. His black cashmere winter coat was folded over his forearm. A fashionable slim dark blue suit looked tailored to his tall, lean figure. The councilman's aide looked like he was walking into a studio photo session for young, aspiring politicians.

Sister Lou paused to smile at the young man. "Good afternoon, Jefferson."

"Good afternoon, ladies." The newcomer slipped his hands into his front pants pockets as he split a look between Sister Lou and Shari. "Is Kerry around?"

Sister Lou's smile faded with concern. What had caused Jefferson to drive all the way from Buffalo to speak with Kerry in person? "She must have stepped away from her desk. I'm certain she'll be back shortly. Is something wrong?"

"No." Jefferson shrugged. "I'm taking her to lunch."

Surprised, Sister Lou could only stare at him.

"You drove all the way from Buffalo to Briar Coast to have lunch with Kerry?" Shari asked the question that was on Sister Lou's mind. "Are you taking a two-hour lunch? Don't you have to get back to work?"

Jefferson's smile seemed forced. "My boss understands."

"Nice boss." Shari turned to continue on her way to the breakroom.

"Enjoy your lunch." Sister Lou nodded to Jefferson before turning to follow her friend. "I wonder if Kerry knew Jefferson was coming to take her to lunch."

Shari grunted again. "If not, the surprise will be on him. She might have made plans to have lunch with someone else."

Good point.

They found Penelope alone in the executive kitchen-cum-breakroom, standing by the coffee station. She appeared to be in a fog as she stirred the hot beverage in her mug. Sister Lou crossed the white-and-silver-tiled floor to the newly appointed finance director. She sensed Shari close behind her.

"Penelope?" Sister Lou repeated the young woman's name when she didn't at first respond.

Penelope jumped. Her whole body shook. She blinked at Sister Lou and Shari as though she was waking up. "I'm sorry." Her laughter was breathy and awkward. "I think I was woolgathering."

Sister Lou put a gentle hand on Penelope's shoulder. The black wool of the finance and management director's sweater dress was soft beneath her palm. "We didn't mean to startle you."

Her woolgathering, as Penelope had called it, was understandable. With Opal's death, Penelope had lost her boss and, by her own words, a good friend. Having to fill in for Opal meant she hadn't had time to grieve her loss.

It had only been eleven days since Opal's accident; four days since her funeral. More than a hundred people had attended the service, according to Shari's article. Mourners had come from other towns and other states to pay their respects. Opal's fiancé had stood stoically with her family. Tears had streamed down his face beneath his sunglasses as Sister Lou, Sister Carmen, Chris and Shari had expressed their condolences.

Penelope looked from Sister Lou to Shari. "Is there something I can do for you?"

Sister Lou exchanged a look with Shari. In silent communication, they agreed this wasn't the time to interview the new director.

With her hand on the younger woman's arm, Sister Lou guided Penelope to the same table where she and Shari had questioned Kerry four days before.

"We wanted to see how you were doing." Sister Lou took the seat beside Penelope. She glanced up as Shari settled onto the chair across the table from the finance director.

Penelope stared into her mug of black coffee. "Some days are harder than others." She took a shaky breath. "Opal meant so much to me. She wasn't just a boss, you know? She was a true mentor. And a good friend."

"I'm so very sorry for your loss." Strangely, those words had never sounded more inadequate to Sister Lou. Then she remembered how they'd brought her comfort when her dear friend Dr. Maurice Jordan had been murdered.

Shari lowered her voice and leaned closer to Penelope. "I wish I had known her better. She seemed like such a great person."

"She was the best." Penelope seemed to get a burst of energy. "I learned a lot from Opal. She was so generous with her time and her knowledge. She wanted to help me advance my career. That was her goal for me."

Sister Lou had a flash of insight. "Do you think she was grooming you to take over the finance and management department?"

"I don't know." Penelope flexed her shoulders restlessly. "I don't think so. Opal loved her job and she loved working for Mayor Stanley."

That seemed to be a common theme among the mayor's team. Sister Lou didn't think the words were just lip service. She had the sense that the sentiment was very sincere. "Do you think Opal was hoping the mayor would be reelected?"

"I think so." Penelope blinked quickly as though

struggling to hold back tears. "Although she used to say that she didn't know whether she'd be able to survive two terms with Mayor Stanley. She meant it as a joke, but looking back, it seems almost prescient."

"That's creepy." Shari sat back on the hard plastic chair. Her cocoa eyes were dark and troubled.

"Yes." Penelope's sigh quavered with unspent sorrow. "I just hope her other prediction doesn't come true."

Sister Lou experienced a cold shiver of trepidation. "What was it?"

Penelope looked up from her mug of untouched coffee and held Sister Lou's gaze. "She didn't think Mayor Stanley would survive two terms, either."

Chapter 24

"Our long Saturday runs make these five miles seem like nothing." Sister Carmen's voice bounced with enthusiasm Monday morning.

"You were right about our taking yoga classes, too." Sister Lou smiled as she jogged beside her friend. "Even though we're the oldest yogis in the class," she added dryly.

"Age is just a number." Sister Carmen spread her arms without breaking stride. "We're young at heart, Lou. We're young at heart."

That description definitely applied to Sister Carmen. Her friend and longtime jogging companion's positive energy—and her fuchsia running wear—made the cold, dark predawn hours much more palatable. It was the final Monday in February, almost two weeks after Ash Wednesday.

Sister Lou tugged on her black knit hat, pulling it down over her ears. They started to warm again immediately. *Ah, the little things.*

They continued their five-mile jog from the congregation's motherhouse and around the campus of the

College of St. Hermione of Ephesus, skirting the
mounds of melting snow that crunched under their
feet and masked the lawns beneath. Thick evergreen
trees and boxy evergreen bushes valiantly strove to
add color to the dauntingly gray and white grounds.
Lights glowing in the old-fashioned lampposts that
outlined the campus added magic to the otherwise
depressing tableau.

Sister Lou breathed in the scent of pine and cold.
They were so alien to the smell of warm sand and surf
from the beaches she used to jog along in Southern
California where she was born and raised. Still she
much preferred jogging outdoors.

"We've cleared all of the people on our suspect list,
every one of them." Sister Lou's comment shattered
the thick silence. The impatience she felt sharpened
her tone more than she'd intended.

"How can you be sure?" Sister Carmen's eyes narrowed with confusion. Her words slipped out on
cold breaths of air. Her electric blue insulated vest
and golden tights seemed to beat back the predawn
darkness.

"Heather was right." A steady, crisp breeze pinched
Sister Lou's cheeks. "Her staff is committed to her
and to Briar Coast. They're convinced that Briar
Coast's future well-being is dependent on the mayor
being elected to a second term."

Sister Lou considered the lights that glowed from
a smattering of dorm room windows in the residence
halls. Those must be early risers, like her and Sister
Carmen. Sister Lou adjusted her gait as she and Sister
Carmen jogged away from the residence halls and
toward the campus oval.

"What about the people who *don't* like her?" Sister

Carmen broke the companionable silence that had carried them through most of their first lap around the oval.

Sister Carmen adjusted her knit hat over her ears and thick, curly hair. The hat was almost a twin to Sister Lou's in style only. Sister Carmen's hat was a startling citrus orange compared to Sister Lou's black yarn.

"Heather's most outspoken detractors are the town council president, Ian Greer, former mayor Owen Rodney and Mister Rodney's biggest campaign donor, Wesley Vyne." Sister Lou matched her gait to Sister Carmen's as they started their second lap around the campus oval. "I don't think any of them are behind the threats to Heather, though."

"Why not?" Sister Carmen's question forced Sister Lou to take a harder look at the reasons she'd initially crossed those three men off of her suspect list.

"Owen and Wesley are excited by the prospect of campaigning against Heather." Sister Lou listened to the silence on the campus grounds as she and Sister Carmen continued their second lap around the oval. It was almost surreal. "Wesley is confident that Heather won't win reelection, and Ian doesn't want to force a primary with Heather because he thinks it would hurt their party."

"It probably would." Sister Carmen fell silent again beside Sister Lou.

Sister Lou allowed herself time to reflect as they moved around the oval. Sister Carmen was right. The physical challenge of their long weekend jogs had made their regular runs during the week even easier. In keeping with their training schedule, they'd run twelve miles last Saturday for their longer run.

In addition, the Friday morning yoga classes worked wonders in stretching their muscles.

"Keep running, Sisters!" The familiar chorus of well wishes came from the women's track and field runners.

Sister Lou greeted the young women as they raced past her. Sister Carmen gave them her standard parade wave and camera-ready smile.

"If no one has a motive to threaten Heather, then how do we know someone's really threatening her?"

Sister Carmen's question confused Sister Lou. What was her friend implying? "We've seen the letters that the stalker sent to her."

"How do we know that Heather didn't write those letters herself to make us think that someone's threatening her?"

Sister Lou's confusion cleared. Sister Carmen must have been watching the mystery movie channel again. The theory may seem farfetched, but Sister Lou wouldn't dismiss it. "If we believe Heather wrote the letters herself, how then would we explain the attack against her while she was jogging?"

"That's right, she's a fellow jogger. That makes me less likely to believe she'd do anything shady."

"Focus, Carm."

"Maybe she tripped." Sister Carmen shrugged. They were approaching the end of their second lap around the oval.

"That's plausible." Everything Sister Carmen was saying was plausible. Still, as with the list of obvious suspects, they were missing a viable motive. "Why would Heather feign these threats? Why would she go to all of that trouble?"

"Maybe she doesn't want to run again." Sister

Carmen shook her head. "If that were true, why wouldn't she just say that she wasn't running for re-election? We're missing something."

Sister Lou frowned. "Or someone."

"You had a job interview this morning? With whom?" Chris sat across the table from Shari during their lunch at the Briar Coast Café Monday afternoon. He sounded as though he was trying to mask his shock. He wasn't succeeding.

Shari lowered her soupspoon. She'd miscalculated Chris's reaction. She thought he'd be curious or even interested. Shari hadn't expected the tension she sensed rushing out of him like a faucet.

She inhaled, hoping the scents of pastries, soups, and coffee would calm her. They didn't. "*Buffalo Today.*"

"The job's in another city?" Chris seemed even more agitated.

"There's only one newspaper in Briar Coast. I have to look outside if I want another job."

"I thought you liked working for the *Telegraph.*"

Shari lowered her eyes to her colorful salad, which was swimming in honey mustard dressing. "I like to be aware of other opportunities so that I can be prepared in case of . . . anything. The managing editor at *Buffalo Today* has been trying to bring me over for about three months."

The silence between them was strained. The bursts of laughter and happy chatter around the café seemed to mock their sudden tension. The care and feeding of personal relationships remained a mystery to Shari. She resisted with all her might the urge to squirm on her chair. Her gaze returned to her chicken and dumpling soup. It was growing cold. Chris's beef and vegetable soup was probably cooling, as well. Neither of them seemed to have much of an appetite anymore.

"I wish you'd told me sooner." There was disappointment in Chris's voice. That was worse than his shock. "I would have liked advance notice that my girlfriend was thinking of leaving town."

Shari had objected to the "girlfriend" label the first couple of times Chris had used it, but now the term was growing on her. At least she liked it in reference to their being together.

"Who said I was leaving Briar Coast?" Shari sampled a spoonful of her soup. She frowned. As she'd suspected, it was lukewarm. "*Buffalo Today*'s offices are less than forty-five minutes away. Besides, I just signed a one-year lease on a new apartment." The thick slashes of Chris's eyebrows leaped up his forehead. Some of the tension seemed to drain from him. "You'd commute between Briar Coast and Buffalo? That's a long drive, back and forth for five days a week—or more."

Shari thought about her drive to the job interview this morning. Compared to her ten-minute jaunt to the *Telegraph*'s office, the almost forty-five-minute sojourn to *Buffalo Today* had seemed like a punishment. But her travel times in Chicago had been even more painful and she'd survived them.

"I've had worse commutes. At least this one would be worth it—*if* I decide to take the job." Shari offered Chris a smile and felt rewarded when he gave her a genuine smile in return. "Did you really think I was breaking up with you?"

"The thought had crossed my mind." Chris finished his soup, then picked up his roast beef and cheddar sandwich on whole grain bread. His appetite appeared to have returned. "How was your interview?"

"It was okay." Shari shrugged a single shoulder as she moved her salad around its bowl. "The people were nice, but they always are during the job interview. They don't start showing their real personalities until about six months after you've taken the job."

"That's a cynical perspective." Chris's eyes twinkled with amusement.

"I'm speaking from vast experience."

"I agree that it's a good idea to be aware of other job opportunities, but you don't sound enthusiastic about this one."

Shari let her gaze wander to the scene outside their window. It was just after noon. What remained of the snow that storekeepers had shoveled a week or so ago ringed the sidewalk and glittered in the midday sun. Maple trees lined the curb. They were bare and swaying in the stiff wind.

"*Buffalo Today*'s office is in great condition. It's newer and much more modern than the *Telegraph*'s building." Shari looked at Chris again. "Unlike the *Telegraph*, their carpeting is thick. The walls have fresh paint, and the kitchen has modern appliances. It even smells better."

"Then what's wrong?"

Shari hesitated. "It's not the *Telegraph*."

Chris inclined his head. "I understand. I'm glad that you're happy at the *Telegraph*. You're right that it's good to have options, but for purely selfish reasons, I hope you don't have to add to your commute."

At least one of them had shaken off their tension. Shari was still spinning her wheels. Should she stay with the *Telegraph* or should she go? Should she wait until they asked her to leave or should she make a dignified retreat?

Shari returned to redecorating her salad. "Let's hope Diego doesn't decide to cut me loose."

Chris gave her a bewildered look. "Why would he?"

An image of Harold—annoying, obnoxious, and *normal*—came to mind. "I just want to be prepared."

Chapter 25

"Can you prove that someone's trying to kill you?" Shari asked Heather late Monday afternoon.

Sister Lou winced beside Shari as they sat in front of Heather's desk. As she'd driven Shari to the Briar Coast Town Hall, Sister Lou had shared with the reporter the conversation she'd had that morning with Sister Carmen. Sister Lou hadn't dismissed Sister Carmen's theory, but she wasn't convinced it was valid. She wanted to approach it with caution. On the other hand, Sister Carmen's proposal excited Shari. The possibility that Heather had written the threatening letters to herself intrigued her.

Heather gave the reporter a questioning look from the seat behind her desk. She tilted her head, causing her thick fall of chestnut hair to slide across the left shoulder of her violet suit jacket. "How would I prove that?"

Sister Lou interceded. "You were right, Heather. It doesn't appear that any of the individuals on our initial suspects list have a motive to want you to leave

Briar Coast. We don't believe any of them is behind the threats to you."

Heather switched her troubled gaze to Sister Lou. There were circles under her eyes. Was the mayor having trouble sleeping? A fresh mug of coffee sat wrapped between her hands on the table. She'd offered Shari and Sister Lou a cup when they'd arrived. Sister Lou had declined, but Shari was always game for more caffeine.

Heather expelled a sigh of frustration—and fatigue? "Well, someone's writing them. Contrary to what our intrepid newswoman thinks, I'm not sending them to myself."

Shari gestured toward the mayor with her white porcelain mug of java. "Can you prove that?"

Heather turned to Shari. "Why would I threaten myself?"

Shari placed her elbows on the wooden arms of the cushioned chair and balanced her coffee mug in both hands. "To make us think that you're being stalked. Sure, your job approval rating is at a historic high for an incumbent Briar Coast mayor, but your popularity rating is dismal. Maybe you don't want to run for re-election or maybe you want to get sympathy votes from people who believe someone's trying to kill you. Their sympathy could boost your popularity numbers."

Sister Lou felt the anticipation rolling from Shari like ocean waves. Hearing Shari verbalize Sister Carmen's theory convinced her even further that the notion, though creative, wasn't valid.

Heather looked amused by Shari's premise. "If I didn't want to run for a second term, I'd simply say so. I wouldn't concoct some elaborate scheme, then inconvenience four other people by asking them to investigate it for me. If you believe that I have a problem speaking my mind, you haven't been paying attention."

"That's true." Shari sounded disappointed. She seemed to consider Heather's point as she drank her coffee. "You never hesitate to speak your mind, even when other people aren't interested."

"We have that in common." Heather didn't sound offended. "Regarding the so-called sympathy vote, that doesn't make sense, either. If I'd wanted sympathy, I'd at least tell the deputies and the media that I was being threatened. Counting myself, you're only one of seven people who know about the letters and I've asked you not to report it."

Shari lowered her mug and settled back on her chair. "That's a good point."

Heather held Shari's gaze. "And my popularity numbers may not be *great*, but they're not *dismal*. I resent that."

Shari inclined her head. "I apologize."

Heather took another sip of coffee. The caffeine didn't appear to be helping her. The mayor seemed tired. "We either have to find other suspects or take a harder look at the ones we have."

"The usual suspects aren't working." Shari looked at Sister Lou before turning back to Heather. "Your opponents are excited to run against you. Your staff admires you, and your party supports you. We need new, more viable names."

Sister Lou caught Heather's eyes. "Is there anything that you're not telling us that could possibly help identify your stalker and the reason for these threats?"

"The reason is clear." Heather's voice was tight with frustration. "He wants me to leave town."

Sister Lou searched her mind for everything she knew about the mayor from what she'd read and what others had told her. "Could it be someone from your past?"

Heather set aside her porcelain coffee mug. "Everyone from my past is either in El Paso, Texas, or Norman, Oklahoma."

Shari shrugged. "We've talked with most of the people in Briar Coast who don't like you. Maybe a frenemy from out of town has caught up with you."

Heather looked wryly amused. "I can't think of anyone I've offended so terribly that they would carry a grudge for all these years, then travel thousands of miles for revenge."

"It's a theory." Sister Lou spread her arms. "If we can't identify a suspect from your present, we have to think about your past."

"I'm feeling desperate, too." Heather unlocked her bottom desk drawer and retrieved her purse. From the front compartment of her black faux leather handbag, she pulled out a plain white business envelope. "I received another letter this morning. I was going to show it to you tonight."

Sister Lou accepted the plain sheet of copy paper from Heather. She leaned toward Shari so they could read the anonymous message together.

Outsider, don't fool yourself. My threats are real. Call off the investigation with Sister Lou. Leave office and Briar Coast. You know I've killed before. I can kill again.

Sister Lou trembled with apprehension. The stalker's rage and hate were undeniable. She sensed it with each word in his latest threat. Beside her, Sister Lou felt Shari's shiver.

"He's getting chattier." Shari's voice was hard with anger. She sat back on her chair. "It might be time to go to the deputies."

"His messages have grown even more ominous." Sister Lou handed back the note to Heather. "Shari's right. We need to ask for the deputies' help."

"No." Heather shoved the letter back into its envelope. She hid the threat inside her purse and locked her purse in her drawer again. "I'm not going to the deputies. I will not allow this psycho to intimidate me."

"Well, he's intimidating me and I'm not the one getting the letters." Shari gestured toward Heather. "And your calling him a psycho makes me think he's having some kind of an effect on you."

Sister Lou silently agreed. "Since you refuse to go to the deputies, what would you recommend we do next?"

Heather pulled her chair farther under her desk and folded her hands on its surface. "My next step is to formally announce my reelection campaign."

"What?" Sister Lou heard Shari echo her reaction. She took a settling breath. "Are you certain that's a wise next step?"

"I'm certain it's *not*," Shari insisted.

Sister Lou nodded in the direction of the drawer that hid Heather's purse. "Your stalker has threatened to hurt you—"

"To *kill* you," Shari interrupted.

Sister Lou continued, "—if you campaign for reelection."

"That's why I'm going to make my announcement."

Heather took a deep breath as though to steady herself. "I *have* to do this. Don't you understand?"

Beneath the steely determination and righteous outrage, Sister Lou saw the desperate plea in Heather's eyes. It was the look of someone who was trying to make amends to those she'd disappointed in her past, and who was trying to live up to a promise she'd made to those who'd more recently taken a chance on her.

Sister Lou sighed. "I think I do."

Shari looked from Heather to Sister Lou and back. "Then explain it to me."

Heather turned to the reporter. Her voice shook with the force of her convictions. "If I can't stand up for myself and what I believe in, how can I stand up for the people of this town? If I turn my back on the commitment I made to them, I won't be able to live with myself."

Shari drummed her fingers on the chair's wooden arm. "Well, you've made a believer out of me."

Heather shared a look with Sister Lou and Shari. "Are we in agreement that we *won't* contact the deputies?"

Shari sighed. "All right."

Sister Lou was hesitant to make a full commitment. "We won't contact them yet, but you'll have to provide a more viable list of suspects. We have to stop this person before he actually harms you—or anyone else."

"I couldn't agree more." Tension crept back into Heather's voice.

"I'll do some more research on the names we have so far." Shari finished her coffee. "Maybe we've missed something."

Sister Lou stood, collecting her purse. "I know that

we have." *And I can't shake the feeling that it's right in front of us.*

Sister Marianna marched into Sister Lou's office at the end of the day Monday. She took a stand in front of Sister Lou's desk. "Louise, this has gone on long enough. It's been almost two weeks. I insist that you tell me why the mayor is staying with us in the mother-house."

This is exactly the diversion I need right now.

Sister Lou checked her crimson Timex wristwatch. It was just a few minutes before five o'clock. During the past almost three hours, Sister Lou had been sitting at her desk, plagued by distractions and uncertainties that had kept her from being as productive as she needed to be. She was worried about Heather. What repercussions would she face from announcing her reelection campaign? Had the public servant painted a target on her back? One member of her executive team already had been killed. Were other members of her staff in peril?

Is the congregation in danger?

Sister Lou forced back her fears and manufactured a brilliant smile for Sister Marianna. "Good evening, Marianna. How was your day?"

She could almost hear the other woman gnashing her teeth. The imagery brightened her mood even more.

"*Why* must we *always* play this game, Louise?" Sister Marianna thrust her fists onto the hips of her brown skirt suit. She'd added a gold and brown handmade silk scarf to her outfit.

How many of Kathy's scarves had Marianna purchased?

Sister Lou gave her guest a genuine smile this time. "Indulge me, Marianna. It's been a long day."

"Must you always have your way?"

"Not always. Just this afternoon."

Sister Marianna turned her grimace into a smile and settled onto one of the chairs in front of Sister Lou's desk. "My day was just fine. How was yours?"

"It's much better now that you're here." The truth of that statement surprised Sister Lou. Sister Marianna was the best distraction from her concern for Heather. Her unexpected guest's obvious disbelief in Sister Lou's response made it even better.

"Are we done with your games now, Louise? Can we get back to more consequential matters?"

With a lighter heart, Sister Lou inclined her head, inviting Sister Marianna to continue. "By all means, Marianna. How can I be of assistance to you?"

Sister Marianna gave her a sour look. "The mayor has just announced at a press conference that she plans to run for reelection."

"I know." The mayor's decision to announce so soon had dampened Sister Lou's spirits. Doubts preyed on her once again.

Did I make a mistake by not alerting the deputies to the threats against Heather? Is her stalker on the move right now while I sit here teasing Marianna?

Sister Marianna continued. "As a resident of the motherhouse, I have a right to know why Mayor Stanley has moved in with us."

"The mayor hasn't actually moved in." On occasion, Sister Lou relished matching wits with Sister Marianna. This was one of those occasions. "That would imply that all of her belongings were at the motherhouse, and they're not."

Sister Marianna blew an impatient breath. "You know what I meant, Louise. Must you always prevaricate? How much longer will Mayor Stanley be with us?"

Sister Lou wouldn't lie to anyone, including and especially a member of her congregation. However, her promise to Heather had come face-to-face with Sister Marianna's near-legendary persistence. Her best strategy was to go on offense.

She drew a deep breath, allowing the scent of her white tea potpourri to center her. "Why are you so fixated on the amount of time that the mayor will be with us, Marianna? Is her presence making you uncomfortable?"

"Why is Mayor Stanley here at all?" Sister Marianna fiddled with her scarf, loosening the garment from her neck. "Is this some political ploy to try to impress Briar Coast's religious voters?"

The suggestion took Sister Lou by surprise. "I believe the mayor is too genuine to use her relationship with our congregation as a campaign tool. That type of strategy would be beneath her."

Sister Marianna gave Sister Lou a skeptical look. "Then what is Mayor Stanley hoping to gain from her stay with us?"

Sister Lou searched her mind and said a quick prayer for inspiration. Her request was answered right on time. "Have you considered that you're asking the wrong question, Marianna?"

Sister Marianna appeared intrigued. She arched a thin, gray brow. "What do you mean?"

"Perhaps instead of asking what the mayor is getting from us, you should instead consider how the congregation could benefit from the attention that we're getting from the mayor."

Sister Marianna leaned forward on her seat. "Are you saying that the congregation is using the mayor's stay as leverage to make her one of our regular donors?"

The idea sounded even better coming from Sister Marianna. "I'm afraid that I'm not at liberty to say, but as you've probably realized, having the mayor spend so much time with the congregation gives her an opportunity to learn more about our mission."

"She can hear directly from us instead of reading about our works in a letter."

"Exactly."

"What a brilliant idea, Louise." Sister Marianna clapped her hands together. Her eyes shone with excitement. "How are you doing with the solicitation? Has she made a donation yet?"

Sister Lou had anticipated Sister Marianna's question. "Actually, Marianna, I could use your help with that. Mayor Stanley hasn't yet made a final commitment."

"Of course, Louise. All you had to do was ask." Sister Marianna rose to her feet. "In fact, I'll take charge of Mayor Stanley's education about our congregation and mission for you, and convert her into a regular donor. You won't have to worry about a thing. Consider this task taken off of your list."

Success!

Sister Lou was thrilled to have found a project that would distract Sister Marianna from further questions about Heather's stay at the motherhouse or her reelection campaign. As an added bonus, Sister Lou had no doubt that Sister Marianna would turn the mayor into a regular donor for the congregation.

She smiled up at Sister Marianna. "Thank you, Marianna. I knew that I could count on you. It's a great relief to be able to leave things in your capable hands."

Sister Lou watched Sister Marianna disappear down the hall outside of her office. "Poor Heather."

Chapter 26

I could get used to this.

Heather buckled her seat belt after Diego closed her passenger door Monday evening. She watched him circle the hood of his SUV. The vehicle may have a lot of miles on it, but it was solid, dependable, and in great shape. Much like its owner.

The aforementioned owner settled behind the steering wheel and shifted his car into gear. It was minutes before seven o'clock in the evening. The parking lot was dark and pretty much deserted. A shiver chased through her. This would have been the perfect night for her stalker to attack her again. Had he been out there, waiting? Had Diego's arrival stopped him? The *Telegraph* editor turned up the heat in his Honda. Had he noticed her shiver?

"I caught your press conference, announcing your reelection campaign this afternoon. Was that wise?" Diego's gaze bounced to her, then back to the windshield as he navigated his vehicle out of the town hall visitors' parking lot.

"I thought it was. Otherwise I wouldn't have

done it." Heather wrenched her gaze from Diego's clean profile and dropped it in the almost empty parking lot.

"That's funny. I thought announcing your reelection campaign would be the wrong thing to do, considering a confessed murderer has threatened to kill you if you run for reelection." Diego's voice was thick with sarcasm and anger. His tone caught Heather off guard.

"I've told you before. I'm not going to let some madman run me out of my town."

"It was that kind of arrogance that got you in trouble in El Paso." Diego kept his eyes on the road even as he challenged Heather.

Heather unclenched her teeth, took a calming breath, then clenched them again as she caught his scent. It reminded her of soap. She struggled to erase a mental image of Diego stepping out of the shower. "It was my decision to make, Diego."

"Why couldn't you have waited until after we caught the person who's threatening you?"

"I wanted to show this worm that he's not going to intimidate me." Heather heard a curious sound like a choking gasp. It seemed to come from Diego.

"Wouldn't it be smarter to learn from your mistakes rather than repeating them?" Diego sounded like the words were being ripped from his throat.

Heather stared at his sharp profile in fascination. "You really are angry, aren't you? Even angrier than you were in El Paso."

"Can you blame me when I see you making the same mistake?"

"It's not the same." Heather turned to stare out of the passenger-side window. "In El Paso, I made the mistake of trusting the wrong person."

"No, you made the mistake of not accepting help." Diego's sigh expressed sorrow and fatigue. "I wanted to help you, Heather. Why didn't you let me? You accept help from your cabinet every day. Because you listen to them, Briar Coast is beating the odds and making an incredible economic recovery. Why can't you accept *my* help?"

Heather's head snapped around to put Diego back in focus. "Are you implying that I'll only accept help from other women?"

"That's not what I said." Diego's voice was strained as though he was making a herculean effort to remain calm.

So was Heather. "They're incredibly smart and obviously capable."

"I know." Diego glanced at her before turning his attention back to the road. "But I think I've proven on more than one occasion that I'm a bit smarter than a rock."

Heather smiled. "Yes, you have."

She returned to the view through the passenger-side window. The scene was proof that winter was holding on with both hands, but it felt comfortably warm in Diego's SUV. It was the last Monday in February. Even though St. Patrick's Day was more than two weeks away, smiling images of the Irish patron saint's leprechaun mascot had taken over the streets and shop windows.

Heather's smile faded. "I read Graham Irsay's obituary a couple of months ago."

"So did I." Diego's voice was low.

Graham Irsay was the political operative who'd set up Heather to take the fall for his corrupt development scheme. He would have succeeded if Diego hadn't intervened, saving Heather from herself. According to his obituary, Graham, who'd served eight years in prison for his transgressions, drank himself to death.

"I wonder what happened to his wife and children."

"Irsay and his wife separated during his trial. After his conviction, she divorced him and moved back to Austin with their son and daughter. She remarried a few years later."

"I remember that Irsay and his wife were born and raised in Austin." Heather recalled a family photo she'd seen several times on Graham's desk. It was the perfect campaign image of a wealthy, successful, attractive dark-haired couple with their awkward-looking dark-haired son and blond daughter. More than one curious observer had privately wondered from where the daughter had gotten her strawberry blond curls. "Their children were very young at the time of the trial, weren't they?"

"Their son was nine or ten. Their daughter was a year younger."

Heather heard the shrug in Diego's voice. "It must have been a confusing and frightening time for them. Their father disappeared, then their mother took them away from everything that was familiar to them."

"None of that was your fault." Diego's tone was firm. "Irsay brought all of it on himself."

"I know." Yet Heather couldn't move past a sense of guilt.

Diego turned his vehicle onto the wide and winding driveway that curved around the congregational offices and rose toward the motherhouse. Heather studied the landscaping as they crawled along the driveway:

the rolling lawns and barren maple trees, the rows of evergreen bushes, and surging evergreen trees.

Diego stopped his car outside the front door of the congregation's motherhouse. He turned to her. "Do you want to attend your Charity Spring-Raiser together?"

Heather had flashbacks of Diego's similar invitations during the time they'd first known each other: lunch, dinner, coffee before work, drinks after work. She'd been tempted fourteen years ago. Not surprisingly, she was tempted now. The newspaperman was even more handsome, charming, and irresistible today.

But resist him, she did. "Why don't we just both go to the event? We don't have to show up together. I don't think either one of us wants to become the topic of town gossip."

Diego gave her a wistful smile. "I wouldn't mind."

"I would." She hated that she always had to be so scrupulous about her private life. She was living in a political fishbowl. "I'd rather people didn't speculate on my personal life. *Who's the mayor dating? Is she getting favorable news coverage because she's sleeping with the editor of the local paper?* I don't want to have to deal with that."

"I understand." Diego's words conflicted with his tone. "I'll see you in the morning, then. Same time?"

"Yes, thank you." Heather climbed from Diego's SUV, dragging her briefcase and purse with her.

A cold wind snatched her breath away as she walked toward the building. Heather huddled deeper into her sapphire wool coat. She was conscious of Diego watching to make sure she got into the motherhouse safely. His chivalry was another thing that attracted her to him.

Heather pulled open the motherhouse's heavy front door, then turned to wave at Diego, letting him know the coast was clear. She watched him drive away. It was too dark to tell if he'd waved back. She liked to imagine that he had.

Heather sighed, turning toward the elevator that would carry her to her room. She was willing to risk her life to follow her political ambition, but she wasn't willing to risk her political reputation to follow her heart. The realization left her feeling cold and empty.

"Are you glad you came?" Chris couldn't take his eyes off Shari. They stood together at the Mayor's Charity Spring-Raiser late Thursday evening. It was the first day of March.

Shari's eyes still sparkled with amusement over Chris telling her she was stunning. That had been an understatement, though. Her flowing sweater dress was a pale green reminiscent of key lime pie. Of course her ankle-high boots were the exact match. How did she walk in those four-inch stilettos? She'd accessorized her outfit with chunky silver jewelry.

Shari's gaze swayed to the nearby dessert table. "The mini cupcakes are delicious. And, since we've been jogging together in the mornings, I won't feel guilty when I go back for thirds."

"I'll probably join you." Chris glanced over his shoulder at the table burdened with cakes, pies, cookies, pudding, and mini cupcakes. "We should smuggle a couple out for Sister Carm." Sister Carmen's weakness for pastries, particularly mini chocolate cupcakes, was well known.

Shari's dark eyes widened with excitement. "That's a great idea. Leave it to me."

The Briar Coast Community Center once again hosted the annual event. It looked as though a flower shop had exploded in the center's large ballroom. Petals were strewn over every table. Bouquets of flowers stood on every counter and table around the room. The arrangements featured yellow daisies, red roses, and orange mums. The floral fragrances mingled with the aroma of the hot and cold hors d'oeuvres, and the fresh pastries from the Briar Coast Café. It wasn't an unpleasant combination. Quite the opposite. Chris felt like he was on a picnic with more than a hundred of his closest friends.

His attention returned to Shari. It wasn't a hardship. Chris loved looking at her. "Have you thought any more about whether you're going to accept the job with *Buffalo Today*?"

Shari's gaze slid away from him. "I haven't been thinking about it *a lot*, but I suppose I should make my decision soon."

"What's holding you back?" Chris's question seemed to make Shari uncomfortable. He sipped the fruit punch one of the servers had offered him when they first arrived. The plastic glass was shaped like a champagne flute.

"It's a big decision." Shari's nonchalance seemed forced. She took a long drink from her own fruit punch.

Chris watched the muscles in Shari's throat work

as she swallowed the liquid. "I know. There are a lot of factors to consider."

Shari pinned Chris with a direct gaze. "What do you think?"

Chris hesitated. "I want you to be happy. That's the most important thing, and I don't want to influence your decision in any way."

Shari gave him a dry look. "Do you think my mind is so prodigiously weak that I'd do something I didn't want to do just to please you?"

Chris couldn't imagine that ever happening. "When you put it that way . . . Have you done a pros and cons list?"

Shari shook her head. "I don't need a list to know there are plenty of things on each side."

"But think about the significance of each point. For example, you're from Chicago. The longer commute won't bother you, but the frequent trips to the gas station will strain your budget."

"*Buffalo Today* pays more than the *Telegraph*." Shari's tone was dry.

"And you'll have to drive more to cover your stories. That will add to the wear and tear on your car."

"It pays *a lot* more than the *Telegraph*."

"I see." For most people, that kind of financial compensation would have been enough for them to accept the job offer within the hour that it was made. Shari wasn't most people, though. Something more was holding her back. "Your workdays will be a lot longer."

She shrugged. "I work long days now with the *Telegraph*—and for a lot less money."

Chris was reluctant to play this next card, but it was

laying there, unspoken between them. "With your longer commute, you'll have a lot less time for Aunt Lou. And for me."

Shari's gaze held his. *"That's* the greatest drawback."

Chapter 27

The annual Mayor's Charity Spring-Raiser was a big thank-you from the local government to the organizations that served the community and the donors that supported them. In Sister Lou's estimation, that was the event's altruistic purpose. In fact, it was another fund-raising opportunity for the organizations that served the Briar Coast community.

The event's registration also raised money for the Briar Coast Community Center, which hosted the event, and the mayor's pet fund-raising project. For the past four years, the Stanley administration's goal had been to break ground on the town's first-ever health clinic.

Sister Lou stood alone for the moment, surveying the community center and the event attendees. She enjoyed the temporary relief from the demands of socializing. Sister Carmen, who was more of an extrovert, would have reveled in that aspect of the evening. Sister Lou didn't. She felt her knotted muscles relax as she sipped her fruit punch. The sweetly tart drink was light and refreshing.

The room was comfortably cool for the large gathering. Sister Lou searched the crowd, picking out each member of the congregation's leadership team with their specific donor assignments.

Their prioress, Sister Barbara, and the president of the College of St. Hermione of Ephesus, Sister Valerie Shaw, stood together. They appeared to be blocking the exit as they stood smiling and chatting with Donald and Sonya Russell. The wealthy retirees were notoriously reluctant donors although Sister Lou was grateful for the couple's response to the congregation's annual appeal. Perhaps with Sister Barbara's and Sister Valerie's combined persuasion—and a small miracle—the Russells would decide to extend their generosity to the college.

Sister Lou wondered if she should join Sister Angela Yeoh and Sister Paula Walton at the hot hors d'oeuvres station. It would give her an excuse to get more of those Swedish meatballs. But the sisters were deep in conversation with Montgomery Crane, one of their donor assignments. The handsome older gentleman was the chief executive of Crane Enterprises, which owned and operated a chain of vacation resorts across the country. A wave of sadness rolled over Sister Lou as she recalled that Montgomery had been a mentor to the late Autumn Tassler. Sister Lou found peace in the knowledge that she'd played a role in catching Autumn's killer.

Sister Marianna had cornered Ian Greer near the pastries. In addition to educating the town council president on the congregation's various service projects, Sister Marianna had planned to voice her objection to several of the town council's legislative proposals, including the tax abatement. Every other member of the leadership team was concerned about combining both messages, but Sister Marianna was confident that she could pull it off. Sister Lou had promised Sister Barbara that she would handle damage control. She also made a note to bring back one or two mini chocolate cupcakes for Sister Carmen.

"You look like you could use something stronger, but I'm afraid all I have is fruit punch." Heather's voice drew Sister Lou's attention away from Sister Marianna. The mayor took Sister Lou's empty glass.

"Thank you." Sister Lou accepted the proffered full glass of punch. "I was lost in thought. Forgive me." She managed a smile for Heather and Diego, who'd joined the mayor.

"There's nothing to forgive." Heather waved a dismissive hand. "I only wanted to make sure you were having a good time."

"Absolutely." Sister Lou's attention was drawn away as Kerry appeared beside them with her boyfriend.

"Excuse me, Mayor Stanley." Kerry offered their small group a blinding smile. "Jeff wanted to pay his respects."

Heather accepted the young man's right hand. "Thank you for coming."

"Thank you for the invitation, Mayor Stanley." Jefferson released Heather's hand but kept her attention. "You know, Kerry told me that you announced your reelection campaign on Monday. Good luck."

"Thank you." Heather's smile was pleasant but perfunctory.

The mayor appeared to be fighting a battle on two fronts. On one front, Heather didn't appear to want to interact with Kerry's boyfriend. On the other front, she didn't seem to want to insult her administrative assistant by cutting her exchange with Jefferson short. She was in quite a quandary.

"Do you know who your challengers will be?" Jefferson glanced around the ballroom as though he could pick out the other candidates on sight.

"No one else has formally declared." Heather sounded resigned to having a lengthy conversation with the budding politico.

Sister Lou masked her smile behind her glass of punch. She drew a sip of the sweet-and-tart beverage. A few of the ice chips brushed against her lips. Diego also seemed to be amused by Heather's dilemma. Kerry didn't appear to be aware of Sister Lou, Diego, or anyone else in the room. She gazed at Jefferson with near adoration. How long had the couple been dating, and were Kerry's feelings returned in equal measure?

Jefferson was still holding court. "You must have some idea who would be running against you. Every good politician has an ear to the ground to find out how the political winds are blowing, you know? They know their allies and their enemies."

Heather's features were hard to read. "As a public servant, I've been too busy serving the public to be a politician. Whoever runs against me will be running against my record, which is the way it should be."

Sister Lou silently applauded Heather's response, but it seemed her message was lost on Jefferson.

He swept out an arm to encompass the ballroom. "Don't you think this large-scale event poses, you know, an unfair campaign advantage for you over your opponents?"

"No, I don't." In a blink, Heather went from irritation to amusement. "The annual Mayor's Charity Spring-Raiser is a decades-long Briar Coast tradition. I didn't start it, but when I'm ready to leave office, I hope my successor continues the tradition."

"I don't know." Jefferson's gaze once again swept the room before he gave Heather a pitying look. "I wish you luck with your reelection, but I think you're facing several uphill battles. You know?"

After making his declaration, Jefferson spun on his heels and stalked away.

Kerry's gaze shot to Heather. "Don't worry, Mayor, I'll find out what uphill battles Jeff is talking about and let you know." The young woman chased after her boyfriend.

Heather's expression was thoughtful. "I know it's not my place, but I really don't know what Kerry sees in that guy."

Sister Lou followed Kerry's flight across the room. "I'm at a loss as well, but he just gave me an idea."

"Guess you really botched the mayor's reelection campaign announcement." Harold's was the last voice Shari had expected to hear tonight.

Standing at the dessert station, she wrapped the mini chocolate cupcakes that she'd pilfered for Sister Carmen in paper napkins before facing the rookie reporter. Harold had been using that unique greeting with her since Diego's piece on Heather's reelection announcement had run in the *Telegraph* Tuesday morning.

"Why do you keep saying that to me?" Shari was more curious than annoyed. "You're responsible for the election coverage. Don't you understand what that means?"

"Of course I know what that means." Harold leaned forward to take a chocolate chip cookie from one of the trays.

"Then you understand *you're* the one who botched the mayor's reelection announcement." Shari considered Harold's expensive black suit and bow tie. "What are you doing here?"

Harold sipped from his champagne flute. Shari didn't think he was drinking fruit punch. "My parents made a significant donation to the Briar Coast Health Clinic project. It's their way of helping me ease into the community."

Shari's eyebrows rose in surprise. "That's nice."

It had been tempting to make a snarky comment about Harold's parents buying friends for him. He'd probably been expecting it. But the proposed health clinic was too important to the community for her to diminish it with an ungrateful comment. Besides Harold's disconcerted expression was worth it.

Harold bit into his cookie as he scanned the ballroom. "I've been watching Sister Lou and the mayor this evening. They've been spending a lot of time together." He turned to hold her gaze. "I was right when I asked the mayor about her association with Sister Lou, wasn't I? What's going on?"

"Why are you so sure that Sister Lou is investigating anything?" Shari watched Harold closely. His persistence had gone beyond annoying to concerning.

Harold scowled. "What other reason could there be for them to spend so much time together?"

Shari crossed her arms over her sweater dress. "Why don't *you* tell *me*? What do you think Sister Lou and Mayor Stanley are up to?"

Harold gestured with his right arm. His movements were jerky with impatience. "Sister Lou is obviously investigating Opal Lorrie's murder."

Chris came up to Shari and put his arm around her waist, making her jump. "Is everything all right?"

Shari smiled up at him before continuing her exchange with Harold. "There's no evidence that Opal was murdered. Do you know something that we don't?"

Harold looked from Chris to Shari. "No, I don't, but I know that there's something going on. I can sense it."

Shari watched Harold stalk away. She could sense something going on, too, but she couldn't quite put her finger on it.

"What was that about?" Chris asked.

Shari turned to him. "Have you heard the theory that criminals try to insert themselves into an investigation so they could learn what the police have discovered?"

Chris's eyebrows knitted. "Yes. Why?"

Shari looked over her shoulder in the direction that Harold had disappeared. "I'm getting a weird feeling about Hal."

"Are you gathering intelligence for your mayoral campaign?" Sister Lou addressed Owen Rodney minutes later. The real estate agent and former mayor stood at the hot hors d'oeuvres station.

"I won't need that much intelligence to beat her."
Owen chuckled at his unfunny joke.

"I believe you're underestimating Mayor Stanley."
Sister Lou put a few Swedish meatballs on a plate.
She used the pause to recall Jefferson Manning's
exact words. "I understand that every good politician
has an ear to the ground to find out how the political
winds are blowing. They know their allies and their
enemies."

"That's right. It's called strategizing." Owen stabbed
a meatball with a tiny silver plastic fork and shoveled it
into his mouth.

"Have you identified your allies and enemies?"
Sister Lou claimed a meatball with her fork. Wafts of
steam carried its flavorful aroma up to her, causing
her mouth to water in anticipation. When she bit into
the hors d'oeuvre, spices exploded in her mouth.

"You bet your . . . Sorry, Sister." Owen rocked on
the heels of his black loafers as he tore apart a chicken
wing with his teeth.

"Who are they?" Sister Lou led Owen a few steps
away from the food station to make room for other
guests.

Owen stilled. He looked at Sister Lou suspiciously.
"Why are you asking?"

Sister Lou cleared all expression from her face and
widened her eyes to simulate innocence. "I'm just
curious. Who would you consider an enemy and who
would you think was your ally?"

Suspicion faded from Owen's eyes. Excitement
replaced it as he talked about his candidacy. "Well,
of course I consider my enemies to be anyone who
doesn't want what I want and my allies are the ones
who support my ideas."

Simple enough. "What about Mayor Stanley? Who would you say are her enemies?"

Owen tossed back his head with a laugh as he resumed his rocking stance. "Oh, she has lots of them."

Why, then, do I have the sense that Heather has just one enemy, and I'm looking at him? "Who would you say they are?"

"I wouldn't want people to accuse me of gossiping, but a lot of her enemies are on her staff."

Sister Lou shook her head. "I've heard those rumors, too. They aren't true. Her staff is devoted to her."

Owen smiled knowingly. "Oh, sure, her *executive* team *loves* her. I'd love her, too. Well, I'd *probably* love her. Still, that doesn't mean that I'd be loyal to her. Her executives get all the pay and all the glory. But the working stiffs who report to them and actually do the work, they take all the sh— Sorry, Sister."

It was Sister Lou's turn to contemplate Owen. His theory sounded plausible. She and her team should at least look into it. They didn't have any other leads. Owen's ideas would give them a place to start.

"Are there any people in particular who you believe are disloyal to the mayor?"

Owen turned to a nearby tray to deposit his empty plate. He rubbed his jawline with the blunt fingers of his now free hand. "Well, one name that immediately comes to mind is Kerry Fletcher, the mayor's admin."

Sister Lou's newly discovered acting skills were not yet strong enough to mask her surprise at such a huge— and false—revelation. "What makes you think Kerry is disloyal to the mayor?"

"I wouldn't want people to accuse me of gossiping, but the rumor is that Kerry resents Mayor Stanley because the mayor forces her to work long days and odd hours." Owen's eyes gleamed with the satisfaction of sharing negative news about his opponent.

This news didn't match her impression of the close relationship between Heather and Kerry. That didn't mean Owen was wrong. Perhaps Sister Lou was mistaken. "Is there anyone else?"

"Why are you asking all of these questions? Are you going to help the mayor clean house?"

"Not at all." Sister Lou's mind moved quickly to create a plausible reason for her line of questioning. "It helps to better understand the candidate if you know the people that they surround themselves with."

Even Shari would agree that my excuse was pretty good for a spur-of-the moment cover story.

"Well, I wouldn't want people—"

"I'm not accusing you of gossiping, Owen. I'm just grateful for any insights you can share with me."

A blush rose up from Owen's neck and filled his cheeks. "Well, thank you, Sister. The thing is I don't have other names to give you right now. I've just heard stories about her abrasiveness and meanness. That's one of the reasons that her popularity is so low. Because she's an outsider, she doesn't have the common decency that longtime Briar Coast residents are accustomed to."

Sister Lou nodded. "I understand, Owen."

"But I'd be happy to get those names for you."

Sister Lou was certain he would be. "Thank you, Owen. That would be very helpful."

"Now you see the mayor in a whole new light, don't you?" Owen nodded with satisfaction. "If I think of anything else, I'll let you know."

"I would appreciate that." Sister Lou placed her

empty plate with Owen's on top of the counter, then turned to leave.

The evening was growing later. Guests were departing. Sister Lou stopped by the dessert station and wrapped two mini chocolate cupcakes in paper napkins for Sister Carmen. She'd taken perhaps five steps from the table when Chris caught up with her. The concern in his eyes was unsettling. "What's happened?"

Chris laid a hand on Sister Lou's upper arm. "The mayor's received another threat."

Chapter 28

Heather claimed to be fine, but Sister Lou didn't believe her. The signs of stress were there. Her eyes were haunted. Her lips were tight. Her hands were clenched on her lap above her black wool dress. She gripped a single plain sheet of paper in her fists.

Diego sat beside Heather on the sofa in Sister Lou's sitting room after the Mayor's Charity Spring-Raiser. He'd barely touched his mug of chai tea. Instead his attention kept straying toward Heather. Sister Lou sensed his unease. The whole room felt swollen with tension.

Heather squared her shoulders and cleared her throat. "Thank you for agreeing to meet with me so late on a work night."

It was after ten o'clock Thursday night. Sister Lou had to get up early the next morning for her yoga class, but she expected she'd have trouble sleeping after tonight's events.

Sister Lou glanced at Chris and Shari, who sat opposite Heather and Diego on the matching love seat. "Chris told me you found the note in your coat pocket."

Heather eased her grip on the sheet of paper; it shook in her hand. Her voice trembled as she read the message aloud. "*Outsider, you announced your plans to run again when you know you should be making plans to leave. Why aren't you taking me seriously? Do you want to be the next to die?*"

Shari looked at each of them. "Is it my imagination or does this note sound angrier and more frustrated than even the last one?"

"It's not your imagination." Diego was grim. He took the paper from Heather and scanned it before offering it to Sister Lou.

Sister Lou reviewed the note. The threat was worded as Heather had read it. The message matched the others in appearance: the plain printer paper, computer print, the neat folds. But there was something about the tone of it that kept running through her mind.

It's as though there's more of his personality in his phrasing.

Sister Lou leaned forward to give the sheet of paper to Shari.

Diego shifted to face Heather. "This has already gone on too long. We have to report these threats to the deputies."

Heather was shaking her head even as Diego spoke. She stood to pace the width of the room from Sister Lou's front door to her kitchenette. Her black stilettos tapped against the hardwood flooring. "How can I sound an alarm now? I've just announced my campaign."

"Who cares?" Diego was incredulous. "You need protection. You need a security detail."

"Absolutely not." Heather slashed her right hand through the air. "I won't let this guy scare me." She spun away from the kitchenette.

"Well, he's scaring me." Diego appeared to be running out of patience.

"And me." Shari passed the note on to Chris.

Heather stopped in front of the door to Sister Lou's apartment. "I'm safe here at the motherhouse. And, Diego, you're driving me back and forth to work."

Diego spread his arms. "What about when you jog? Who's with you then?"

"I've been using the treadmills in the college's fitness center instead of running through the streets." Heather made an expression of disgust. Sister Lou could empathize. She didn't enjoy running indoors, either.

"Diego has a point." Chris held up the message that Shari had passed to him. "For your own safety, we should call in the professionals."

Heather stopped pacing. She stood with her arms wrapped around her waist as she considered Chris. Then she lifted her gaze. "What do you think, Sister Lou?"

Sister Lou took another sip of her chai tea as she put together the pieces of this puzzle. The warm cinnamon taste was soothing. "Your stalker is deliberately playing a game of cat-and-mouse with us."

Shari cradled her mug in her palms. "How do you figure that? I think it's just mouse."

Sister Lou considered the note Chris still held in

his hand as she visualized their most recent sequence of events. "Heather announced her campaign on Monday afternoon. Why did the stalker then wait three days before contacting her? If he's really so angry that she's not taking him seriously, why didn't he rush this threat to her on Tuesday?"

Shari spoke to Heather. "He probably wanted to lure you into a false sense of security."

Chris turned to Heather. "Either that or he wanted to increase your tension."

"He was toying with you." Sister Lou considered Heather. "You did the one thing he told you not to do, so he punished you by making you wait to see what he would do next. I'm curious. Did you put him out of your mind or did you worry about his reaction?"

Heather looked away, pulling her fingers through her hair. "As much as I hate to admit it, I was worried."

"That settles it," Diego said. "We're calling the deputies now."

Sister Lou interrupted. "Actually, Diego, I would have been more worried if Heather had put these threats out of her mind."

"That's somewhat comforting." Shari crossed her arms over her sweater dress.

Diego sent Heather a disgruntled look. "I want to go on record that I disagree with your decision."

"Me, too." Chris gave Heather a concerned look.

"Me, three." Shari raised her left hand, palm out.

Heather waved a dismissive hand. "Duly noted."

Sister Lou inclined her head. "In the meantime, we have to consider the message he was sending when he left that note at the event."

"What do you mean?" Heather resumed her pacing. Her movements seemed even more stiff and agitated.

How can I get you to admit that we need to go to the deputies? "Why did he leave the message at the event rather than your office or even your home as he's done in the past?"

"I have no idea." Heather rubbed her hands together. Her voice was thin and distracted.

Diego rubbed the back of his neck. "He must have been at the event. We may have even spoken with him."

Heather looked at each of them. "Let's think about who was there."

"Everyone on our list." Chris spread his hands. "Every member of your executive team, Owen, Wesley."

"Hal." Shari's new addition drew everyone's attention. "He's been asking a lot of questions about Sister Lou's investigations."

Heather shook her head. "I've never seen Hal before in my life. Why would he threaten me?"

Shari threw up her hands. "Why is he fixated on the idea of Sister Lou investigating Opal's murder?"

Diego inclined his head. "It's worth looking into."

Shari nodded. "I'll take care of that."

Sister Lou contemplated her guests. She sensed Diego's anger, Chris's frustration, Shari's confusion, and Heather's fear. "Whoever he is, he wants Heather to know that he can reach her wherever and whenever he wants to, whether it's her office, her home, or an official event attended by hundreds of members of the community."

The blood drained from Heather's face. She

collapsed back onto the sofa beside Diego. The room was silent as she stared blindly at the hardwood flooring. No one seemed to be breathing.

Finally, Heather turned to Sister Lou. "Let's bring in the deputies."

Chapter 29

The temperature in the congregational office's small conference room had dropped several degrees since Sheriff's Deputy Fran Cole and her partner, Deputy Ted Tate, had joined Heather and Sister Lou late Friday afternoon. It didn't show any signs of warming up this millennium.

"We still don't understand *why* we weren't called when you first started this investigation." Fran's voice was cool. Her bottle green eyes were glacial.

Sister Lou turned her attention to Ted, who was seated on Fran's left across the ash wood table from Sister Lou and Heather. As Sister Lou had expected, Ted's expression of displeasure could curdle milk.

Sister Lou addressed Fran. The female deputy was usually more receptive to reasoning. "I apologize. I wanted to gather as much—"

"It's my fault," Heather cut in. She looked from Ted, seated across from her, to Fran. "I repeatedly told Sister Lou that I didn't want to involve the sheriff's office. Last night, she convinced me to change my mind."

Ted gave the mayor a sullen look. "Why didn't you want to call us in right away?"

Heather's words dripped with sarcasm. "Oh, I don't know, Deputy. Maybe because bringing you in would make me look weak and persecuted, and I'd lose the confidence of the community?"

Sister Lou raised both of her hands. "Excuse me, Deputies, but you mentioned you'd found some information that could be helpful in identifying Mayor Stanley's stalker."

"Thank you for bringing us into the investigation, Sister Lou." Fran opened the thin manila folder that lay on the table in front of her. "We did background checks on all of the people on your suspect list. We found some troubling information on Kerry Fletcher."

"What troubling information?" Heather sounded defensive at the implied criticism of her administrative assistant.

Ted took a sheet from his manila folder and slid it across the table to the mayor. "Your admin has a record. Didn't you do a background check before you hired her?"

Sister Lou pictured Kerry's big blue eyes and doll-like features. Past experiences had confirmed for Sister Lou the error of judging people by appearances. Still there was something about the effervescent assistant that didn't seem to match a criminal past.

Sister Lou glanced at the page in front of Heather. Presumably it was a duplicate to the document in Fran's folder. "What was the charge?"

"*Charges.*" Ted made the correction. He seemed to enjoy delivering the bad news. "Breaking and entering, and assault."

Heather stared fixedly at the document in front of

her. "These charges are more than eight years old. We don't typically go back further than five years for positions that don't require a security clearance."

Ted seemed disappointed. "You should change that policy, especially since it seems that Fletcher could be behind your threats."

Sister Lou found the accusation farfetched. "As I explained on the phone this morning, we interviewed the mayor's executive team. We don't think any of them could be behind the threats. They're too loyal."

"Or they want you to think that the mayor has their loyalty." Fran sat back on the cushioned conference chair.

"I know my team." Heather's violet eyes darkened with temper. "No one can fake that kind of loyalty. We never should have given you that list. You just took it and ran with it without checking in any other directions."

"Look, Your Honor." Ted stabbed the sheet in front of Heather with his hefty index finger. "The facts speak for themselves. You didn't even know your admin had a sheet. What else don't you know about her?"

Heather's gaze wavered. She turned to Sister Lou. "What do you think?"

Sister Lou slid the so-called rap sheet closer. "I think there's a better explanation behind Kerry's record than we'll find on this single sheet of paper." She looked up at Ted first, then Fran. "Were there any leads on similar threats in your crime database? Are there any recent stalking reports or threats against other public officials?"

Ted again gestured toward the sheet Sister Lou

held. "Why would we search the database when we've got our suspect right here?"

Perhaps a search would result in a better suspect. Sister Lou returned the printout to Ted. "I see."

"We have the information you gave us." Fran counted each point on a different finger on her left hand. "First of all, the stalker knows the mayor's schedule, which means she has access to the mayor's calendar. So does Fletcher. Secondly, the stalker has access to the mayor's mail. So does Fletcher. Third, the stalker knew where the mayor kept her spare key." She turned to Heather. "Does Fletcher know you kept the spare under your planter?"

Heather crossed her arms over her pearl gray sweater. "Yes, she does, but she wouldn't need to use the spare key. I gave her a copy in case I needed her to retrieve something from my home."

Sister Lou considered the mayor. Heather cared a great deal for her administrative assistant. And she trusted her completely. "What can you tell us about Kerry?"

Heather didn't hesitate. "She's intelligent, dependable, honest, resourceful, and efficient. She also has a great nature." She frowned at the deputies. "I can say that about all of my staff. These are dedicated professionals who gave up lucrative opportunities in the private sector to do some good in their community."

Ted grunted. "Yeah, well maybe they think getting you out of office would do some good."

Only time would tell, but Sister Lou suspected that keeping the deputies out of the investigation may have cost Heather the support of the sheriff's office during the next election.

"According to Sister Lou's notes, Fletcher's even

dating some political staffer, which could give her motive. Add that and her B-and-E to the other evidence and we have a compelling suspect." Fran pushed back from the table. She collected her brown felt campaign hat as she stood. "Let us do our job. We'll bring Fletcher in for questioning this evening."

Heather rose. "Deputies, I'm counting on your discretion. I don't want these threats to become public knowledge."

"We can do discrete." Ted collected his hat and followed Fran from the conference room.

"When will you have an update for us?" Sister Lou escorted the deputies down the hallway to the front lobby of the congregational offices. Heather joined them.

"We'll call you in the morning." Ted tossed the response over his shoulder.

Heather waited beside Sister Lou and watched the deputies disappear through the congregation's dark wood doors. "I hope we didn't make a mistake by calling in the deputies."

I fear that we did.

"Good morning, Mayor Stanley." Sister Marianna settled onto a chair across the table from Heather during breakfast Saturday morning. "I see we're both early risers."

Heather struggled to switch mental gears. She was worried about Kerry. What questions had the deputies asked her? Had it been an interview or an interrogation?

Was Kerry really involved with these threats?

Heather pulled her mind off the torturous loop it

had been on since she'd spoken with the deputies yesterday evening. "Good morning, Sister Marianna. Yes, I find the morning hours to be very productive, even on the weekends."

Sister Marianna gave her an approving nod. "I hope you're enjoying your stay with us."

Now that she was no longer deep in thought, Heather was aware of the activity around her. It seemed that most of the sisters were early risers. Heather scanned the other tables in the formal floral dining room. They were full of women breaking their fast. Their conversations and laughter floated around her.

Heather glanced at Sister Marianna's breakfast tray. The large glass of water, small white porcelain bowl of oatmeal, and an even smaller bowl of fresh fruit seemed lost on the powder blue surface. In contrast, Heather had capitalized on the tray's space with a plate of scrambled eggs, turkey sausage and hash browns, a separate plate of buttered whole grain toast, a bowl of blueberry yogurt, and a large glass of orange juice. She'd also managed to accommodate two cups of coffee. After a fitful night and an early morning run on the treadmill at the college's fitness facility, she was too tired to even think about returning to the coffee station for a refill.

Heather managed a smile in response to Sister Marianna's question about her time at the mother-house. Sister Lou had warned her about the other woman's insatiable curiosity. "Yes, I have enjoyed my stay. The residence is lovely. Everyone is so warm and welcoming, and the accommodations are very comfortable. Everything was perfect for my needs."

"I'm happy to hear that." Sister Marianna glowed

with pride. "If I may ask, what have your needs been while you've been with us?"

Heather shrugged with studied casualness. "My needs haven't been out of the ordinary, eating, sleeping, and of course some work. The motherhouse is quiet enough to allow me to concentrate."

"I'm glad." Sister Marianna filled her spoon with more oatmeal. "We want to ensure that our guests are comfortable. It's extraordinary to have such a prominent government official with us. I trust we haven't infringed on your privacy?"

"Not at all."

Sister Marianna nodded. "Good, and how long did you say you would be with us?"

"I didn't say, Sister Marianna. Sister Barbara was very generous. She said that I could stay here as long as I liked, but I won't impose on the congregation's hospitality much longer." Heather's tension returned with a vengeance.

When did the deputies intend to contact her with an update on their meeting with Kerry? She checked her rose gold wristwatch. The seven o'clock hour continued at a snail's crawl.

"You're certainly not imposing on us, Mayor Stanley." Beneath Sister Marianna's smile, curiosity shone in her gray eyes. "We enjoy having you here. It's a privilege and an honor. We're glad that you chose to stay with us at the motherhouse instead of more public accommodations such as the Sleep Ease Inn Hotel, for example. How did you make your decision?"

Heather smiled at Sister Marianna's lack of subtlety. "The answer to that is obvious. Look around you. The motherhouse is charming. You must love living here. How long have you been with the congregation?"

Sister Marianna seemed pleased with the mayor's interest. "I've been with the Briar Coast Motherhouse for almost six years. I arrived just a few months after Louise and Carmen. Were you able to tour the mother-house?"

It took Heather a moment to realize that "Louise" was "Sister Lou." "Yes, Sister Lou gave me a tour when I first arrived. Where were you before you came to Briar Coast?"

"I was teaching at one of our schools in Nigeria." Sister Marianna set aside her now empty bowl of oatmeal.

Nigeria? Heather was intrigued. "I hadn't realized that the congregation had schools in other countries."

Sister Marianna looked up from her bowl of fresh fruit. "Yes, we have ministries all over the country and around the world. In fact, congregations of Catholic religious women have founded many of the hospitals, educational institutions, and organizations that serve communities in need in this country and abroad."

"I wasn't aware of that. I'm very impressed." Heather looked around the room again, this time seeing these unassuming women with different eyes. A lot of the preconceived—and admittedly negative—notions she'd had of nuns and sisters were being dispelled the more she learned about this congregation.

A movement toward the front of the dining room drew Heather's attention. Sister Lou was crossing the room toward Heather, weaving around tables and exchanging only brief greetings with the other sisters. Speaking of early risers, Sister Lou looked as though she'd been up for hours. She was well dressed, and her movements were brisk and purposeful. What gave Heather pause, though, was Sister Lou's expression of concern. Even from a distance, Heather could tell the other woman wasn't coming toward her to share good news. Quite the opposite. Heather took a deep breath and almost forgot to exhale.

Sister Lou finally reached their table. "Good morning, Mayor Stanley, Marianna."

"Good morning, Louise." Sister Marianna spoke with a calm confidence that Heather envied in this moment. "I was just telling Mayor Stanley about our ministries."

"What a wonderful idea, Marianna. Thank you for sharing that information with the mayor." Sister Lou turned toward Heather. Her eyes were clouded with concern. "Are you ready to go, Mayor Stanley?"

Sister Marianna interrupted them. "Where are you going?"

Sister Lou's smile seemed tight and unnatural. "We're going to see a friend." She turned to Heather. "She's waiting for us."

"Is it Kerry? What's happened?" Heather hurried to catch up with Sister Lou after detouring briefly to return her dishes and tray to the serving area.

Sister Lou shared a worried look with Heather. "The deputies arrested her this morning."

Chapter 30

Sister Lou tried but failed to convince the mayor to first try diplomacy. Instead, in a manner reminiscent of Shari's, Heather marched into the sheriff's office Saturday morning and confronted the deputies. "Why is my administrative assistant in your jail?"

Seated behind a desk burdened by coffee-stained papers, Ted rocked back on his chair. "Is this how you thank us for finding the person who threatened to kill you and may have killed your finance director?"

Heather set her hands on her hips. "If you *had* found the stalker, I *would* thank you, but you've arrested an innocent person."

"Kerry Fletcher isn't innocent." Fran interrupted them.

Sister Lou turned to Fran who was typing something into her computer. "What evidence do you have to support your charges?"

Fran hit a few more computer keys before looking up at Sister Lou. "We found one of her letters to the mayor."

Heather's jaw dropped. "What?"

Sister Lou was speechless. She took the large plastic evidence bag that Fran offered her. The bag held a plain white sheet of paper. The paper was completely wrinkled as though someone had balled it up to throw away and someone else had retrieved it and attempted to smooth it out. The latest threat had been typed onto the paper: *Outsider, do not run for office again. Leave Brair Coast now or face the consequences.*

"'Briar Coast' is spelled wrong." Sister Lou made the observation almost absently. "That doesn't seem like an error that someone who works in the mayor's office would make, does it?"

Ted rolled his eyes. "It's just a typo. Big deal. It's probably the reason she didn't send that one."

Sister Lou passed the evidence bag to Heather. "Where did you find this note?"

Fran turned, pulling her chair under the desk. "It was crumpled up and tucked into a corner of one of the drawers in her nightstand. We got the warrant to search her apartment this morning."

Sister Lou frowned, trying to follow the deputies' logic. "What prompted you to ask for a search warrant?"

"It didn't take a brain surgeon to figure it out." Ted crossed his arms over his deep chest, rocking back on his seat. "When you finally accept the truth, you're going to kick yourselves for not catching the other clues sooner."

Sister Lou gestured toward the evidence bag that Heather still held. "Does it strike you as strange that Kerry crumpled this anonymous, threatening letter allegedly addressed to her boss, then hid it in a corner of her nightstand drawer?"

Ted rolled his eyes again. "As opposed to doing *what* with it?"

Sister Lou tilted her head in question. "Why didn't she throw it away? I'm certain she has trash receptacles in her apartment. If she didn't want the letter to be found, she could have burned it. Why hide it in a drawer?"

Fran shook her head. "Who knows her motivation? Maybe she didn't want to destroy it. Maybe she wanted to keep it as a memento."

Heather looked up from the evidence bag. Her eyes, shadowed by pain and confusion, locked on to Sister Lou's. "I can't believe this. I just can't believe it. This doesn't even sound like Kerry."

"Then perhaps it's not." Sister Lou turned to Fran and Ted. "Can we speak with her?"

Fran shrugged. "It couldn't hurt."

Sister Lou, Heather, and even Fran ignored Ted's disapproving growl.

Minutes later, Sister Lou sat with Heather and Kerry in one of the interrogation rooms. It looked nothing like the interrogation rooms in television police procedurals. It was small, but comfortable, with gray tiled flooring and pale yellow walls. The faint scent of wildflowers came from a scented plug-in affixed to the corner socket. Sister Lou glanced over her shoulder at the two-way mirror again.

If I were a betting person, I'd lay odds that Fran, Ted, or both are listening to this conversation.

"I haven't done anything." Kerry's plaintive words claimed Sister Lou's attention. The young woman's voice was tight with fear. Her eyes were wide with panic and wet with unshed tears. "Heather—Mayor Stanley—I swear to you. I don't know anything about threats against you."

Sister Lou wanted to embrace the young woman

and assure her that everything would be all right. However, that required more confidence than she had right now. "Kerry, how did that note come to be in your nightstand?"

"I don't even know." Kerry swallowed hard.

Sister Lou tried another angle. "Most of the threats Mayor Stanley received were delivered through her office mail. You handle her mail. Do you have any thoughts on how or when those messages could have been added?"

Kerry shook her head. "I'm sorry. I don't know anything about that, either. I just collect the mail that's sent up to the mail room in those plastic tubs."

Sitting back against the hard gray plastic chair, Sister Lou considered Kerry. The young woman looked lost and frightened out of her mind. Kerry stared down at her hands, which she'd gripped together on the polished surface of the oak wood table. One tear traveled over her round pink cheek and bounced against her knuckles. She quickly wiped her hand over her face. Either Kerry was an excellent actress or she was innocent.

Heather hadn't said a word since they'd entered the room. She'd sat beside Sister Lou, looking at her administrative assistant as though Kerry was a stranger to her. Sister Lou felt a chill.

Please, Heather, don't lose faith now. I could be wrong, but I truly don't believe Kerry is our villain.

Sister Lou recalled her conversation with Owen during the fund-raising event. "There are rumors that you resent Mayor Stanley because she forced you to work odd hours."

"What?" Heather and Kerry reacted at once. They both stared at Sister Lou as though she had two heads.

"Where did you hear that?" Heather dug a packet of tissues from her purse and handed them to Kerry.

Sister Lou didn't hesitate to reveal her sources. "Owen Rodney said that you made Kerry work late hours and weekends."

"That must have been when I was taking classes to complete my master's degree in finance," Kerry explained. "Heather allowed some flexibility with my work hours to accommodate my class schedule. I graduated last May."

"Congratulations." Sister Lou was amazed that the public had twisted such a generous gesture on Heather's part to appear to be something negative— and all because they lacked the facts.

"Thank you." Kerry wiped fresh tears from her cheeks.

Sister Lou contemplated the administrative assistant. "I have one last question for now."

"Yes, Sister?" Kerry spoke around a hiccup.

Sister Lou reached across the table to cup the younger woman's hand. "Who would want to frame you for threatening the mayor?"

Kerry's eyes widened. "No one." She turned her attention to Heather who regarded Kerry without comment. Her face was expressionless. "Who would want to threaten you?"

Heather broke her silence. "I'm posting your bail and taking you home. We'll get this straightened out."

Kerry wiped away more tears. "Thank you, Heather. I don't know why this is happening."

Heather reached across the table to squeeze Kerry's hand. "We'll figure that out, too."

Sister Lou closed her eyes. *We're going to need a miracle.*

* * *

"Kerry can't be behind the threats to Heather." Sister Lou jogged beside Sister Carmen. They seemed to be moving faster than usual in the predawn Monday hour. It was probably their relief at the warmer weather now that they were several days into March.

"Why not?" Sister Carmen tugged her neon citrus orange knit cap farther down over her thick curly hair and ears.

They were approaching the oval on the campus of the College of St. Hermione of Ephesus. The college's fitness center stood across the street in their direct path. Through the glass façade, Sister Lou watched several familiar staff, students, and faculty members using the treadmills and stationary bicycles. Several of them she recognized as the early morning joggers who joined her and Sister Carmen outside in the spring, summer, and early fall. The colder climes had driven them to the indoor exercise equipment. *The room for the faint of heart.* Sister Lou smiled to herself.

Sister Carmen seemed oblivious of the facility. Sister Lou gave it a speculative look before deciding that it just wasn't cold enough to warrant running on those treadmills. She preferred the natural scenery. If she could survive jogging outdoors during December, January, and February, she could handle March.

This past Saturday, for their long training run in preparation for their Memorial Weekend marathon, Sister Lou and Sister Carmen had logged thirteen miles. It had been difficult. Sister Lou was relieved that next Saturday, their training schedule allowed them to decrease their distance to ten miles.

Sister Lou clapped her hands to keep her blood flowing. "There are several issues that keep me from accepting that Kerry is Heather's stalker. The stalker claimed he mistook Opal for Heather. Kerry wouldn't have made that mistake. Besides, she knew that Opal had attended that meeting in Heather's place."

"Presumably Kerry was in the office during Opal's attack." Frosty breaths of air trailed Sister Carmen's words. "She can't be two places at one time."

"That's another good point." Sister Lou led them onto the campus's oval.

The space was deserted for now, but soon the women's track and field team would join them. The student-athletes always exchanged enthusiastic greetings with Sister Lou and Sister Carmen, cheering them on as they sprinted past the duo on their way to the dirt trail that led from the college to the center of Briar Coast.

Sister Carmen blew into her cupped hands through her citrus orange knit gloves. "You seem certain that the stalker is a man."

"We believe the stalker is the same person who attacked Heather about three weeks ago while she was jogging." Three weeks and they still had no idea who the stalker could be, and bringing in the deputies hadn't advanced their investigation. "Kerry wouldn't have the strength to pick up Heather."

"I haven't met Kerry, but I'm sure you're right."

"Heather has the impression that her attacker was a man."

Sister Lou fell silent beside Sister Carmen. The cold pinched her face as she neared the end of their first lap around the oval. Winter's scent—metal and moist earth—surrounded her. Their rhythmic footfalls were like white noise keeping her thoughts company. Who was Heather's stalker? What was his motivation, and how was he adding his threats to Heather's mail?

"Good morning, Sisters!" The staggered choruses cut across the cold air to claim Sister Lou's attention.

She looked up to find that the women's track and field team had joined them right on schedule. Their synchronized steps covered the pavement at a rapid pace with seemingly boundless strength, energy, and enthusiasm. Sister Lou returned their greeting. As usual, their appearance lifted her spirits and gave her an extra boost. They had the same effect on Sister Carmen. Sister Lou chuckled at her friend's red-carpet-worthy smile and vigorous wave. She watched the nine young women disappear among the trees, bushes, and undergrowth that bordered the dirt trail that led deeper into Briar Coast.

Sister Carmen touched Sister Lou's arm. "You're speeding up again."

"Oh. Sorry." Sister Lou forced herself to slow down.

"What do you want to do about Kerry?"

"I'm not sure." Sister Lou frowned into the distance as she and Sister Carmen continued their second lap around the oval. "Kerry is at the center of this. Everything keeps coming back to her: the letters, the break-in."

"I can understand why the deputies suspect her. Kerry as the stalker is an easy answer, which makes her the perfect suspect. The fact that she handles the mayor's mail would explain how the threats are being delivered."

"But it doesn't make sense that a person would deliver her own anonymous threats."

"Not if she wants to remain anonymous." Sister Carmen's tone was dry.

Sister Lou agreed. "Heather also mentioned that she gave Kerry an extra set of keys to her house in case she needed Kerry to retrieve something for her. If that's the case, why would Kerry use the spare key instead of her own?"

"Maybe she wanted to give the impression that a stranger broke into Heather's house?"

"Would a stranger have *known* that Heather kept a spare key hidden beneath one of the flowerpots on her porch?"

"Probably not." Sister Carmen sounded as frustrated as Sister Lou felt.

"If you're breaking into someone's house, would you take the time to search for a spare key when you're not even certain there is one?"

"No, I would want to get in and get out as quickly as possible so that no one would notice me."

"Of course, which means the only way a stranger would know to look for the spare key is if someone told him there was a spare and where he could find it."

Sister Carmen turned wide eyes to Sister Lou. "Who did Kerry tell?"

Sister Lou frowned. "I think I have a name for Shari to check."

Chapter 31

"How can you be sure Kerry isn't behind the threats? Her loyalty could be an act to maintain your trust." Diego had been repeating variations of this warning since Heather had settled onto the passenger seat of his black SUV. He'd picked her up from the motherhouse early Monday morning to take her to work.

Heather glared through the windshield. Diego was part of this particular amateur sleuth team, but maybe it hadn't been a good idea to share How I Spent My Weekend with the newspaper editor. She was tired of repeating herself. "As I said, you didn't see her. Sister Lou and I did, and we *both* believe that Kerry isn't acting."

Diego stopped at a red light. "The deputies have pretty compelling evidence against Kerry with that letter they found in her nightstand."

Heather considered the view through the side passenger window. Perhaps she should get out and walk. They weren't that far from town hall.

"I trust every member of my team unequivocally."

She glanced at Diego. "I'm grateful to you for not reporting that the deputies arrested Kerry."

The light turned green. Diego continued on his path to town hall. "The public isn't in danger. That's my first concern. And we've agreed that Shari will cover this story once we've caught the stalker, but what about the other news outlets? If they get a tip on this story, how will you handle them?"

"I met with my executive team yesterday to plan our strategy." Heather rubbed her forehead between her eyebrows. The tension during that long Sunday meeting had been almost unbearable. Her team had been angry that she hadn't told them about the messages and the threats' connection to Opal's death. Their reaction had been justifiable, but if she could go back in time, she'd make the same decision. "If we get a lot of media inquiries, we'll release a statement that my office is looking into rumors of these threats and that it's absurd to think that anyone in my office would be involved."

Diego seemed satisfied. "That'll fly. Let's hope you won't need it."

Silence settled into the SUV as Diego continued toward town hall. Rush hour in Briar Coast—both morning and evening—was nonexistent compared to the traffic Heather had navigated in El Paso, Texas, and even Norman, Oklahoma. She hoped it would always be this way.

Being chauffeured to work had its perks, including the luxury of soaking in the scenery. Heather loved Briar Coast. She loved the architecture's understated grandeur, and the landscaping both natural and designed. Most of all, she loved the people and the way they loved their town. They'd made it through the near economic crisis brought about by the previous administration's policies with determination, self-sacrifice, and good humor. This community was the definition of good neighbors.

Heather sank deeper onto the cloth bucket seat. The vehicle was warm and toasty. This made it even easier to forget that the weather outside was cold and biting. As late as last week, these buildings, sidewalks, and streets had been covered in pure white layers of snow. Those beautiful layers had been shoveled, then froze into abstract blocks of ice.

Trees that lined the sidewalks were brown and bare. Their arms were raised as though in surrender to the cold climes. Their acquiescence was a ploy, though. In a matter of weeks, these same trees would fight their way back, shooting buds in acts of defiance, much like the occupants of the buildings and residences beyond those tree lines.

"I'll miss this." Diego's statement made its way into Heather's reverie.

She switched her attention to her companion's chiseled profile. A deep breath drew in his clean soap and sandalwood scent. "Miss what?"

"Driving you to work in the mornings and bringing you home in the evenings." Diego made the admission without fuss or fanfare. "Once we find this stalker, we won't need to do this anymore."

"I'll miss it, too." Heather's gaze touched on the thick dark slashes of his eyebrows, then dropped to his coffee brown eyes when he glanced at her.

"If we both enjoy the carpooling, I wouldn't mind continuing it."

"All right." Heather's mood brightened. "But your driving me around doesn't mean I'll stop busting your chops over articles in your paper if I disagree with them."

"I wouldn't expect you to." Diego's quick grin bought a flash of his perfect white teeth. "In exchange, I'll keep reminding you that my newspaper isn't the town's promotional brochure."

"Deal." Heather turned back to the view outside of the windshield. "You know my political opponents will use our relationship to trash your paper."

"Does that bother you?" Diego pulled into the town hall parking lot, stopping in front of the building's entrance. Door-to-door service; Heather definitely would have missed this.

She looked over at Diego. "It's not my job to defend your newspaper."

"And it's not my newspaper's job to defend your administration."

Their banter was new and yet familiar. It transported Heather back fourteen years into the past. She'd looked forward to matching wits with the newspaperman. His mind had challenged her. His humor had entertained her. His looks had turned her on. She had the same reactions to him now that she'd had all those years ago. Apparently, he felt the same.

The car's interior was suddenly warmer. And smaller. The scent of soap and sandalwood surrounded her. The look in Diego's hot brown eyes sharpened. Heather caught her breath. Her smile faded. Her heart beat slow and steady.

Diego leaned forward just a little bit, asking his question. Heather leaned forward a little bit more, giving her answer.

The metal-on-metal snick let Heather know that Diego had unfastened his seat belt. His beautiful eyes traced her features as he shifted closer. Then he covered her lips with his own. With a sigh, Heather melted against him. His lips were firm, his body warm, his taste intoxicating. This was the kiss that they'd waited fourteen years for. It was well worth it.

Slowly, Heather drew away. A pulse fluttered in her throat. Her mind was mush. Diego's breathing was shallow and fast. He dragged his gaze from her lips to meet her eyes.

"I'm going to be watching the clock all day until I can see you again." Diego's husky tone made her want to forget her obligations.

Instead, Heather traced his lips with a trembling index finger and imagined what five o'clock would bring. "If anyone asks about our relationship, tell them that we're definitely dating."

Heather tossed him a smile as she hopped out of his car. She welcomed the crisp cold air that followed her up the town hall steps.

After more than a decade—and three states—she was finally embracing her long-denied feelings for Diego. Heather's sense of well-being at her decision surprised her. She pushed through the town hall entrance and turned toward the staircase.

How would her public relationship with the editor of the town's local newspaper affect her reelection campaign?

I don't care.

She no longer felt cold or empty. At the end of the day, that's all that really mattered.

Sister Lou froze, shocked at the sight of the college's director of food services walking the campus oval with

Unnamed Calico Monday morning. "Corny, is that your cat?"

The cat was docile, even friendly, as she wound between the feet of her tall, slender companion.

Cornelius Ferguson paused to look down at his four-legged companion. He bared bright white teeth in a brilliant grin. His long dreadlocks were banded together behind his shoulders. "Sister Lou, this cat doesn't belong to anybody." His slow Southern drawl bounced with good humor.

"She's made that clear to me as well." Sister Lou leaned down to offer the calico her hand. "But she must have a home. Look at how healthy she is."

The cat stepped forward. Her green eyes were cool, almost condescending. She sniffed Sister Lou's fingers before giving her approval to be petted. The calico withstood a few strokes along her warm, snow white fur with its gold and brown markings, then resumed her serpentine movements between Cornelius's feet. The food service director didn't seem concerned that the calico was leaving a trail of hairs on the hem of his black pants.

"This cat doesn't need a home." Cornelius shoved his hands inside the pockets of his black winter coat. "She's a survivor. She showed up outside of the dining hall in December, and used her feline wiles to get food and shelter for the winter. Now that the weather's warmer, she stops by for a meal but spurns any other hospitality."

That solved the mystery of where the calico had spent the cold. "It was kind of you to take her in for the winter, and that you continue to feed her."

Cornelius chuckled. "She reminds me of my older cousin, Isiah."

Sister Lou blinked. "In what way?"

Cornelius returned his gaze to the calico. "He was always nice when he wanted something. The minute he didn't need you anymore, he'd disappear. Once we realized that was the way he was going to be, we started ignoring him." Cornelius looked up at Sister Lou. "The past always comes back to get you, Sister Lou. The past always comes back."

Sister Lou frowned, thinking about Heather. "You're right. You can't always escape your past or the people in it."

"You were right, Sister Lou." Shari placed her hand over the manila folder she'd prepared for her Monday lunch meeting with Sister Lou and Chris at the Briar Coast Café.

"What did you find out?" When Sister Lou had agreed to meet Shari and Chris, she thought Shari had seemed a little paranoid. The reporter had insisted that they take a table away from the front and rear café entrances. To humor her young friend, Sister Lou had chosen a table for four away from the windows.

Shari tapped her manila folder. "As you know, my research didn't find any connections between Hal and Heather besides their both being from Texas. As you requested, I did a search on Jefferson Manning." She pulled a sheet of paper from her folder and slid it across the table to Sister Lou. She handed a copy of the same printout to Chris, who was seated beside her.

As Sister Lou studied the color copy of Jefferson Manning's biography complete with a photo of a stranger, she had a better understanding of the reason behind Shari's caution.

Chris looked up from the paper to frown at Shari. "This isn't the Jefferson Manning you introduced me to during the mayor's fund-raiser."

"No, it's not." Shari tapped his copy of the printout as it lay in front of him on the café table. "But it is the Jefferson Manning who is the aide to Buffalo Councilman Brice Founder. I triple checked."

Sister Lou was stunned. "How did you come by this information? Is your source reliable?"

Shari spread her arms. "My source is the Buffalo City Council's website. I didn't have any reason to check it before you suggested we look at Jeff."

Sister Lou studied the photo again. This Jefferson Manning was at least ten years older than the one they knew. His dark brown hair was bone straight and cut military short. His gray eyes were set deep into a broad, angular face. He had a prominent nose, high cheekbones, and a square, cleft chin.

Chris frowned at Sister Lou. "What made you ask Shari to check into Manning and Beckett?"

Sister Lou sighed. "Someone is framing Kerry, and neither Jefferson nor Harold are on our list."

Shari turned to Chris. "I thought it was odd that Jefferson worked for a councilman in Buffalo, but his schedule still allowed him to take Kerry to work in the mornings, surprise her for lunch in the afternoons, then pick her up after work at the stroke of five o'clock. What political aide do you know who has such a flexible schedule?"

"None," Chris admitted.

Sister Lou caught Shari's gaze. "Then who has Kerry been dating?"

Shari shook her head. "I don't know, but maybe Fran and Ted can help us figure this out."

"No." Sister Lou's interjection cut off Shari's suggestion. She sent a cautious look around the café, then lowered her voice. "I have a feeling you've found Heather's stalker."

Shari corrected Sister Lou. "*We* found him. I wouldn't have done this research if you hadn't suggested it."

Sister Lou waved a dismissive hand. The fact was this was the best lead they had for their investigation. "Kerry as the stalker didn't seem logical until I realized someone must be using her to take the blame if investigators got too close to the real culprit. The question I couldn't answer was who."

All of the pieces were starting to fit. After feeling as though she'd been running in circles, Sister Lou had an enormous sense of relief.

Chris sipped his iced tea. "Jefferson—or the person we know as Jefferson—must have found a way to add his threatening letters to Heather's mail when he drove Kerry into work. He used her as his cover."

"The poor thing." Shari sighed. "You must be right, but I feel so sorry for her, being used that way."

"So do I, but we're obviously dealing with a sociopath." Sister Lou felt grim. "Jefferson must also be behind Opal's accident. He didn't know Heather wasn't going to attend that Board of Education meeting."

Shari drummed her fingertips on the table. Her soup and salad remained untouched on the tray in front of her. "Kerry must have mentioned where Heather hid her spare key. It was probably just an innocent remark that she didn't realize her fake boyfriend would use to terrorize her boss."

Chris looked from Shari to Sister Lou. "The fake

Jefferson probably also attacked Heather. He looks strong enough."

"I agree." Sister Lou stared blindly at her black bean soup and green salad. "But who is he and why is he threatening Heather?"

Shari dragged her spoon through her cooling chicken noodle soup. "Can't the deputies bring him in on identity theft or something? If we find out why he's using someone else's identity, that could help us figure out his motive for threatening the mayor."

Chris shook his head. "If the deputies bring him in for questioning, he'll realize that we're getting close to him. He's gone to a lot of trouble devising this detailed plan, targeting Heather. We can't risk his having a backup plan in case he gets caught. We could be endangering Heather and possibly Kerry."

"Then what do we do?" Shari asked.

"I can only see one solution." Sister Lou folded her hands on her tray. "We have to make the fake Jefferson think we're falling for his plan. We have to arrest Kerry."

Chapter 32

"You came!" Kerry leaped from her gray hard plastic chair in the sheriff's office's interview room late Monday afternoon and threw herself into Jefferson's embrace.

She wasn't acting. Kerry was enormously relieved to see him. During her meeting earlier with Sister Lou, Heather, Shari, Chris, Diego, and the deputies—so many people—they'd made it sound as though Jefferson was the villain behind the threats to Heather. They claimed that, if he thought his nefarious plan was discovered, Jefferson would let her rot in jail while he skipped the country or something.

But his being here proved that he cared about her. That he loved her. The deputies and all of those other people were wrong. Jefferson wasn't some crazy psycho stalker killer. So his name wasn't Jefferson Manning. And he didn't work for a councilman in Buffalo. Big deal. Kerry was certain he could explain those things if they'd just ask him.

Jefferson stepped back to look at her. "Of course I did. Why wouldn't I?"

Kerry kept her hands on his shoulders. They were so broad and warm beneath the jacket of his dark brown suit. "I was afraid you wouldn't be able to get away from work this early. It's not even four o'clock yet."

Jefferson pulled her hands from his shoulders. "I came as soon as I got your call. What's going on? I thought the mayor had posted your bail."

"She did." Kerry drank in his handsome features. His wavy golden hair gleamed beneath the fluorescent lights. She was sure she saw concern in his beautiful brown eyes. For her. "The deputies had more questions for me."

"What did they ask you?" Jefferson led her back to the interview table. He sat on the chair beside hers and kept her trembling hands in his.

"They wanted to know if I'd hired someone to attack Heather that night while she was jogging." Kerry was shaking so badly. Jefferson would think she was nervous about her future. In fact, she was nervous because she was lying to him. She hoped he would forgive her once he realized that she was trying to prove his innocence.

"What did you tell them?" Jefferson's grip tightened on her hands.

Kerry stilled. She'd been ad-libbing this exchange based on Sister Lou's suggestions, but she thought she knew how Jefferson would react. That wasn't the reply Kerry had been expecting. Where was his disbelief? Where was his outrage on her behalf? Instead of either of those responses, he asked how she'd answered the deputies' imaginary question. What did he think she'd say?

Kerry shot a quick look toward the two-way mirror

across the room. The deputies—if not the entire Briar Coast Magnificent Seven: Heather, Sister Lou, Shari, Chris, Diego, and the two deputies—were watching from the other side.

"I told them that I hadn't hired anyone to hurt Heather and that I never would." Kerry was starting to feel uneasy. "Heather's not only my boss, Jeff, she's my friend. You know that, don't you?"

"What else did they ask you?" Jefferson ignored her question. His eager request for information seemed like morbid fascination and smelled like desperation.

Kerry's stomach muscles knotted. Was Jefferson trying to figure out her defense strategy? She'd rather he offered to hire a real lawyer for her.

"You're crushing my hands." Kerry tugged free of his grasp.

"Sorry." Jefferson fisted his hands on his lap. "Tell me what else they wanted to know."

Kerry heard his urgency. She saw his tension. "Why are you asking these questions? I wanted you to be here to reassure me. Instead you're making me feel like I'm being interrogated by one of those villains in a James Bond film."

Jefferson's laughter didn't sound real. "I'm asking because I care, dear. I want to help you, you know?"

"Well, you're starting to freak me out."

"Come on, honey, let me help you. Tell me what they asked."

Kerry still hesitated. How could she prove that Jefferson wasn't involved in these threats or in Opal's death? "They asked me about Opal's accident." *Tell me that you're not responsible for that, Jeff. Please tell me and stop these doubts.*

Jefferson's body jerked as though he was surprised.

He stood to pace, turning his back to her. "What did you say?"

Oh, no. No. "What do you mean?"

Jefferson spun toward her. His expression was mean and ugly. His tone was gruff and angry. "Come on, Kerry. I shouldn't have to drag every word out of your mouth. *What* did you *tell* the *deputies*?"

For the first time, Kerry felt alarm. She snuck another quick look toward the two-way mirror to reassure herself that she wasn't alone.

Jefferson caught the direction of Kerry's gaze. He froze. Kerry held her breath. She watched as Jefferson pulled himself together. His demeanor changed, morphing back into the caring companion with whom she'd spent the past several weeks. Kerry shivered— with cold? With fear? With revulsion? All of the above? *Who is this man?*

Jefferson returned to the table and took her hands again. "Come on, baby. I'm only trying to help you. You know that, don't you? Just tell me what you told the deputies."

Kerry freed her hands. Her skin crawled at the possibility that she'd helped a sociopath who'd already killed one of her friends and was trying to harm another. "It doesn't matter what the deputies asked me or what I told them. I'm innocent, Jeff, and I can prove it."

"Well, that's great, sweetheart." Jefferson's smile didn't erase the worry from his eyes. "How?"

How did he get me to fall in love with him? "I have the last copy of the old key to Heather's house. The psycho who broke into Heather's home and left behind that lame threat that didn't even work, by the way, used the spare key that Heather kept under a fake flowerpot."

"Won't the deputies believe that you're, you know, trying to pass the spare key off as your key to Heather's house?"

"Heather can confirm that my key looks different. The flowerpot key is green to match the pot. My key looks like a regular key."

Jefferson looked distracted. "I see."

So do I. I see everything, *including how stupid I've been.* "I mentioned that flowerpot key to you, didn't I, Jeff?"

Jefferson stood to pace again. "No, I don't believe you did."

"I'm pretty sure that I mentioned it, but maybe you forgot." Kerry's temper stirred. She wasn't certain she could control it. "Anyway, the fact that I still have my key while the spare key is missing should help prove my innocence."

Jefferson stood to pace. He shot a quick look toward the two-way mirror. "Where is your key?"

Really? Can you be *any more obvious?* "You don't have to worry about my key. It's somewhere safe just waiting for the right time for me and my lawyer to give it to the deputies to prove my innocence. Because I *am* innocent, and soon everyone will know that."

Jefferson faced her with his arms outstretched. "I know that you are, darling. I just want to check on your key, you know, to make sure that it's okay. I can bring it to you so that you can keep it safe with you."

"You don't need to do that."

"I insist. I want to help. Please, let me do this for the woman I love."

You mean the woman you duped. "All right. It's in my desk at work. The center drawer." Kerry struggled to keep the anger from her voice. "If anyone stops you, just tell them that you're checking on my key."

Jefferson crossed to her. "I'll do that."

He bent, appearing intent on kissing her. Kerry was horrified. If his lips touched hers, she'd start screaming and wouldn't be able to stop. At the last minute, she turned her head so that his lips landed on her right cheek. Jefferson straightened, giving her a questioning look.

Kerry jerked her head toward the two-way mirror. "They may be watching."

Jefferson gave her the indulgent look that used to make her knees weak. He cupped the cheek he'd kissed. "You're so modest."

"You should leave now. They're going to lock the building soon." Kerry fisted her palms until he dropped his hand.

"All right. I'll be right back." Jefferson turned to hurry off.

"I can't wait."

Jefferson disappeared behind the door. Kerry let the tears flow, anger, sorrow, shame.

The door opened again, allowing Heather, Sister Lou, and Shari into the room.

Kerry lowered her eyes. Her voice was thick with tears. "How could I have been such a fool?"

Heather stood beside Kerry, putting a comforting arm around her shoulders. "He tricked all of us."

Sister Lou pulled a fistful of facial tissues from her oversized purse. "You aren't to blame for his actions."

The deputies announced their arrival with a knock on the door. Ted stood with his back to the group as though afraid to witness Kerry's tears.

Fran crossed into the room. "We should get going if we're going to catch this guy in the act. Kerry, thanks for your help."

Heather helped Kerry to her feet. "Are you up to joining us?"

Kerry looked at Heather, grateful for her assistance. She didn't think her knees would support her. New tears blinded her. "No, I'm not. I'm going to ask Penny to come get me, but could you do me a favor?"

"Anything." Heather's response was prompt. She guided Kerry past the deputies through the door. Sister Lou fell into step on Kerry's other side.

Kerry's knees were shaking. Her teeth were starting to chatter. "Could you let Jefferson—or whatever his name is—know that I helped catch him?"

Sister Lou's hand on Kerry's shoulder stopped her. "Kerry, we couldn't have done this without you."

Kerry gave the older woman an unsteady smile. "Thanks. That goes a long way toward making me feel better. Now go get that sociopath." She turned to Shari behind her. "And I want to read all about it in tomorrow's paper."

Chapter 33

Sister Lou's muscles stiffened as Fran and Ted escorted the man they all knew as Jefferson Manning into the large conference room in the mayor's suite on the third floor of the Briar Coast Town Hall.

Jefferson's arms were handcuffed behind his back. Sister Lou's eyebrows arched in surprise. It was after five o'clock, but she could hear movement in the hallway outside of the room. How had the town's government employees reacted to seeing two sheriff's deputies lead their suspect into one of their conference rooms?

The polished walnut wood table accommodated up to ten people. Heather was seated at the head of the table. Sister Lou was seated on Heather's right. Diego was beside her. Shari sat across the table from Sister Lou on Heather's left with Chris next to her. The deputies had brought Jefferson in through the door at the back of the room. Now they sat him on the chair at the foot of the table with Fran on his right and Ted on his left.

Despite its lack of windows, the room was bright

with eggshell walls and blue-gray carpeting. The temperature was comfortable. Sister Lou almost forgot that outside winter still gripped Briar Coast.

Jefferson smiled mockingly at the five people arranged around the other end of the table. "Are these your bodyguards? Are they supposed to intimidate me, an old lady, an old man, and a boney chick?" He nodded toward Chris. "I'll give that guy some credit."

Sister Lou glanced around the table. Her companions wore various expressions of irritation, annoyance, and anger. Sister Lou wasn't angry or offended. There were plenty of days when she did feel old. Today wasn't one of those days.

Heather gripped the wooden arms of her black cloth chair. "Who are you?"

Jefferson's smile widened. "Don't you recognize me, Madame Mayor?"

Heather didn't blink. "No."

Jefferson tsked. "I'm hurt." He locked eyes with Heather. His expression mocked her. "In fairness, it's been a long while since we've seen each other and my hair had been brown. I was ten at the time."

Shock moved over Heather's elegant features. "Benji?" Her question was a disbelieving gasp.

"Ben?" Diego spoke at the same time.

"So you do remember me . . . both of you. How nice." Their mysterious stalker's gaze moved between Heather and Diego. "I prefer Benjamin."

Sister Lou shivered at the hatred that marred Benjamin's otherwise handsome features. How did Heather and Diego know the young man?

Fran narrowed her eyes. "Benjamin who?"

Benjamin's attention remained fixed on Heather. "Benjamin Irsay. My father was the former chief of staff to an El Paso councilman. Your esteemed mayor framed him for crimes she'd committed."

"I did not frame your father." Heather spoke through her teeth. "Graham Irsay was guilty of abusing the position of his office—"

"You're lying!" Benjamin's roar cut off Heather's response and nearly shattered Sister Lou's eardrums.

Ted clamped a bearlike hand on Benjamin's shoulder. "Simmer down there, tiger. You may not be a fan, but she's *our* mayor. Show some respect."

Ted's defense of Heather was a good sign. The last thing the mayor needed—personally or professionally— was to lose the support of the Briar Coast County Sheriff's Office.

"Respect?" Benjamin redirected his anger toward Ted. "Why should I respect a liar and a cheat?"

Beside her, Sister Lou sensed Diego's growing temper.

The newspaperman shifted on his seat toward Benjamin. "I don't know where you're getting your information, but every word of it is wrong."

Benjamin jerked his chin toward Heather. "My father told me on his death bed that *she* made those deals with the development company. *She* framed *him* for the crimes *she'd* committed."

Diego started shaking his head even before Benjamin completed his last sentence. "The evidence showed otherwise. If you don't believe us, ask the court to let you review the case files."

"I don't need to," Benjamin barked. "I know that my father wouldn't lie to me, especially not with his dying breath."

Sister Lou felt sorry for the young man whose

father's deception had ruined both of their lives. "Why do you want Mayor Stanley to leave Briar Coast?"

Benjamin's eyes darkened with anger. He shoved his response through clenched teeth. "I want to end her political career just like she ruined my father and *his* career."

"I want to make one thing perfectly clear." Heather never raised her voice. She leaned into the table, holding Benjamin's eyes. "I never gave a thought to leaving Briar Coast, but even if I had, leaving this town wouldn't have ended my political career."

"Maybe. Maybe not." Benjamin's brown eyes glowed with venom. "But one thing I'm certain of: leaving this town would have broken your heart the same way being blackballed from politics in the state of Texas broke my father's. You love Briar Coast. Everyone knows that."

Heather shrugged. "I've never denied that."

Benjamin didn't seem to hear Heather. "People here admire you. I've seen that and it's turned my stomach. They treat you like you're some kind of local hero. I know that leaving this town would've *killed* you."

Heather didn't respond. Her expression remained closed, but Sister Lou sensed that Benjamin's words had found their intended target.

Shari regarded Benjamin with open contempt. "In your obsession with Heather's political career, you killed Opal Lorrie."

Benjamin frowned. "I grabbed her and she struggled. I told you I didn't mean to kill her, although I did find some interesting information in her briefcase. She fell, but none of this would have happened if your mayor hadn't framed my father."

Shari raised her voice in outrage. "Opal had nothing to do with any of this."

Benjamin shrugged. "Collateral damage."

His eyes were devoid of guilt or grief. Sister Lou's heart broke for Opal, and her friends and family again.

"Heather would never have left Briar Coast," Sister Lou said. "She didn't campaign to be mayor to advance a political career. She ran because she wanted to serve. Your plan failed because you didn't understand that."

"Did my plan fail?" Benjamin gave Sister Lou a humorless, spiteful smile.

Heather arched an eyebrow. "Did you miss my reelection announcement?"

Benjamin nodded toward Shari. "What do you think will happen to your campaign once that reporter breaks this story and tells people what I tried to do and why?"

"You're missing the point, Benjamin." Heather settled back on her seat, appearing as though she didn't have a care in the world. "As Sister Lou said, regardless of whether I'm reelected, Briar Coast will always be my home. Nothing you can do will ever change that."

Benjamin's face reddened with fury. "Get me out of here."

Shari crossed into her cubicle at the *Telegraph*'s office Tuesday morning. She finished skimming her news story on the mayor's accused stalker. The article appeared on the front page of Tuesday's edition of the *Telegraph*. Shari was relieved that the copy was accurate and error free, despite the wild race to complete it before the news deadline last night. She also was satisfied with the accompanying photo, which Diego had taken. It showed the deputies escorting Benjamin Irsay out of the Briar Coast Town Hall. All in all, it was a solid news package.

With a satisfied and somewhat relieved sigh, Shari reached for her CAN I QUOTE YOU? mug, which stood beside her computer keyboard.

Her phone rang, interrupting her morning coffee. "*Telegraph.* Sharelle Henson."

"Sharelle, it's Becca Floyd with *Buffalo Today.*" The voice that crossed the phone line was slightly amused and very familiar. "I had to call to compliment you on another great news story. I knew that if there was anything more to Opal Lorrie's death than a simple fall, you'd find the truth."

Shari was a little uncomfortable with Becca's enthusiasm. "I was just doing my job and following the story."

"That's what good reporters do. They go where the news takes them and don't give up until they get to the end." Becca's words were a verbal nod of approval. "I don't suppose there's any chance that you'll change your mind about joining our team here at *Buffalo Today?*"

"No chance at all." Shari's gaze moved lovingly over the *Telegraph* office's aged carpeting and stained walls. "This town and this newspaper are home."

"Remember the door's always open here if you do change your mind down the road." Becca's sigh signaled her surrender. "What's next for you? Are you going to interview the mayor about that El Paso corruption case?"

"That's old news." Shari settled onto her chair at her tan modular desk and turned on her computer. "The online version of the story has a link to the original article on the corruption case if anyone wants to read about it."

"Are you sure that's enough? The case could become a campaign issue, especially since the threats were about her reelection."

Diego hadn't asked Shari to interview Heather about the corruption case. Even if Diego hadn't been the reporter who'd covered the trial, Shari bet he still would have recommended only adding a link to the original article. She couldn't imagine him being interested in a fourteen-year-old case that didn't have any relevance to their town.

Shari logged on to her computer. "Briar Coast residents are focused on local issues: education, jobs, infrastructure, and access to health care. That's the coverage the *Telegraph*'s going to give them. Anything else would be a distraction from the real concerns that are affecting our community."

"Then you wouldn't mind if *Buffalo Today* covers this story?"

"Actually, I would." Shari sat back on her chair in frustration. She could really use another cup of coffee. "Have you read the original trial coverage?"

"Not yet." Becca sounded reluctant to make the admission.

"Read that story first. I'm betting you'll realize your resources would be better served on something else."

"I'll take your advice, and I wish you all the best for your future."

"Thanks. You, too." Shari smiled as she disconnected

the call. Becca's attention was flattering, but she hoped the managing editor had said her final good-bye. Shari was running out of ways to say no to the other woman's job offers.

"Who were you talking to? Did they ask you why you stole my story?" Harold's questions came from behind her.

Startled, Shari spun her chair to face her cubicle entrance and the rookie reporter. "How long were you eavesdropping on my call?"

"Not long." Harold waved his copy of the *Telegraph*. "But the real question is why did you steal my story?"

"*Your* story? How are the threats against the mayor *your* story?"

Harold scowled at her. "It's about her reelection."

"Seriously?" Shari considered Harold. In his navy pinstriped suit complete with handkerchief in the jacket pocket, and black wingtip shoes, he looked as though he was on his way to a bankers' convention.

Harold's expression darkened. "Of course I'm serious."

Shari shook her head in amazement. She glanced at her still-empty coffee mug. "I suppose that if you squinted, turned your chin to a certain angle, then stood on your head, you could interpret threats of bodily harm against another person as a reelection issue. However, the state of New York considers it a Class A misdemeanor."

Apparently undaunted, Harold shifted his glare to the newspaper gripped in his right hand. "I should have done a better job of keeping you off my beat. Then this article would have had *my* byline."

"I doubt it." Shari crossed her arms and legs. She spun her chair from side to side.

Harold gave her a sharp look. "It doesn't matter anyway. You can take as many stories off of my beat as you'd like."

"That story wasn't on your beat. As much as you'd like to think otherwise, I'm not here to do your work for you. You can—"

"It's not my work anymore. I'm giving up the newspaper business."

"You are?" Shari was surprised. "Why? Have you realized that you're not cut out for it?"

"*It's* not cut out for *me*."

"What does that even mean?"

Harold ignored her question. "I gave Diego my two weeks' notice. I'm leaving the *Telegraph* and good riddance."

Shari bit her lips together and squeezed her eyes shut to keep from squealing with joy. They were three weeks into the Lenten season, but this news made it feel like Christmas morning. Should she pinch herself to make certain she wasn't dreaming?

She did, then opened her eyes. "You're leaving the *Telegraph*?"

"That's right." Harold nodded his confirmation. "You're a really good reporter."

"Oh yeah?" Shari eyed Harold curiously.

He grinned at her. "I don't blame you for being suspicious, but I'm serious. You make it look so easy. I thought that if I could get a silver bullet like Sister Lou, I could be just as good a reporter as you are. I was wrong. It's not about Sister Lou. It's all you. You're really good."

Shari was overwhelmed. She'd never expected to hear such words from Harold. And she'd never expected them to mean so much. "Thanks, Hal."

He shook his head with a smile. "You're never going to stop calling me that are you?"

"It's better than the other nicknames."

"Are there a lot of them?"

"Oh yes."

"Do I want to hear them?"

"Oh no." Shari called after Harold as he turned to leave. "What are you doing to do?"

The soon-to-be-former reporter gave her a smug look. "I'm going to be working on Owen Rodney's communications team. I'm helping him with his mayoral campaign."

Shari blinked. "I didn't see that coming. I hope you'll be happy with your new job."

"Oh, I'm sure I will be." Harold grinned. "*You'll* have to come to *me* when Owen wins the election and becomes the next mayor of Briar Coast."

Shari laughed. "Do you *really* think Owen Rodney's going to beat Mayor Stanley?"

"Absolutely!"

Shari collected her coffee mug and stood to leave her cubicle. "It wouldn't be the first time you were wrong."

Chapter 34

Sister Lou set down her glass of water. "What will you do if you don't win reelection?" She asked the question of Heather who was seated diagonally across the table from her in the motherhouse's dining area.

"Isn't it bad luck to ask a question like that?" Sister Carmen looked up from her seat across from Sister Lou.

Sister Lou, Sister Carmen, Heather, Shari, Chris, and Diego were dining in the motherhouse Tuesday evening to celebrate successfully—and safely—resolving the threats against the mayor.

Sister Lou gave her friend an indulgent look. The dining room was fragrant with the mouthwatering scents of the congregation's main entrée: savory blackened chicken and spicy red beans and rice. Despite such temptation, Sister Carmen kept to her habit of delaying her main course in favor of starting with dessert. For tonight's selection, Sister Carmen had chosen the apple pie à la mode and added hot fudge, caramel, and maraschino cherries from the ice cream station.

Heather held a forkful of red beans and rice. Like

most normal people, including the others around the table, the mayor had chosen to honor custom by starting with her main course.

"It's all right, Sister Carm. I don't mind the question." Heather gave Sister Lou a thoughtful look. "If I'm not reelected, I'll return to practicing law. I'm not interested in corporate law anymore, though. I want to work with community groups, defending people whose rights are being violated."

"I voted for you last time, and you didn't disappoint me." Sister Carm sipped her ice water. "But now that I know your other option, I don't know whether I want you to win or lose."

"Neither do I." Chris smiled as he sliced into his blackened chicken. "I know of several nonprofit organizations that could use your legal services."

Heather chuckled. "I want to finish the work my administration started for Briar Coast: balancing the budget, fixing the roads, improving Internet access. But I admit that my three weeks with the congregation have had a positive impact on me. Sister Marianna told me so much about the congregation and its mission. I had no idea how much good the sisters do in the local community and around the world. I'm inspired."

The mayor's words filled Sister Lou with a warm glow of pleasure and pride. "That's very nice to hear."

Sister Lou gazed around the dining area at the other members of the congregation. Their joyous laughter and lively conversations danced around the bright, cheerful room.

Sister Carmen swallowed another bite of apple pie. "Spread the word. We can use all the support we can get."

Heather waved her fork toward Sister Lou. "If you need help with fund-raising, Sister Lou could consider charging for her sleuthing services. I bet she'd bring in a lot of money."

Sister Lou shook her head with a smile. "I could never do that."

"I didn't think so." Heather inclined her head. "Anyway, thank you again. I knew that I'd made the right decision in asking for your help."

Sister Lou's cheeks warmed with a blush. "Thank you, but I wouldn't have been able to solve this mystery without you, Shari, Chris, Diego, and Carm. These investigations are always a team effort."

"I knew from the beginning that Lou would get to the bottom of this." Sister Carmen finished her pie and started on her red beans and rice. "If it weren't for Lou, those deputies would have charged Kerry on the flimsiest of evidence."

Heather sliced into her blackened chicken. "I never should have doubted Kerry. I feel terribly that I did, however briefly."

Beside her, Diego squeezed Heather's shoulder. "You had a moment of doubt, but you supported her when she really needed you, and you're supporting her now."

Shari was seated between Sister Lou and Chris. "How is Kerry?"

Heather expelled a heavy sigh. "She's still blaming herself for trusting Benjamin."

Chris forked up more of his beans and rice. "No one can blame her. Benjamin had planned to fit in. He wanted to be overlooked."

Sister Carmen chuckled. "Little did he know that our amateur sleuth team doesn't overlook *anything*."

"No, we don't." Shari lowered her water glass and turned back to her main course. "I think we work pretty well together."

Sister Lou swallowed a bite of the chicken. Its spicy seasoning exploded on her taste buds. "Fran and Ted may be challenging to work with, but they always come through for us in the end. This time, their participation was critical to our plan to catch Benjamin."

Chris shook his head. "I can't understand why Benjamin's father would make a false deathbed statement. Didn't he realize how much that would hurt his son?"

"Graham Irsay was a coward." Diego's voice was low with anger. "He went to great lengths to frame Heather for his crimes, and never admitted to any of his wrongdoings. I'm not surprised that he'd lie to his son on his deathbed."

Sister Lou stared at her forkful of beans and rice. "Benjamin and his sister were Graham Irsay's remaining legacies. In that context, it's not surprising that a man like him would lie to preserve his legacy."

A pensive silence settled over the group. Sister Lou sneaked several glances at her friends gathered around her. Working with them to solve this case had been rewarding. They'd all gotten to know each other much better. Chris and Shari's relationship had been strengthened, and Diego and Heather had resolved old hurts. She couldn't have asked for more.

Sister Lou set aside her empty entrée plate and drew her dessert closer. Like Sister Carmen, she'd chosen the apple pie à la mode, but without the hot fudge, caramel, and maraschino cherries.

"Working these investigations is obviously part of

your charism, Lou." Sister Carmen's words startled her. It was as though her friend had read her mind.

Sister Lou let her gaze move over the table again, touching on Chris, Shari, Diego, and Heather before returning to Sister Carmen. "Perhaps. Especially in light of the Lenten season, the investigation reinforced for me the message that the sacrifices made for friends truly are the most meaningful."

Connect with Us

Visit us online at
KensingtonBooks.com
to read more from your favorite authors, see books
by series, view reading group guides, and more.

[Join us on social media]

for sneak peeks, chances to win books and prize packs,
and to share your thoughts with other readers.

facebook.com/kensingtonpublishing
twitter.com/kensingtonbooks

Tell us what you think!

To share your thoughts, submit a review,
or sign up for our eNewsletters, please visit:
KensingtonBooks.com/TellUs.